Barrettsport Mysteries

Tilting at Windmills

by

Alan Kemister

A grisly murder introduces newly-recruited detective Simon Goodyear to the less salubrious underside of Barrettsport, Nova Scotia. It sends Simon and Constable Diana Jackson on a three-month-long search for a devious manipulator who entangles much of the town in his nefarious schemes. Along the way, the town, a school teacher, and a young graphic artist draw Simon into their much more personal intrigues.

Acknowledgements:

I thank members of theNextBigWriters, an online writing workshop, and the Dartmouth Nova Scotia based Evergreen Writers Group for the encouragement that pushed me past my frequent bouts of writing inertia. Numerous members of both groups also provided constructive criticism that made this book much better than it would have been without their help.

Thanks also to my long-suffering wife who put up with me spending countless hours hunched over my computer when I should have been more productively employed. She also provided a final read picking up spelling and grammatical errors that persisted despite the dozens of times I read and reread the text.

Map of Barrettsport and environs

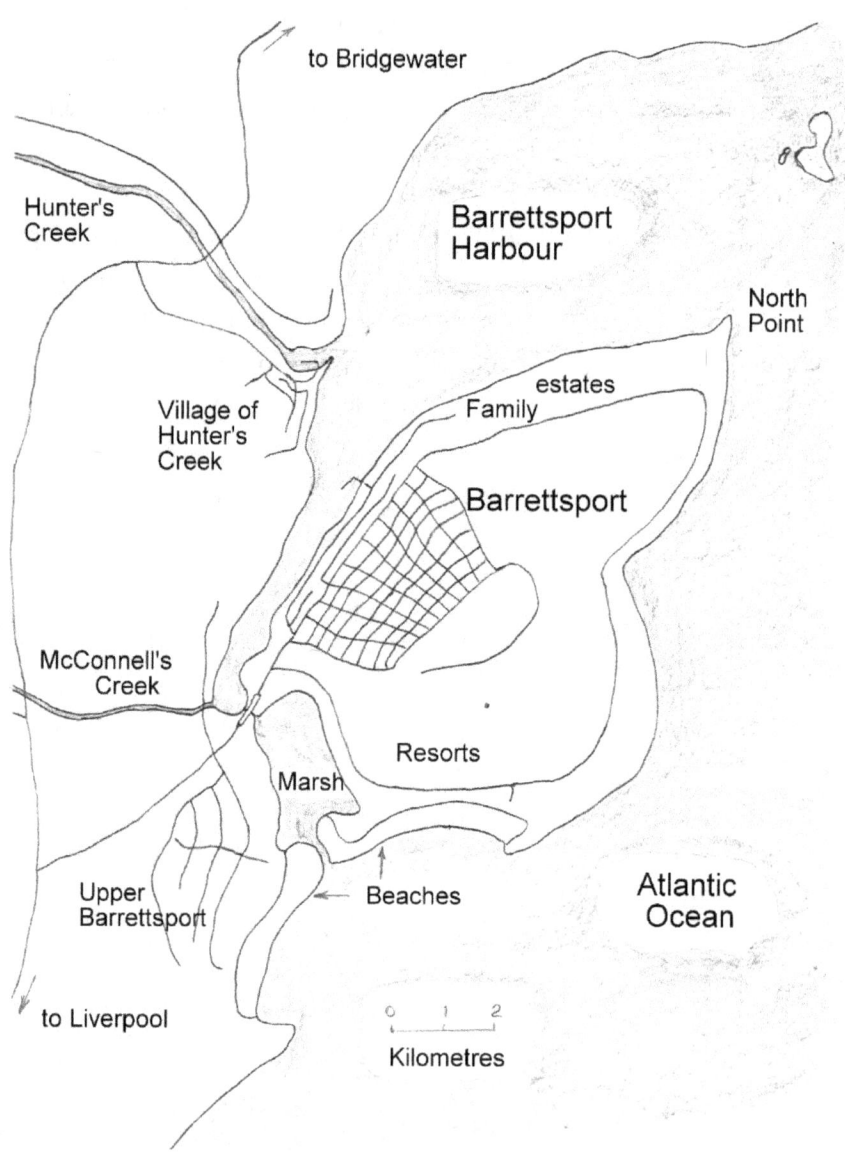

to Bridgewater

Hunter's Creek

Barrettsport Harbour

North Point

Village of Hunter's Creek

estates

Family

Barrettsport

McConnell's Creek

Resorts

Marsh

Upper Barrettsport

Beaches

Atlantic Ocean

to Liverpool

0 1 2

Kilometres

Street map with locations of places featured in the text

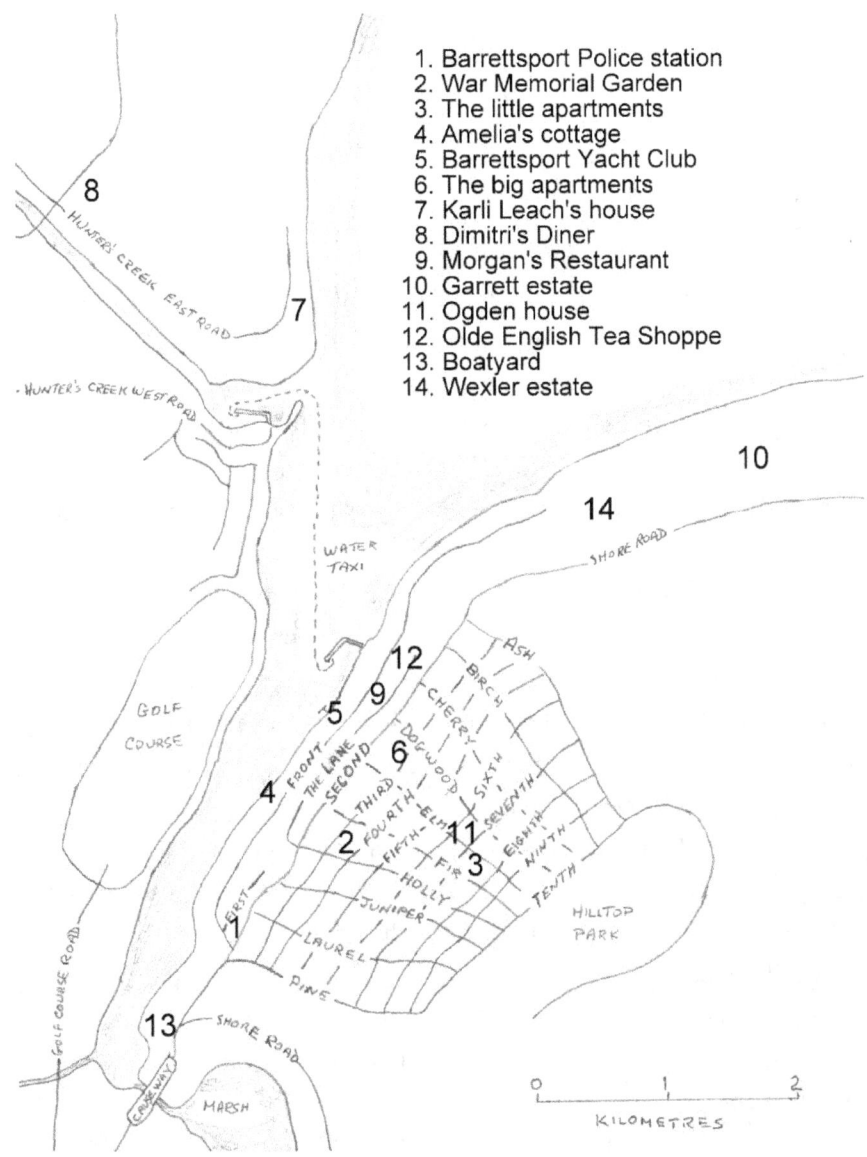

1. Barrettsport Police station
2. War Memorial Garden
3. The little apartments
4. Amelia's cottage
5. Barrettsport Yacht Club
6. The big apartments
7. Karli Leach's house
8. Dimitri's Diner
9. Morgan's Restaurant
10. Garrett estate
11. Ogden house
12. Olde English Tea Shoppe
13. Boatyard
14. Wexler estate

Chapter One

Detective Simon Goodyear pondered his future as he drove through the rocky terrain and stunted trees dominating the landscape along Nova Scotia's Atlantic coast. He'd lived in Barrettsport for five months. Time to cut the crap and admit his move east was a long-term commitment.

His job was working well, but his social life needed improvement. He drew mental parallels between the barren-looking landscape and the restricted social opportunities for a thirty-two-year-old bachelor in his new hometown.

A deer grazing near the road and an eagle, or large hawk, circling caught his attention. Were they omens suggesting social opportunities should be less bleak than he suspected?

His cell phone's ringtone broke into his reverie. Simon was enjoying the stress-free drive home and considered ignoring the call on this sunny Saturday morning but decided against it.

"Thank God you've picked up," Margaret Summerville, the usually unflappable woman who managed day-to-day activities in Barrettsport's police station exclaimed. The panic in her voice suggested he'd made the correct decision.

He pulled onto the shoulder. "What's the problem?"

"Thank God, you picked up," she repeated. "All hell's broken loose. We need you here."

Thoughts of his future, and the land denuded of soil and vegetation during the ice age ten thousand years earlier, no longer held his interest. Simon returned to the road and accelerated, covering the remaining sixty kilometres in record time.

"The chief wants to see you," Margaret announced as he strode into the station thirty minutes later.

Simon stopped by her switchboard. "What's up?"

The matronly woman with grey-speckled hair gestured toward their two holding cells. "Sorry, strict instructions to send you in without discussion."

Simon took the hint and detoured toward the cells. Six topless women, two he recognized as members of the pseudo-aristocratic families dominating the town's social and political life, occupied the nearer one. Simon looked back at Margaret. She shook her head and pointed at the chief's door.

As he drove the final kilometres into town, Simon had wondered what problem demanded his urgent attention. The behaviour of the citizens of his new hometown often surprised him, so he anticipated something unusual. None of his speculations, however, included half-naked wives of the town's dignitaries in their lock-up.

Police Chief Reginald DeWolfe was in an animated telephone conversation when Simon knocked and entered his office.

"The mayor," the chief mouthed, holding his hand over the phone and pointing it at a chair. Simon nodded and remained silent while the chief stammered his replies.

The chief sighed as he cradled the phone and focused on his visitor.

"Glad you're back. I need you to lead this investigation, so I can deal with the mayor and council." He paused, drumming his fingers on his desk. "We arrested six women parading naked in the War Memorial Garden near the bandstand. One is Selectman Garrett's wife."

"Naked, or topless like the women in the holding cell?"

"Topless, like they are now. What difference does it make?"

"A lot. Public nudity is against the law, but topless is a grey area."

The burly, grey-haired chief shook his head. "I can't worry about that. Our bylaws make their behaviour illegal."

"We should consult the lawyers. We could charge them under our bylaw, but I doubt it would stick."

7

"Forget about charging anyone. Just make the problem disappear!"

Simon rose and turned toward the door. "I'll handle it. Anything else?"

"Constable Jackson was with us. She'll fill you in. And we apprehended a seventh woman."

Simon didn't question the chief's parting shot because everyone knew he enjoyed ending conversations with apparently extraneous comments that contained hidden stingers. His overall message was clear, solve the topless women problem, and do it quickly. Step one was finding Diana Jackson.

The tall black woman with a noticeable British accent was the small force's solution to the minority and female representation problems. Constable Jackson was born in Nigeria but raised in England where she trained as a police constable. After working for a few years on a regional force, she and her husband moved to Nova Scotia. She'd been a member of the Barrettsport Police for five years.

Diana sat before her computer, scowling at a woman sitting outside his office.

Simon wondered what generated her sour expression. Could it relate to the chief's stinger? "I need an explanation."

"We received two anonymous calls warning us of a protest supporting National Go Topless Day. The chief organized a response, and we detained the six participants. They were by the bandstand with placards declaring their right to go topless wherever and whenever men can."

A noise from the cells interrupted her. When the noise died down, she resumed her report. "We picked them up and put them in a holding cell. They're still topless if you're interested."

Simon shook his head. The station apparently harboured a childish fascination with toplessness. "I've noticed. Why didn't someone find them something to wear?"

"We offered them rain capes in the van. They rejected them, saying they were beneath contempt. In the station, we provided the orange jumpsuits we have for prisoners, but they were no more popular."

"And the woman outside my office?"

"One caller mentioned her, so we asked her to accompany us. She was wearing red shorts like the others but still had her shirt on."

"What have you done since arresting them?"

"No sign of their tops, and they won't tell us where they left them. I suggested they get someone to deliver them, but they declined. I've recorded names and addresses. None had ID."

Simon nodded toward the young woman sitting outside his office. "And that one?"

"She had ID. I said she could go, but we'd be around. She chose to wait, so I plunked her outside your office."

"We've no grounds to detain them, but we can't let them go in a state of undress. What might they wear without a struggle?"

"T-shirts we made for a fundraiser last spring?"

"Sounds promising. I'll do some fund-raising. How much we selling them for?"

"Twenty bucks. I'll get you a bunch."

She pushed back her chair, but Simon held up his hand. "Are we sure they've given you accurate personal information?"

"Three are prominent Barrettsport citizens, so we know them. The others are actresses at the Chester Playhouse. You know the place, a small town an hour's drive to the northeast." Diana paused, pointing at a photo on her computer screen. It was from the theatre's publicity blurb for their current play. "Those three are definitely our actresses. The address they gave is a rooming house where they're staying during the run."

"Okay, I'll offer them T-shirts stressing it's for a good cause and let them go. Do they have money to pay for them, and what about car keys and keys for their rooms?"

Diana shook her head. "I checked for weapons and had them empty their pockets but that's all. Some had money."

Simon turned toward the cells. "Once we get the six sorted out, I'll talk to the woman outside my office."

Mrs. Caroline Garrett stood at the front of the cell posed like a Greek statue. The imposing blonde with the upright posture of a runway model was strutting her stuff in a way her stuffed-shirt husband, Selectman Matthew Garrett, would not appreciate. The rest hovered near the back of the cell. Mrs. Cynthia Ettinger, the only one Simon recognized, appeared to be shielding another. Orange jumpsuits were piled on the floor outside the cell.

Over the next few minutes, he sorted out the actresses, selling them T-shirts on credit before releasing them into Diana's care. Simon was less successful with the three Barrettsport women. Mrs. Garrett, who claimed she spoke on their behalf, refused his offer and insisted on making a phone call.

Simon addressed the constable talking to Margaret in the public part of the small police station. "Let Mrs. Garrett talk to her lawyer, but don't let her go anywhere."

Moments later, the half-naked woman was in a lively conversation in full view of the building's glass entry doors. She replaced the phone, and the constable escorted her back to the cell.

"Mrs. G. didn't talk to a lawyer," Margaret said when Simon returned with a mug of coffee. "She talked to someone named Lisa about their belongings. Didn't sound too happy."

"I'm not surprised. Tell us when Lisa arrives."

Simon stopped at Diana's desk and interrupted her conversation with the actresses. "Any of you know someone named Lisa?"

One actress responded. "She's a friend of Cynthia's who was at the park this morning."

"That's what I figured," Simon replied. "I'm confident she'll soon arrive with your stuff."

"I planned to drive them to Chester," Diana said. "Should they wait?"

Simon nodded and put three twenties on Diana's desk while looking at the women. "Why don't you have lunch on us?"

He then strode to his office to talk to the seventh woman.

The young woman stood, extending her hand before Simon greeted her. "Thank you, Detective Goodyear, for talking to me." It was a good ploy if she wanted to prevent him from suggesting they talk later.

"Hello, Ms.... I'm sorry; I don't remember your name. But I've seen you around. One of our school teachers, aren't you?"

She appeared to be in her late twenties, about five-foot-nine, and thin with brown eyes and short light brown hair. Not a striking beauty like Mrs. Garrett, more like the deceptively pretty tomboy from next door who doesn't get the notice she deserves. She wore white sandals, red shorts, and a white T-shirt with extensive embroidery done with barely noticeable ivory-coloured thread.

"Craddock, Amelia Craddock. I want to relate my side of the story before you decide I was part of this morning's stunt."

Simon maneuvered into the cluttered space behind his desk and pointed toward his visitor's chair. "Tell me the story from your perspective."

"Someone I'd rather not name phoned at eight o'clock. She asked me to arrive at the bandstand by nine forty-five dressed as I am and watch what happened. She claimed it would be interesting." Amelia paused for a breath as she gazed around Simon's office. "When I sounded doubtful, she begged me to go, so I agreed. That's it. I was sitting there, and Constable Jackson insisted I accompany her to the station."

"Why won't you identify her?"

"I will, I promise, but I must tell her first."

Simon pushed his phone across the desk. "I suggest you phone her."

Amelia held up a cell phone. "I've tried several times. She isn't answering."

"I can't force you, but please, tell me as soon as you can. Anything else you want to say?"

"No."

"Do you have any dealings with Mrs. Garrett, Mrs. Ettinger or Miss Campbell?" He'd learned Beverley Campbell's name from Margaret after Mrs. Garrett made her call.

11

Amelia shrugged her shoulders. "Well, yes, we're a small community and they're prominent citizens, but our lives rarely intersect."

This didn't surprise Simon. The descendants of the five families that established Barrettsport in the early 1800s behaved like landed gentry and led lives separated from those of the common citizens. The class distinctions had featured in the major case he'd solved during his short tenure as Barrettsport's only detective.

"What about the other three?" he asked.

"Never seen them before, but I'm going to their play. Want to accompany me?"

Simon couldn't miss her coquettish look, but he, foolishly perhaps, played along with her banter. "Not until you tell me who phoned you this morning."

"Deal! I'll be back this afternoon. See you then." Amelia scurried out before Simon could tell her she was free to go. She appeared too happy for the circumstances, and how did she know they were actresses performing at the Chester Playhouse?

And Simon was unhappy with the implied commitment to attend the play.

Simon checked his watch as he walked towards Diana's desk. It was only twelve fifteen; he'd been at the station for less than an hour.

"Any sign of Lisa?" he asked.

"Not yet. Margaret will tell me when she arrives."

"I wish she'd appear. We need to discuss the case. I'd even buy your lunch."

"From the way you've been throwing your money around, I'd guess you've come into a fortune. If I counted correctly, you've funded our actresses to the tune of $120."

"I'm confident they'll pay me back."

Diana snorted. "Good luck. You'll never see that money again!"

"Wanna bet? I'll bet you lunch at the Traveller's Inn they'll pay for the T-shirts and return any change from my sixty dollars."

She stood and extended her hand. "It's a bet, but we must postpone lunch. I brought food for today and you should eat while I wait for Lisa and the actresses."

"Okay, I'm off. See you in half an hour."

When Simon returned forty-five minutes later, seventy-two dollars sat in the middle of his desk with a note that read *Lunch is on me. D.*

A few minutes later, Diana stood in his doorway.

"Everything's cleared up. Lisa Powell arrived with their kit. I recorded Ms. Powell's story, and our six lovelies departed. We prepare a report, and we're done."

"Sounds good," Simon replied. "Draft up what you can, and I'll finish it."

"I assume you found the money. They offered to come up with the forty-eight dollars for their lunches, but I said you'd claim it from the department. Is Tuesday okay for lunch?"

"Tuesday's great, but you don't have to buy me lunch."

"Yes, I do. We made a fair wager, and I lost."

Simon's phone rang as Diana turned to leave. "Hello, Detective Goodyear."

"Detective, it's Amelia Craddock. She's been murdered."

Chapter Two

Simon waved Diana back into his office before responding to Amelia's shocking pronouncement. "Are you sure?"

"Of course I'm sure! Her head's totally bashed in."

"Where are you?"

"Outside number three in the little apartments."

The three-storey tall little apartments were on Seventh Avenue near the top of the Hill, a minor summit that provided a backdrop for the town. Barrettsport's other apartment building, seven storeys high on Third Avenue, was called the big apartments.

"We'll be right there. Don't touch anything."

"I'm not going back, and I'm too weak to run away."

Five minutes later, Simon leapt from the squad car as Diana brought it to a screeching halt before the building's main entrance. Amelia sat on the top step.

She cringed as Simon charged up the stairs. "I'm sure I touched nothing, but the door may have locked when I closed it. If I'd stayed, I would have been sick."

Simon stopped to question Amelia as Diana rushed into the building. "Who's the victim and are you sure she's dead?"

"Holly Craig. There's blood everywhere."

"The door isn't locked," Diana yelled from down the hall.

Simon glanced into the building before turning back to Amelia. "You can wait here, or sit in our car, but don't leave until we understand the situation."

"I'll wait here until I feel better."

She shivered despite the summer day's early afternoon warmth.

He fetched her a blanket. "If you feel faint, put your head between your knees."

Diana waited in the apartment doorway. "It's definitely a homicide. Rigor suggests she's been dead for several hours."

"Okay, I'll check things out while you stand guard and keep an eye on Ms. Craddock. Call the chief and tell him what you've seen, and the Mounties to request forensic support."

"We'll also need the coroner," Diana added.

"Yeah."

Simon donned latex gloves and plastic shoe covers before entering the apartment. A young woman wearing black shorts and a pale blue top sat at the dining room table with her torso and head slumped into her breakfast. Unseeing eyes stared at him, and shards of bone protruded from the back of her skull. He scanned the room for a potential murder weapon but saw nothing.

Next, he checked the ground floor suite's patio door and discovered it was unlocked. He found a half-full bottle of milk near room temperature on the kitchen counter and a full pot of cold tea on a stove burner. A small but functional kitchen table with two chairs occupied a corner. The state of the bedroom and bathroom suggested only one peaceful sleeper spent the previous night in the apartment.

"Do we have a positive ID?" Simon asked Diana when he returned to the hallway. "No purse and I didn't want to disturb the body before the coroner arrives."

"The apartment's rented to Holly Craig, a freelance reporter who works for the big Halifax daily. I've seen her around town, and I'm confident it's her."

"Ms. Craddock may have something to add. She apparently knew Ms. Craig quite well."

Diana motioned toward the open door with her head. "Don't ask her to return. I doubt she's up to it."

Simon approached Amelia. She remained huddled under the blanket but appeared less pale. "You okay?"

"Better," she replied, sounding tentative. "Not much use, am I? Totally freaked out by a little blood?"

"It's a gruesome scene and lots of blood."

"Still, I should be tougher."

"You're sure it's Ms. Craig? It couldn't be someone else?"

"Definitely Holly. She was looking straight at me."

Amelia turned pale again, and Simon reminded her to put her head down if she felt faint. She did so, and he waited until she recovered.

"You up to answering a few questions before Officer Jackson takes you home?"

Amelia slowly nodded her head. "I guess."

"Was Ms. Craig the mystery caller you wouldn't identify earlier?"

"Yes."

"You left my office at twelve fifteen. It's now one thirty. That's an hour and a quarter?"

"I returned home, made a sandwich, and phoned Holly again."

"Then?" Simon asked as Diana approached.

"I hiked up from my cottage."

"And when you arrived?"

"Her door was ajar—"

Simon raised his right hand. "What about the main entrance?"

"Wedged open as it often is. I didn't stop to call." She paused, gazing at Simon. "Is that a problem?"

"For us, yeah, but not for you. So, you got to her door..."

"I pushed it open without knocking, stepped into the entranceway, saw her almost immediately, turned, and fled. I think I screamed, but it's all blurry."

"Did you hear anyone?"

She shook her head, her expression puzzled. "I don't think so."

"Okay, that's enough for now. We'll visit later this afternoon for the rest of your story."

Amelia stood, folded the blanket, and handed it to Simon before following Diana. He scrutinized her clothes as she turned away. She was wearing the same red shorts and T-shirt with embroidery around the neck. He saw no bloodstains.

While Diana took Amelia home, Simon greeted the doctor who doubled as the local representative of the medical examiner's office. Dr. Pike rather huffily commenced his examination after making pointed comments about the RCMP forensic unit Simon awaited.

The Royal Canadian Mounted Police provided routine policing in areas without local police forces, and investigative capacity to other forces. Barrettsport didn't have the manpower or expertise for detailed forensic examinations, but that didn't stop townspeople from disparaging the Mounties' incursions into their space.

Another Barrettsport constable arrived after the coroner returned to work. Diana was right behind him. With their help, Simon secured access to the apartment's two doors and the garden outside the sliding door. They made a tour of the building's perimeter while they waited for the forensic unit. After their tour, the medical officer joined them, passing Simon a wallet he'd taken from the victim's pocket. It confirmed their identification.

Simon and Diana left to interview Amelia Craddock after the forensic team took control of their crime scene. The short trip took them down the hill to the T-intersection at Second Avenue. They drove along the main commercial street to the police station where they turned onto Front Street. Amelia's house was a one-and-a-half storey waterfront cottage nestled behind a tall hedge.

Nice spot, Simon thought as they walked through a gap into an isolated front garden dominated by a flagpole created from an old yacht's wooden mast. *How could a young school teacher afford such a prime piece of waterfront real estate?*

Amelia answered the door wearing a silky red bathrobe. Its colour reminded Simon of the shorts Amelia and the six other women wore at the protest.

"Please excuse my appearance," she said. "I was sick after I returned home. I've just finished cleaning the bathroom and having a shower, and now I'm having tea. May I get you some?"

"Yes please," Diana replied. Simon nodded his agreement.

"We have more questions," Simon said once they were seated at her kitchen counter.

"You'll let me get dressed if you must take me to the station?"

"We're not planning to arrest you; just a few questions you can answer in your house. We can wait while you get dressed."

She wrapped the robe more tightly around herself before pouring the tea. No sign of a belt to keep it properly closed. "I'm okay. Fire away."

Simon began. "I'll start with this morning when Ms. Craig asked you to visit the park wearing red shorts."

"She phoned me at eight with the request as I told you before. I was reluctant, but she convinced me."

"Why wouldn't you tell us who she was?"

"When we talked, I promised not to tell anyone."

"Are you okay? You're looking pale again."

"I'm responsible for her death, aren't I?"

She fainted and would have tumbled from the stool if the vigilant Officer Jackson hadn't caught her and laid her on the floor. Diana repositioned the robe that slipped open as Amelia fell. A quick glance at Simon confirmed they both noticed she wore nothing under it.

"Should we continue this conversation tomorrow?" Simon asked after Amelia recovered.

"No, I want it done."

"Then we should move into your living room. You won't have as far to fall the next time you faint."

Amelia sat on her sofa with Diana beside her. Simon chose a chair facing them.

"I'm responsible, aren't I?" Amelia repeated. "If I'd told you earlier, none of this would have happened."

Simon sighed before looking at Diana. "Let's try to get past this misconception. You picked her up at what, ten thirty?"

"Close," Diana replied. "Ten forty-five when we arrived at the station."

"And when did we ask her why she was there?"

"You asked around twelve."

"But I could have volunteered the information at ten thirty or eleven," Amelia interjected, reaching for a Kleenex to dab away tears.

Simon shook his head. "We suspect she died while she was having breakfast, probably between eight and nine. You couldn't have saved her life by telling us sooner. We should focus on how you *can* help us?"

"Okay," Amelia said, sounding far from convinced.

Simon returned to his interrupted line of inquiry. "Did she tell you what to expect?"

"Just that it would be interesting."

"Can I assume you and Ms. Craig were good friends?"

"We socialized, but I wouldn't say, great friends. Not the kind you share your secrets with. The few young people in this town, especially ones who are outsiders, gravitate together."

Simon understood her meaning. Restaurants and shops were located on Second Avenue and the Lane, a pedestrian mall between Second Avenue and Front Street. They catered to Barrettsport's 'landed aristocracy' and the wealthy old-fashioned tourists who favoured the Victorian style resorts on the south side of the peninsula. There wasn't much social interaction between this group and the rest of the citizens. And options for a younger, less formal crowd were limited. A pub and several less expensive restaurants were located in a commercial area between the coastal highway and the causeway joining the town to the Nova Scotia mainland. Barrettsport only had a population of four thousand, so not surprising members of these isolated groups gravitated together.

"What can you tell us about Ms. Craig?" Simon asked. "Did she have a boyfriend?"

"She was seeing a married man but kept his name secret."

Simon straightened. "Can you describe this man?"

"I never met him. No idea what he looks like."

"Was he a local?"

"Barrettsport or one of the nearby communities."

"Why's that?"

"From their comings and goings, they met on too short notice for someone from Halifax."

"Did he come to her apartment?" Simon asked next.

"Not to my knowledge."

"Did she normally eat in her kitchen or her dining room?"

"Kitchen, I think." Amelia gazed around as if searching for an answer to his question. "Unless she had visitors, then she might eat in the dining room."

Simon paused while he considered her reaction to an innocuous question. "If you visited for breakfast, where would you eat?"

"I was never there for breakfast, but we had lunch together in the kitchen a few times."

He shook his head, thinking this wasn't getting him anywhere. He altered his approach. "Did she carry a purse?"

Amanda shook her head. "She often carried a large bag with her notebook and a tape recorder, and maybe a small computer."

"Can you describe it?" Diana asked.

"Brown leather with a shoulder strap, rather masculine. More like a laptop computer case than a purse. She kept keys and wallet in her pockets like a guy."

Simon resumed the questioning while Diana recorded the description in her notebook. "Back to this morning. Why did she want you there?"

"I've been considering that. She must have heard about the protest and wanted my opinion for a quote in the article she expected to write."

"Why the red and white outfit?"

She fidgeted and tugged at her robe. "I don't know."

"One other thing. You said you tried to phone Ms. Craig twice. When did you make the first call?"

"Outside your office, eleven fifteen or thereabouts."

Simon stood and motioned to Diana. "Okay, let's leave it there. Will you be okay?"

"I can call my neighbour if I need help. She'll know what to do."

"Then we'll be off, and really, you're not to blame for what happened. Don't beat yourself up."

"You better watch out for her," Diana said as they strode to the car. "She may be in shock, but it's not preventing her from making a play. You're another single, young outsider in Barrettsport, and she wants you to gravitate together."

"That was so obvious I wondered if her exhibitionist display was intentional."

"You think she has something to hide?"

Simon turned and gazed at the cottage. "Can't rule it out. Traces of blood on her clothes would contradict her story."

"Already in hand. When I took her home, I suggested her clothes and shoes might be useful for our investigation, and she volunteered them."

Difficult situation, Simon thought as he followed Diana to their car. Amelia claimed she'd talked to the deceased at eight and discovered the body five hours later, so they would need to investigate her movements. And during part of that time, she'd essentially been working for Ms. Craig.

Also, some of Amelia's actions appeared downright suspicious. He didn't appreciate the way she'd manipulated their initial interview in his office, or the ill-fitting robe she insisted on wearing when they interviewed her again. On the other hand, her reaction to finding the body and her fainting fit appeared genuine. She was either a suspicious character or an important witness, so they needed to establish her story.

Diana's suggestion Amelia was making a play for him was discomforting. If she was an innocent witness, Diana's suggestion fit the facts, but that was no consolation. A romantic relationship with anyone associated with a case was a bad idea, and he wanted to approach relationships in his new hometown more carefully than he had previously.

A complex and manic personal life with wild parties and too many women contributed to his decision to leave his job as an undercover cop in the Vancouver Police Department. He now sought a simpler life. No matter how desirable Amelia Craddock was, he needed to keep her at arm's length. But it would be difficult; she'd committed him to a trip to the theatre in Chester, and somehow, he knew it wouldn't end there.

"And what about that cottage?" he asked. "How can she afford waterfront property?"

"I'll look into it, and the rest of her story. Then you needn't worry about the fact she's got your knickers in a twist."

Diana, apparently, could read his mind.

Chapter Three

Chief DeWolfe accosted Diana and Simon as they entered the station. "Constable Kerry's searching for a murder weapon."

Before Simon's arrival in Barrettsport, Reginald DeWolfe had been both chief and detective. His intervention suggested his struggles with relinquishing the secondary role continued.

"Do you want me to join him?" Diana asked.

The chief shook his head. "I've called out an additional constable, and four RCMP officers are on site. The Mounties will dissect the crime scene and share their forensic report with us. You two will lead our investigation." The chief paused, looking at Simon. "You okay with that?"

"Yeah, fine," Simon replied. He welcomed Constable Jackson's contributions to another case but was less comfortable with the chief's testy reaction to RCMP involvement. He'd rather avoid squabbles with the national police force.

"Kerry will seal the crime scene once the Mounties clear out, and report any success finding the murder weapon," the chief continued. "Get working and solve this crime. The remaining staff will handle everything else, and I must visit the mayor."

"We need a plan," Simon suggested, stepping into his office after the chief stomped away. "But first, contact Kerry and give him the description of her purse."

After talking to Kerry, Diana stood with her hand on the back of Simon's visitor's chair. "Shouldn't I be interviewing the neighbours?"

Simon pointed at the chair as he turned on a tape recorder. "I'll start this evening. First, we should determine where we stand."

Diana shrugged her shoulders as she sat. "Okay, Mr. Detective, describe the situation, and I'll take notes." Her sarcastic tone showed Simon she sought action.

"First, Ms. Craig was alone last night. The bed suggests only one person slept in it."

Diana looked up before writing anything in her notebook. "The perpetrator might have straightened it."

"Possibly. Forensics will find evidence of a co-occupant if there was one. We should assume she slept alone unless forensics tells us otherwise. Next, she was up before 8 a.m. because she phoned Amelia Craddock at eight."

Diana looked up again. "Assuming Ms. Craddock is telling the truth."

"I appreciate your skepticism. Keep questioning my assumptions, but phone company records will provide confirmation."

"Should I request them?"

"Later. First, where do we stand?"

"She was eating breakfast in the dining room when someone bludgeoned her."

"The coroner will give us the time, but I'd bet it was before nine."

"Another wager? Maybe I could cancel my promise to buy lunch but not this time. She planned to be at the bandstand before ten."

"Anything else?" Simon asked. Soliciting Diana's views may not have been the quickest way to review the situation, but a worthwhile exercise for investigators formally working together for the first time. *Her answers would help him gauge how she approaches a problem.*

"The intruder was there between eight and nine."

Simon shook his head. "We can't be that specific. He or she may have arrived before eight and had to leave before one. That's the window."

"If he was there before eight, he was someone she knew. What you're saying broadens the time frame, but it also raises new questions."

"That's why we must think before we gather the wrong data."

"Yes, sir, I get the message."

"What's next?" he asked.

"Someone bludgeoned her with the proverbial blunt instrument, but there's no sign of it."

"That's correct, and we should soon have a better idea what we're after. Finding it will be important."

"And hard to do."

Simon stood and began pacing in the confined space behind his desk. "We'll augment our list of facts after we receive the coroner and forensic reports. What questions should we ask?"

"Are the topless protest and the murder linked?"

"Good question. We must dig into the politics behind the protest to answer it."

"I'll add it to my to-do list."

"Why was she eating breakfast in the dining room?" Simon asked.

"Because she wasn't alone and having breakfast with someone, her married lover perhaps. And if he wasn't the murderer, he's an important witness."

"What sort of visitor suggests breakfast in the dining room? We know she would eat in the kitchen with friends like Ms. Craddock. Wouldn't breakfast with her lover be similar?"

Diana shook her head. "What if the lover was a formal upper-class person? He might prefer the dining room."

"Like in one of those Agatha Christie manor house mysteries?"

"And most of the pretentious old families in town maintain old-fashioned upper-class traditions. They might prefer the dining room."

Simon stopped pacing and gazed at Diana sitting by his desk clutching her notebook. She was the picture of the detached assistant recording the details. From the questions she asked, he knew she was involved.

"So, a lover turned murderer from one of Barrettsport's premier families? Might be right, but without evidence, we must tread carefully."

"But we can assume she wasn't eating alone, so someone—presumably the murderer—cleaned up before he left. He wanted us to think she was alone."

"Must it be a he?"

"It doesn't look like a female crime."

"Why not?" he asked.

"Too violent, needed too much physical strength, and the wrong psychology."

"Okay, male or atypical, strong female. Any more questions?"

"The usual ones—motive and opportunity—and we can't address those yet."

"Let's wrap up. Go home and sort out your kids." Diana was a single mother with two small boys, but Simon didn't know the details of her domestic arrangements. "I'll visit our crime scene, assuming the forensic people have departed, and knock on the neighbours' doors."

"The kids are under control, so I can stay."

He raised his eyebrows. "Okay, accompany me. A second perspective can't hurt."

They spent an hour in Holly's apartment developing a picture of their crime scene. After Diana left, Simon interviewed neighbours. An overweight middle-aged woman in typical shop assistant's attire opened the door to the next apartment.

"A man visited her this morning around seven thirty," she said while standing in her doorway. "He was still there when I left at nine forty-five."

She was obviously a nosey-parker who hoped to observe Holly's visitor when he left, but Simon wasn't convinced he could rely on her assertion. The visitor might have departed by another route, and his witness must have abandoned her observation post for short periods. But there was no point in annoying her by questioning her veracity.

"Can you describe him?" he asked.

She shook her head. "He was past my window when I noticed him, and he'd disappeared into her apartment before I got to my door."

"Tall or short, young or old?"

She stared at the six-foot-two detective. "Tallish, but not as tall as you. Brown hair and somewhat overweight."

"What about clothes? Was he wearing a jacket or a hat?"

She paused for a moment, her brow furrowed. "Beige windbreaker and darker brown trousers, but no hat."

"Glasses? And his voice? Did you hear him speak?"

"I don't think he was wearing glasses, but I only saw him from the back. You can't pick up voices through the walls, but she played loud classical music at one point."

"Oh, when was that?"

"Eight-thirty and it continued for forty-five minutes."

"You're sure of the time?"

"It interrupted my radio program."

Simon paused, hoping she might volunteer additional information, but she said nothing. "Did she often have visitors?"

"Seldom, and never early in the morning. That's why I noticed."

His witness mentioned dealing with something on her stove, so Simon gave her his card with the standard request to phone if she thought of anything. He departed, wondering why she insisted on talking in the doorway.

None of his conversations with Holly's other neighbours yielded as much information.

Diana entered Simon's office at seven fifty-five Sunday morning. He'd filed everything on his desk and mounted a large whiteboard on one wall. His office wasn't large, but he'd turned it into an efficient control room by removing extraneous material.

She gazed at the information he'd listed under the headings of Craddock and Craig before turning to Simon, grinning. "Ms. Craddock has her evil eye on you, but I don't see any mention on your list."

"Forget that. Let's start with Ms. Craig," Simon replied, brandishing a felt marker and ticking off the points he'd recorded.

"My interviews last night gave me one observation of an early morning visitor with a partial description, and three mentions of loud classical music, Beethoven apparently, from eight thirty to nine fifteen. Unfortunately, no one else saw the visitor."

"Forty-five minutes is the usual length of a CD. We should check for a Beethoven disc in the machine."

"I got no answer at three apartments, including the one opposite Ms. Craig's. We need to interview the occupants."

"I can do that," Diana suggested. "And I could ask around at nearby houses to determine if anyone saw our mystery man."

"We also need to identify yesterday's two anonymous callers."

"What do the tapes tell us?"

Simon started his tape recorder. They listened to the incoming messages from two different youngish-adult-sounding female voices.

"I don't recognize them, and Constable Evans who's on duty this morning did no better. I'm wondering if one might be Ms. Craig, so I'll ask Ms. Craddock if she knew either of the voices." He paused, watching for Diana's reaction to the second tape's contents. "And I'm suspicious of Ms. Garrett and her three friends. I need someone who recognizes their voices."

"Chief DeWolfe might."

"Good idea," Simon replied, nodding.

"And what about Kerry's search for the weapon? Any luck there?"

"None. We've not found the weapon or the bag with the tape recorder."

"Next of kin?"

"I phoned her parents in Ontario last night after interviewing the neighbours. Her father's coming to Halifax today at the behest of the Medical Examiner's Office."

Diana pocketed her notebook and stood without saying anything about the tape's contents. "Anything else?" She was obviously eager to get on with the investigation.

"We should talk to Ms. Garrett and company again, and we need to find Ms. Craig's mystery lover. Someone must have seen them together. Take her photo to motels and restaurants and ask the staff if they've seen her with anyone."

"Do you want me to start after I interview neighbours?"

Simon held up his hand while he consulted the notes on his desk. "Start on the motels. I'll continue the interviews and chase up the identity of the voices. That way I can be in town to pester the chief and handle calls from Mr. Craig. And I'll get Kerry working on the house-to-house."

"Okay, I'm on it."

While Diana surveyed motels, Simon interviewed the rest of Holly's neighbours without learning anything. He then went to ask Amelia about the voice on the second tape. He was unprepared for the surprise she had in store for him.

Chapter Four

Simon greeted Amelia at her front door. "Hello, Ms. Craddock. I hope you're feeling better this morning."

She stood, properly dressed, blocking his way with one hand on the doorknob and the other on the frame. Her smile said his tall, muscular physique and ruggedly handsome face beneath short cropped ash-blond hair met with her approval.

Simon was thirty-two, heterosexual, and unattached. He'd been living in Barrettsport for five months without establishing a romantic relationship. Amelia Craddock might be the one to rekindle his interest, but not before they proved she was an innocent witness.

"Please, Detective, call me Amelia. After yesterday, we're like old friends, there's no need for formality."

Old friends seemed a stretch and another indication she hadn't abandoned her flirtatious behaviour.

"May I come in? I have a problem you might help me with."

She nodded as she stepped aside. "Would you like coffee? Mine's better than the stuff you make at the station." She led him to the kitchen and fussed with an elaborate machine before passing him a cup. "What's today's problem?"

"I thought you might recognize one of yesterday's callers."

Simon played the short message. It said 'Watch for another woman at this morning's bandstand protest. She will be dressed like the protesters but not participating.'

"It's Holly's voice, but why would she draw attention to me?"

"You're sure."

"Yeah." Amelia disappeared into her living room and called out a few minutes later, "I've found a video with Holly's voice on it. You can compare for yourself, but I don't want you to watch. Stay where you are and listen."

Simon's brow furrowed. How could he identify a voice on a video without seeing her? He shrugged his shoulders. "Okay."

She started the video but stopped it almost immediately. "This is silly. It's only a video we made at Crystal Crescent Beach. You might as well watch. Holly wouldn't worry." She smiled as he approached.

More nudity, Simon thought as he watched the video of Amelia and Holly undressing and teasing each other on Halifax's nude beach. *This damn case is awash in nudity.*

For several seconds he wondered about Amelia's mischievous smile, one that reminded him of her coquettish behaviour when she cornered him about the play, but he soon caught on. Amelia's friends were teasing her because she refused to strip at the nude beach. Holly stripped and mugged for the camera, but despite the teasing, Amelia remained in her swimsuit. Amelia's bikini left little for Simon's imagination, but she wasn't naked when the clip ended. The video, however, proved it was Holly's voice on the police station tape.

"Fooled you, didn't I?" Amelia said. "You expected to see me naked, didn't you?"

"I admit it, I did," he replied, trying to laugh off the embarrassment she'd caused him before getting back to business. "We'll need the disc, at least the audio portion, for our records. Can we run it again, and I'll record the audio onto my tape?"

She pulled the disc from her machine. "Take it. You'll need the video to match up the voices."

"If you're sure. I'll make a copy and get it back to you."

After passing Simon the disc, Amelia returned to the police tape.

"She set me up, didn't she? She wanted to get me arrested."

"Sounds like it. Probably trying to manufacture a story."

Amelia nodded. "If I'd made a fuss after being arrested and mistreated, she'd have a better story."

"That may have been her intention."

"Jesus, that's annoying. I refused to give you her name to protect her when she was pushing me into something I feared."

"Please, explain?" Simon asked.

"I have a phobia about being arrested, strip-searched and mistreated. She tried to make that happen."

"People who fear the treatment they might get in custody often behave in inappropriate ways." He paused, wishing to take back his words. He sounded like he was blaming the victim.

She ignored the implied criticism. "But instead I got you and Diana, and you treated me really well." She reached over and gave him a kiss on his cheek.

"What was that?" he asked, mentally, if not physically, recoiling from the unexpected familiarity.

"A thank you for you and Diana. And when are we going to Chester?"

Simon smiled. He should have known she wouldn't forget his foolish agreement to attend the play. Dating a witness was asking for trouble, but Chief DeWolfe had acknowledged the police in their small community couldn't always keep an arms-length relationship with everyone involved with their cases. Best to agree without complaint and hopefully learn something on the trip. He'd handle the flak after he returned.

"This week? What day works for you?"

"Thursday," she said without hesitation.

"Okay, Thursday it is. I'll pick you up around five and we can eat in Chester. Thank you for the video."

Simon shook his head as he walked away from her cottage. His chances of keeping this relationship from boiling over were almost nonexistent.

One down and one to go, Simon thought as he returned to the station. He was confident one of the protest participants or an unidentified co-conspirator made the other call. It wasn't Caroline Garrett's distinctively husky voice, but it could have been Cynthia, Lisa or Beverley. He could contact them as part of the murder investigation and listen to their voices.

"Have you seen the chief?" Simon asked Constable Evans.

Evans nodded. "He took it home. Says Marge will know if either is from Barrettsport society."

"Sounds good. Is he expected back?"

"He'll call if she recognizes them."

Simon paused in his office doorway. "Tell me if you hear anything." He disappeared inside to begin cataloguing information about their murder victim.

Their data indicated Ms. Craig was a journalist who generated most of her income as a stringer for the Chronicle Herald newspaper in Halifax. She reported on a broad range of South Shore activities. Amelia's evidence suggested she wasn't always the most ethical journalist.

She was twenty-eight and single, with no acknowledged romantic attachments, and a Barrettsport resident for two years. She had no known involvement in local social activities. Amelia said she was a fun-loving individual, which raised the question of why she lived in such a structured community. Simon also generated many questions related to her life before moving to Barrettsport. He searched for answers while waiting for Diana.

Diana returned from her motel quest at eleven thirty.

"What do you have for me?" Simon asked when she poked her head into his office.

"One good lead, a motel between Liverpool and Shelburne, two towns southwest of here."

"I know where they are." Simon hadn't lived in Nova Scotia for long, but he had been out getting the lay of the land.

"Young fellow at the motel thought he recognized Ms. Craig as one of their customers, but he wasn't sure. He didn't have access to registration records that might confirm her presence."

"Any progress with her mystery lover?"

"He thinks she checked in on her own, but he didn't appear convinced. I left Ms. Craig's photo and asked the owner to contact the station at his first opportunity. Our mystery lover may show up on the motel's registration records, or the owner may have seen him."

"Other positive IDs?"

Diana shook her head. "Seven motels and that was my only hit."

"Okay, stay on top of the owner. This afternoon you can dig into Amelia Craddock's story because we need to confirm what she's told us."

"Or refute it," Diana suggested.

"That's not likely but talk to her neighbours. I want to follow up another lead before I meet Mr. Craig in Halifax."

The identity of their second mystery caller would wait because Simon was heading to the beach, the one where clothing was optional.

Chapter Five

Simon arrived at the isolated Crystal Crescent Beach at two twenty after several wrong turns on back roads near Sambro Harbour. He changed into less conspicuous sandals, shorts, and T-shirt and ventured toward Nova Scotia's only clothing optional beach. The path traversed 200 metres of the rocky ground with the scrubby growth so common on Nova Scotia's Atlantic coast. It wound its way around huge granite boulders left behind by retreating glaciers thousands of years earlier.

He caught up with a group making their way toward the nude beach and explained his quest. Several recognized Holly and Amelia from the photos he provided. One perceptive woman asked if they were involved in the murder reported on the morning news.

He nodded without comment.

"Is Amelia a suspect?" Simon's informant asked. She appeared well informed considering the brevity of the news report.

"She was Holly's friend. I'm here to learn about Holly and her friends."

A second woman pointed toward the ocean. "Are you heading for our beach? We might be more forthcoming if you weren't so overdressed."

"I'd rather talk here, especially if I must describe anything in court."

"I don't want you mentioning me in court," another woman said.

"Don't worry," a man interjected, "we're doing nothing wrong."

That wasn't true; the nude beach relied on an informal agreement between the civic authorities and the local naturists' society. Nudity was no more legal on Crystal Crescent Beach than it was in Barrettsport's town garden.

The scene reminded Simon of his druggies in Vancouver's Gastown area. Many were willing to talk, but none wanted their names mentioned. "You're welcome to remain anonymous. So, how often did you see them?"

The woman who initially mentioned the news report broke several seconds of silence. "Holly is often here. Amelia came a few times. They're both very friendly."

"With each other?" Simon asked.

"Not that. With others on the beach," she continued. She was well into middle age, and decidedly overweight. Not the type of person Simon expected on a nude beach.

"Amelia's an inherently friendly person, but Holly's a reporter. She always asked questions, getting stuff that might appear in the newspaper."

"Did they come here with other people?" Simon asked.

"Vera and Caroline came more often than Amelia."

"It wasn't Caroline, it was Christine."

"That's right. Christine."

"Do you know their surnames?"

"Sorry," replied the middle-aged mama who first spoke when Simon caught up with them. She'd answered most of his questions. He made a mental note to get her name. "They never said," she added, gazing around.

"Any others?"

"Didn't that purple-haired girl come with Holly?" suggested a younger woman, a more striking one who fit Simon's chauvinistic image of female visitors to a nude beach.

"What can you tell me about her?"

"Not much. She had short, spiky, purple hair, piercings, and tattoos so she looked outlandish, but she was shy and said almost nothing. I only saw her once, and I don't remember her telling us her name." Others nodded their heads.

"What about men?" Simon asked next. "Did they come with men?"

"I never saw them with men. Vera and Christine are lesbians."

"What about Holly and Amelia? Are they also lesbians?" Simon asked.

"I'm not sure. Georgie can answer better than I. Oh, sorry Georgie, I shouldn't have mentioned your name."

"It's okay, I planned to tell Mr. Goodyear anyway."

"Please," Simon interjected, "call me Simon."

"Okay, Simon," Georgie continued. "She thinks I can answer the question because I'm gay, and she's right, we can usually tell. Holly's bisexual, but Amelia's straight. She stood out from the others."

"I should tell you my name and stop this silly secrecy, it's Joyce, Joyce McGrath," said the woman who'd been the main spokesperson.

Simon made a mental note of her name but didn't record it. In fact, he wrote nothing down. Later, he would scribble down the relevant facts.

"Amelia and Holly were friends," Joyce continued, "because they lived in Barrettsport. It's the weirdest place straight out of *the Great Gatsby* with unfriendly rich people. Amelia told me they were among the few young people who weren't part of this impenetrable elite. It's not surprising they got to know each other." She stared at Simon with her head cocked to one side. "She said another was a new detective. Is that you?"

Simon nodded. "I've only been there for a few months and rather busy, so I haven't met everyone. Barrettsport may be odd, but I like it."

"Neither hated the place. But its unusual character brought them together."

"Okay, anything else anyone can tell me?"

"They made a video," noted someone who'd previously said nothing. "We don't like it when people make videos, but they only recorded themselves."

"I've seen it. Ms. Craddock kept her swimsuit on. Is that normal?"

"It doesn't bother us if sympathetic people are reluctant to get undressed. It's our opponents and the voyeurs we try to exclude."

"Anything else?" Simon repeated. No one said anything. "Thank you, everyone. I would appreciate names, addresses, and phone numbers if you're willing, but I won't pressure you. You've been a big help." He pulled out his notebook and distributed copies of his business card. "Phone me if you think of anything."

After collecting a few names and addresses, he drove into Halifax to meet Mr. Craig. At this early stage of the investigation, their murder victim remained an enigma. He hoped her father might fill some gaps.

Simon cooled his heels in the Dr. William D. Finn Centre for Forensic Medicine while RCMP officers and staff from the Medical Examiner Service interviewed Mr. Craig.

Simon understood the role of the ME's office—interviews with family members could aid in their medicolegal investigation of the cause of death—but why were the Mounties butting into his case? Barrettsport Police Department had requested a forensic unit to pick apart the crime scene. The investigation should have been Simon's problem.

Finally, he got his chance to delve into Holly's background.

"She worked in London Ontario as a journalist, her first job after graduating from Ryerson. She was spinning her wheels doing the kind of crap jobs they give to junior reporters," Mr. Craig said. "She got involved with an unsuitable lover at the paper and escaped to Nova Scotia."

"Unsuitable?" Simon asked, "what do you mean by unsuitable?"

"The guy was a jerk, a freelance journalist who used Holly to get his articles past the editors."

"Would she have influence if she was a junior reporter?"

Mr. Craig smirked. "The jerk expected her to use her feminine wiles. And she was prepared to try before I set her straight."

Sometime later, Simon concluded the interview without learning anything about Holly's alleged bisexuality. He'd discovered, however, that her father was an uncaring man who showed none of the sadness he'd expected for someone who'd just learned of his daughter's violent death. The guy was a first-class jerk who appeared oblivious to her interests. *Could a difficult family relationship have contributed to her decision to leave Ontario?*

When Simon arrived at the station Monday morning, Diana Jackson was sitting in his office reading the information he'd recorded on his whiteboard. After his visit to Halifax and a solitary late supper at the Causeway pub, he'd documented everything they had on Holly Craig and Amelia Craddock. His impressions were coming into focus by the time he went home to assemble the furniture he'd purchased two days earlier. Until then, a recliner was his only piece of living room furniture. Now, he also had two tables and another chair.

"Should I add what I've learned?" Diana asked as he entered.

"Tell me first," he replied, tossing his rucksack into a corner.

"I haven't heard from the motel owner, but he wasn't expected until evening. If he doesn't contact us in the next hour, I'll give him a bell."

"I'd like his input before I talk to the Mounties."

"Isn't it early for the forensic report?"

"Yeah, but they were throwing their weight around yesterday, pushing in to talk to Holly's father before I got to him. They told me to expect something this morning."

"What's their angle?"

"No idea. What did you learn from Amelia's, Ms. Craddock's, neighbours?"

Diana consulted her notes. "They've confirmed what she told us Saturday. Two different neighbours saw her between eight and nine, and both saw her leave dressed in the red and white outfit at approximately nine thirty. She talked to one of them, so solid unless there's a massive conspiracy, and these two old dears don't fit my idea of conspirators."

"Anything else?"

"She leads a quiet life with few visitors other than her parents. One confirmed Holly Craig had been there a few times. She's had a few other visitors, both men and women, but no noisy parties. Until about a month ago, she spent most evenings and weekends working on a sailboat at the bottom of her garden. The boat's been moved to the yacht club. Should we be asking around the yacht club?"

"Yeah, but let's keep it low key. We don't want you stomping around like the Keystone Kops. She's not a primary suspect now that we have her whereabouts on Saturday morning nailed down. I don't want to cause her unnecessary trouble."

"You sure? Until we get a precise time of death, we're relying on Ms. Craddock's statement she talked to Ms. Craig at eight. She could have been murdered earlier."

Simon shook his head. "We have her call to the station just after eight and independent evidence the caller was Ms. Craig. Her phone records should confirm it." He looked up and waited until Diana met his gaze. "Ms. Craddock did not bludgeon Holly Craig, but I don't like her behaviour. She's hiding something, so some discrete investigation of her activities and those of their friends Vera and Christine would be in order."

"One more thing. The money to pay for her house."

"Yes?"

"She inherited it from her paternal grandfather. My sources say the grandfather didn't like her father choosing to be a church minister and bypassed him. He left the inheritance that might have gone to the father to be shared by his children. Amelia's an only child, so she inherited the lot, something in excess of five hundred thousand dollars."

"Has it caused a falling out between Amelia and her parents?"

"Apparently not. The neighbours say they get on fine."

"You got all this from the neighbours?"

"Yeah, there aren't many secrets in a small town."

"Well, that gets us to Holly. She was definitely keeping secrets from her neighbours."

"True, but that's why we're here," Diana responded.

"We need to find Holly's lover," Simon said after recounting what Mr. Craig told him. "Keep on top of our motel owner. If the chief's wife doesn't recognize the voices on the station tape, we need to identify the first caller. And find out if one of the protesters tipped Holly off on their plans. But before you start, fill me in on this go-topless organization."

40

"Nothing underhanded or illegal about them. They're an American organization that thinks women have a constitutional right to go topless anywhere and anytime men can. They organize an annual event in a number of cities where women do something to get publicity for their cause."

Simon flipped open his laptop. "Are they all US cities.?"

"They have a website with a list of cities where they expected protests. They're mostly big US cities."

"The constitutional situation in Canada and the US is similar, and we've had protests?"

"Basically, the same, but protests in Canada aren't linked to this group."

"So, our six were tagging along hoping to gain from publicity spin-off from the US activities?"

"It would appear."

"I wasn't here last year, but I understand from the chief that this is new and a complete surprise."

"Totally unprecedented."

"Simon," Chief DeWolfe called out as marched to his office. "I have an answer for you about your tape."

"He doesn't sound too happy," Diana pointed out unnecessarily as the chief's door slammed.

"Can't be about our tape. He might know why the Mounties are messing in our case."

41

Chapter Six

The chief glanced up when Simon entered his office. "Right, Marge says the first caller is Cynthia Ettinger, but why focus on their stupid performance?"

"Because our murder victim planned to attend their protest and cause trouble," Simon replied. "We must establish her rationale."

"Go easy on the three ladies. The mayor's made it abundantly clear he wants the whole issue buried *tout suite.*"

"There were four prominent women, not three. Lisa Powell also participated. Knowing who called will help resolve the remaining loose ends."

"But you don't think these three, sorry four, women could be involved in a grisly murder."

"No, sir, I don't, but we've found too many links between the protest and the murder for us to ignore it."

"I trust you to do it right. Just get it done." The chief paused, scanning Post-it notes Margaret had affixed to his computer. "Are you making any progress on the murder?"

"Yes sir, we're making progress. We're pursuing a solid lead on an unknown male lover."

"And you've heard from the Mounties?"

"I've been told to expect a call. Any idea why?"

Chief DeWolfe shook his head. "Make sure they stay off our turf."

"If they balk, I'll let you know."

"Right. You best get back to it."

Simon strode to Diana's desk. "He's washed his hands of the protest and expects us to promptly solve the murder case. He's providing no insights into why the Mountie's are meddling, but he must know something."

"Consider his perspective. He probably spent Saturday afternoon and Sunday listening to the mayor and the rest of the establishment. Be thankful he's imploring you to solve it without suggesting what sort of villain we must find."

"I'll try, but he's not being helpful. Makes me realize we had an advantage in big bad Vancouver. A simple detective was more isolated from the political crap than he is here."

"We need to ignore the politics and solve this case. I'm counting on you to rescue me from the drudgery of routine policework."

Simon grinned. "Yes, ma'am, we'll solve our mystery and ensure Officer Jackson gets all the credit."

Diana smiled. "No sir, only the portion she deserves."

"Okay, back to work and cut the 'sir' crap, we don't need that."

"Yes, Guv," she muttered as she refocused on her computer screen.

After the call from the RCMP, Simon sauntered to Diana's desk trying to fathom the Mountie's motivation. "Have you heard from our motel owner?"

"I was sorting out my notes before reporting."

"Give me a summary before I leave for Bridgewater?"

"The Mounties phoned. Who are you meeting?"

"Detective Cavanaugh from Halifax, but no indication of their agenda. He okay?"

"I suppose he's okay, not one of the pretentious toffs you often encounter." It sounded like a guarded endorsement.

"What did you learn from the motel owner?" Simon asked.

"Jamal Kasim. He confirmed Holly Craig had been a guest at his motel several times over the past year. He has records of the visits paid for with a credit card. She always arrived alone, but he remembers a male visitor on several occasions. He didn't have a name to associate with this visitor but gave me a good description. It fits with the one you got from Holly's neighbour."

"Sounds like our first positive lead. Visit the motel and get a written statement and copies of any relevant records. Then, cross-reference them with the receipts we found in her desk. There may be credit card chits that identify other hotels."

"Thank God for expense claims and income tax deductions," Diana muttered as she jotted notes.

"And ask about her visitor's car. Someone must have seen his car."

Simon arrived at the Bridgewater RCMP detachment half an hour before his scheduled meeting with Conrad Cavanaugh. He introduced himself to the officers on duty and asked a few questions about interactions between Barrettsport's Police Department and the two closest RCMP detachments. He received polite and helpful responses. When he changed topic and asked about Detective Cavanaugh, their responses became guarded. Were they protecting one of their own or hiding problems between the Bridgewater detachment and the headquarters in Halifax? Or did they have specific problems with Conrad Cavanaugh?

Detective Cavanaugh's arrival ended the discussion. He was as tall as Simon, thirty pounds heavier, and quick to establish a friendly, informal tone that contrasted with the stiff formality of the Bridgewater officer making introductions.

After what seemed like too much forced camaraderie, Cavanaugh plunked a thick folder on the table in their meeting room.

"Preliminary report from our forensic investigation, a narrative of what they saw and did, and copies of photos they took. Results from the various tests are coming, and we'll get them to you. But before we go into details, we need to discuss general guidelines for this investigation."

"What's on your mind?"

"I've worked with the Barrettsport police and your chief got snotty about your jurisdiction. I don't want that to impede us. We'll leave you to conduct your investigation if it's a local crime of passion or any other localized incident. We'll provide you help in areas we're better equipped to deal with, and all we ask in return is that you share information with us. If we discover it's a crime that's external to your community, large-scale fraud, organized crime, drugs or whatever, we'll take over and expect your cooperation."

Cavanaugh tapped the report and charged on before Simon could respond. "This is step one. I've instructed our people to inform you of anything else we learn, and we'll give you copies of any reports we get. You'll be free to inspect the physical evidence in the lock-up here in Bridgewater. So that's my offer. In exchange, I expect your cooperation if we discover it's a non-local crime."

Simon hesitated, trying to hide his consternation. Someone had pressured the forensic people to generate a preliminary report in record time, and Cavanaugh's elaborate explanation of their interaction was unnecessary. He was repeating himself while describing the standard interaction between the Mounties and smaller police forces.

He decided to bide his time until he understood the underlying story. "Sounds good. Unless I'm overruled, I agree."

Simon described their investigation to date and concluded by saying evidence of a male visitor in her apartment was high on his priority list. He also mentioned help investigating Ms. Craig's life before she arrived in Barrettsport two years earlier.

"I'll mention your concern about male visitors to our lab people, and we'll share whatever we dig up on Ms. Craig's past. We'll forward copies of the autopsy report and anything else we come up with, but I can't simply drop things at your station. Will you be working with anyone?"

"Anything sensitive should either go to me or Officer Jackson. And if we're not there, Margaret Summerville in the reception area is entirely reliable. She'll guard material you give her with her life."

Conrad smirked. "Officer Diana Jackson, an imposing black Amazon with a British accent if I remember correctly but very competent. And I bet she's real feisty in bed."

"Yes, that's her, and I agree she's very competent. I'm learning how much I can rely on her, but I know nothing about her amorous proclivities."

"Proclivities! I bet you learned that word from Jackson. If you have no immediate questions, we should adjourn. Time for coffee at Tim's before we hit the road?"

At a corner table as far from the other Tim Hortons donut shop customers as possible, Conrad leaned forward after glancing around. "There's something I wanted to tell you outside our formal meeting. It may have a bearing on your murder case, so you should be aware. Don't even tell our friendly Amazon unless it has direct relevance to the murder."

He gulped half his coffee before continuing. "We've been investigating shady central Canadian property developers who've been operating in Halifax for three years. The town of Barrettsport has come up several times during our investigations, too many times to be a coincidence. But it doesn't fit. There are no Provincial or Federal government buildings other than the post office, and the whole scam revolves around overcharging for government buildings."

"But what's the connection to Ms. Craig's murder?"

"We don't have a solid link. I've been given this murder because it gives me an excuse to poke around Barrettsport. If we find anything relevant to your murder, I'll communicate personally when I'm in town."

"Sounds like a real undercover job. I thought I'd gotten away from that when I left Vancouver."

"We're aware of your Vancouver past and your health problems." Conrad was referring to two periods of stress-related sick leave that contributed to Simon's decision to move east. "If we weren't convinced you could work undercover, we wouldn't trust you with this. I hope we don't cause a recurrence of your ulcers, but it would be unfair and perhaps unsafe to keep you in the dark. And we might need your input."

"Well, you've caught my attention. I hope I get a retainer."

Conrad laughed. "You have your murder case with numerous sweet young things including several society babes in various states of undress. You must console yourself with that as your reward."

"Do I detect a touch of jealousy?" Simon asked, smirking.

"You bet. All I get are the sex workers and strip joint dancers whose tits and heads and demeanours are equally hard. You're getting some nice wholesome ones."

"We'll see, but mine may not be as soft and pliable as you're implying."

Conrad nodded. "It's time to hit the road. I'll keep in touch."

As he headed home, Simon mind was full of divergent thoughts. First, a quick look at the forensic report suggested it was thorough with much useful information, and he'd been promised more in the coming days. Second, he'd discovered a different and more conspiratorial crime that might be occurring under his nose in Barrettsport. And third, he'd received another lesson in the attitude toward nudity in Nova Scotia. Vancouver was blasé about public or private nudity; nudity just didn't excite anyone. But here public toplessness, not even nudity, caused a major fuss. It was rather naïve.

On another level, it seemed less innocent. Detective Cavanaugh's attitude may have been insincere locker room talk he thought appropriate for two officers getting to know each other. If so, it showed an immature high school or university student approach to nudity. And the reaction of the Barrettsport police staff to the six women in their holding cell had also been childish. Given Mrs. Garrett's performance, she probably deserved the negative attention she attracted, but the whole business made him uncomfortable. It brought him back to his misgivings about his promise to take Amelia to the play in Chester.

Chapter Seven

Tuesday, Simon interviewed the women from the topless protest. Cynthia Ettinger provided the information he sought.

"So, the protest was your idea," he suggested after a formally dressed maid brought them tea in a beautifully appointed sitting room overlooking the ocean. The house was less majestic than the homes of other Barrettsport pseudo-aristocrats but still impressive.

"Caroline and I developed the idea together. She wanted the limelight, but it was my idea."

"Why would you conduct such a provocative stunt? You must have known we'd respond."

"We expected a response, but we must bring Barrettsport into the modern world. You should join us, and together we can turn Barrettsport into a Shangri-La on the Atlantic Ocean."

"And Beverley Campbell, Lisa Powell, and Caroline Garrett are part of this grand experiment in social engineering."

"Caroline was also motivated by personal reasons, but yes, Beverley, Lisa, Caroline, and I are committed."

"So, what went wrong? I trust you didn't anticipate spending three hours in our lock-up?"

Cynthia Ettinger calmly poured the tea. "We didn't anticipate the ferocity of Chief DeWolfe's response and Lisa, who was in charge of our stuff, panicked. We expected a confrontation and after we'd made our point, Lisa would have brought us our shirts and we would have dispersed."

"But the chief brought in the cavalry and herded you into our paddy wagon and hustled you off."

Cynthia grinned. *Did she think the episode had been a harmless lark?* "And Lisa couldn't drive a manual transmission car. Funny, don't you think? Caroline's trophy car with six forward gears stymied Lisa, and our plans disintegrated."

"Yeah, I guess, but what about Ms. Craddock, how does she fit in?"

"She doesn't. She agrees with us, but we excluded anyone like Amelia whose career could be damaged."

"And Ms. Craig?" Simon asked.

"I phoned her because we wanted publicity."

"So, you were disappointed when she didn't show up?"

"Actually, I didn't notice. The chief intervened too quickly."

"Let's review where we stand," Simon suggested after he and Diana returned to the station from their various investigations.

Diana plunked herself down and flipped open her notebook. "First, we must remove Ms. Craddock from our list of suspects. Nothing incriminating on the clothes she was wearing when she found the body. I've asked questions at the yacht club and the school where she works, interviewed other neighbours, and proprietors of various businesses. She's an open book, and I've found nothing that contradicts anything she's told us. She's an important witness, but her behaviour isn't suspicious."

Simon shook his head. "Most of it seems kosher and finding the body definitely upset her. No way she faked that. But then sometimes, it's like she's playing with us, treating everything like a big joke."

"I've already explained that. She's flirting with you."

"Then she's succeeding because Thursday night we're going to the play in Chester, but I'm still less than comfortable with her behaviour."

"The way she switches between youthful flirtation and distress is unusual but, I'd say, sincere. I suspect she's been eying you for months and couldn't resist the opportunity to pounce."

Simon considered Diana's comments. "Her friendship with Holly Craig is also hard to understand. Is she someone who's uncertain about her sexual orientation, or just someone between regular romantic attachments?"

"If I'd known you wanted more dirt on Amelia's social life, I should have taken you to lunch at Mildred Wexler's cafe instead of the Traveller's Inn."

"Why is that name familiar?"

"She owns Mildred's Olde English Tea Shoppe. I interviewed her when we checked on Amelia's alibi for Saturday morning."

"I'm aware of the tea shop, but I hadn't made the connection with the witness statement. She's Amelia's neighbour and a member of the families?"

Diana nodded. "She's a real character and a useful source for information on social activities. She's a sort of Miss Marple, but until now she's had no propensity for walking into murder mysteries. And she's as smart as a whip."

"Okay, Amelia's in the clear. What about Holly?"

"That's not been as easy. People recognized her and knew she's a reporter, but none really knew her. And no one links her with a potential lover."

"So, the town's Miss Marple couldn't fill you in on Holly?"

Diana laughed. "Miss Wexler had no insights. Holly's an enigma, seen about town but known by no one."

Simon shuffled papers on his desk. "The forensic report confirms what we suspected. Someone cleaned up thoroughly, leaving no incriminating evidence. A blood trail to the patio door but none outside."

"That suggests he took the murder weapon to the door but wrapped it before taking it outside."

"They also found blood residue in the sink drain, all of Ms. Craig's type. Other than that, he covered his tracks very well."

"Or she," Diana added.

"True, it should still be he or she."

"What about the murder weapon?"

Simon held his hands a metre apart. "Wooden club, cylindrical, approximately ten centimetres in diameter. Wood fragments were sent to the lab."

"And the autopsy report says she was three months pregnant."

"We need to work on that," Simon said as he strode to his whiteboard. "What's next?"

"Consider possible explanations for Holly's murder and eliminate or confirm them."

Simon stood with marker ready. "What would they be?"

"Three possibilities and only one makes sense. First, the murder could be a direct consequence of the protest, but I see no evidence linking them."

"I agree. What's number two?

Diana paused. "Holly's lover murdered her because of something related to her pregnancy or another reason we haven't yet discovered. This is the best possibility."

"We haven't identified the lover or established the motive. But I agree, it's our most promising lead. But before we get into it, what's your third possibility?"

"The violent breakdown of an intimate relationship with Vera, but we have no evidence. It's totally supposition."

"Why Vera? What about Christine, or the girl with the purple hair?"

"Because Vera's number appears in the phone records."

"I doubt it's a lesbian crime of passion, but we haven't followed this lead. It's something we need to do. Any other ideas?"

Diana shook her head. "Where should I start?"

"Contact Vera and investigate her relationship with Holly. We also need to locate the other two and confirm their alibis for Saturday morning."

"We need a drawing of the man who visited Holly in Mr. Kasim's motel."

"You chase Vera and her friends," Simon said. "I'll talk to the Mounties about an identikit expert and proceed with that tomorrow. I'd like to talk to Mr. Kasim, and this will give me a chance. Once we have our picture, we can work on other motels.

Wednesday and Thursday were devoted to the drudgery of police work. Diana called Vera Cruz and others acquainted with Holly and gathered the information to complete their picture of events surrounding their murder. By Thursday afternoon, they had a drawing of their prime suspect, someone who spent time with Holly at several motels and restaurants over the previous few months. He had also been tentatively identified as the visitor to her apartment on the morning of her death. Putting a name to this individual topped their list of high priority tasks.

At four forty-five on Thursday afternoon, Simon arrived at Amelia's cottage on Front Street.

"You look marvellous," he said when he observed her stunning red party dress complete with spaghetti straps and an elaborate sheer overskirt with a black floral pattern. "I'm early. I made the dinner reservation for six fifteen and I didn't want to be late. Is it okay?"

"I'm ready. I've been sitting here like an impatient school girl for at least fifteen minutes, so you're just saving me more anxious waiting." She grabbed a black shawl that matched the overskirt from a hook by the door and hustled him to his car. "I've also been worried we might be cutting it too tightly."

During the drive, they talked about Barrettsport and life for youngish single adults who weren't members of long-established families. They also discussed the frustrations of the younger family members and the general need for changes in the social structure.

"You'll see significant and positive changes in our little town over the next few years," Amelia concluded as Simon parked the car. "You've arrived at an interesting time, and we need to get you involved in our social revolution."

"Something specific?" he asked as he helped her from her seat.

She grinned mischievously as she had during their interview in his office. "The times are achangin'…"

They were early, so they sat in the bar and each ordered a glass of white wine. The bartender brought over a bottle of their house white, an Ontario chardonnay. He suggested they save themselves a few dollars by ordering the bottle and taking it to their table. They accepted his offer, and Simon joked that the waiter must not think he was wealthy enough to afford four glasses.

"It's not like that," Amelia replied. "He was just being helpful."

"You're from around here, aren't you?"

"I grew up a few miles away in Mahone Bay. It's famous for the three large colourful churches you've probably seen along the waterfront. I went to Dalhousie and the Mount, Mount St. Vincent, for university and then I got my job in Barrettsport. So, I haven't ventured far from home."

"What did you study?"

"Bachelor of Arts degree at Dal and then teacher training at the Mount. My real interest at Dal was volleyball. I was on the varsity team and pretty much all my travelling was team trips."

"And you enjoyed yourself?"

"I wasn't a party girl, but I had a good time. At least I did until a disastrous falling out with my boyfriend during my second year at the Mount."

At this point, the bartender generated an untimely break in their conversation by telling them their table was ready. Simon's hopes of learning why Amelia had lived in Barrettsport for three years without any sign of a boyfriend were dashed. Once they were seated, she insisted on hearing about Simon and why he came to Barrettsport, and before they realized it, it was time to leave.

The informal comedy described three middle-class couples who started with very conventional lives. Cracks and crevices developed as they transformed into more interesting and unusual characters. It reminded Simon of Barrettsport's five families. They presented an image of propriety and privilege with noblesse oblige responsibility to the rest of the citizens. Cracks were showing in their public exterior. The topless protest was an obvious crack, and he confidently predicted close examination would reveal others.

He also saw parallels to Amelia. Simon initially saw a proper young schoolteacher interested in establishing her place in Barrettsport society. A different Amelia emerged on Saturday. And tonight, she clearly identified with the actress who let her sexual nature blossom as the play progressed.

After the final curtain, the cast mingled with the audience. Amelia identifying herself to one of the actresses from the protest. Moments later, the three protest actresses and Amelia were having quite a natter. They even dragged Simon into the conversation, joking about the lunches he'd bought them.

Simon pried Amelia away from the chatty actresses, and they returned to Barrettsport. When he pulled up in front of her cottage, she invited him in.

He glanced at his watch before responding. "It's past midnight and I must be up early tomorrow morning."

She turned in her doorway. "You're not unhappy?"

"No, no, I had a great time. But we have a murder to solve."

"We can go out together another time?"

"Of course, I'd love to."

"Then you can sail on my Bluenose in the Saturday afternoon race."

"We'll see. I'm not trying to avoid you, I just can't guarantee I'll be free. I'll phone tomorrow and we'll sort it out. You may want to rethink this offer because I'm really a novice sailor."

"No way, I'm counting on you, Saturday at noon."

"I'll call in the morning," he said reaching down to give her a kiss before returning to his car.

He had a problem. He could no longer pretend he was reluctant to romance Amelia. She had him tied in knots, or as Diana expressed it, she had his knickers tied in knots, and he had to accept it. Tomorrow, he'd ensure he was free Saturday afternoon. And he had one day to remember at least a little of his limited sailing knowledge.

He hadn't crewed on a sailboat in years, and what did Amelia mean by a Bluenose? As far as he knew, Bluenose was a slang term for Nova Scotians or the name of the huge sailing ship on the back of the dime. He'd seen the full-size replica of the schooner *Bluenose* taking tourists for cruises in Halifax Harbour. He doubted it would fit in Barrettsport's inner harbour, definitely not at the yacht club.

Chapter Eight

Friday morning, Simon buried thoughts of romance and returned to his investigation. While Diana searched for the doctor managing Holly's pregnancy, Simon tackled the RCMP crime lab. The DNA analysis of Holly's foetus would generate an irrefutable link between Holly and her lover providing the lover was the baby's father. His contact refused to give the analysis priority claiming they'd expedite the analysis when Simon provided the father's DNA sample.

"But the DNA results will aid our search," Simon insisted. "If nothing else, we'll learn the father's race and perhaps other characteristics that would focus our efforts."

Their reluctance left Simon in a bad temper. The few hundred-dollar job might save days of searching, but petty concerns for costs were inhibiting progress. And the bill would be the Barrettsport Police Department's responsibility, so they weren't even discussing RCMP funds.

After coffee and a brief word with the chief, Simon phoned Amelia.

"Great," she replied after he announced he should be free Saturday. "A short morning sail will give you familiarity with the boat."

Friday evening, Simon discovered a Bluenose was a small sloop-rigged keelboat, a twenty-three-foot-long daysailer designed by William Roue, the designer of the schooner *Bluenose*. Bluenose sloops carried main, jib, and spinnaker handled by three-person crews. The website photographs showed an old-fashioned, narrow boat with minimal freeboard. No wonder Amelia suggested he bring rubber boots and wet gear.

He arrived at Amelia's for his crash course in Bluenose sailing Saturday morning at nine. She invited him into her kitchen.

"Tell me your sailing experience," she suggested after declining help preparing their picnic lunch.

"One summer, I crewed on a small cruising boat, a San Juan 24, out of Vancouver's Kitsilano Yacht Club. It was older than our competition, but nothing like a Bluenose. Four crewmembers, and I was the bottom guy on the totem pole, so mostly there to weigh down the windward rail. If only three showed up, I'd have a more active role."

"Did you carry a spinnaker?"

"Yeah, a main, one of two jibs and a spinnaker. Deciding which jib was a big deal."

Amelia packed the sandwiches and water bottles into a small cooler. "On *Pallas Athena,* we'll want your help keeping the boat flat, but you'll be responsible for the mainsail when we're going upwind. On the off-wind legs, you'll help Jenny Smith, our other crewmember, with the kite."

"The main will be something new."

"You'll get the hang of it."

She passed Simon the cooler and stepped outside after collecting her sailing boots and kitbag.

At the club, they headed straight to the dock. A young man hurried down the gangway behind them. "To the golden goddess?" the yacht club's tender operator asked as he hopped into the launch.

"*Pallas Athena* is an interesting name," Simon said as they manoeuvred around several moored boats. "I think I understand the Athena part, goddess of wisdom was she not, but Pallas?"

"Pallas Athena is another name for the same goddess, one with a darker connotation. In the Greek legends Athena kills her childhood friend Pallas and afterwards, in remorse, takes on her name and becomes Pallas Athena. I thought naming my boat after the goddess of wisdom was appropriate for a teacher, and one with a dark side suited me particularly well."

Amelia stowed their gear in the space under the foredeck. She removed the cover from the main and attached the jib to the forestay while giving Simon a running commentary laced with nautical terms. As she rattled on, Simon recalled the sailing words he once knew. They weren't forgotten, just buried in his memory.

As she raised the main, the breeze blew the boat around until it pointed into the wind, straining on the rope attaching it to its mooring ball. When Simon released her from the mooring, the golden goddess drifted backwards until the sail filled. They were off, maneuvering under mainsail through the mooring field. When they were clear, Simon raised and trimmed the jib, and they were really sailing.

"We're not here for a leisurely Saturday morning sail," Amelia said when Simon relaxed, gazing around. "Cleat the jib, perch on the windward side, and take the mainsheet."

Amelia was a demanding teacher. As they beat back and forth across the harbour for the next hour, Simon learned exactly how she wanted him to handle the main during the windward legs.

Finally, she relented. "Enough for your first lesson. Back to the club where we can relax until we do it again for real."

With *Pallas Athena* tied to the club's dock, they repaired to the clubhouse for coffee and pastries while they waited for Jenny. Simon sat with Amelia in Adirondack chairs on the yacht club lawn enjoying his late morning snack. He checked out the activity around them as more members arrived for the Saturday afternoon race. Amelia talked with many of them and Simon was polite when introduced to various people, but mostly he watched and compared this yacht club to his Vancouver one. The ostentatious Barrettsport Yacht Club was part of the staid old Barrettsport society. Kitsilano Yacht Club, the third biggest club in a large city, was a much more modest creation of regular folk who were interested in sailing.

Simon noticed Selectman Matthew Garrett, the husband of one of the women they'd arrested the previous Saturday, talking to David Adams, the second of the town's three selectmen, and two others. They looked like a group of delinquent schoolboys sneaking smokes while watching for teachers. Their furtive appearance caught Simon's attention, and he wondered what they were discussing.

"Who's with Matthew Garrett and David Adams?" Simon asked Amelia when he perceived a break in her conversation with various passers-by.

"One is Mr. McGuire, the town's legal counsel, and the other is Richard Campbell, another lawyer."

"You should watch them for a minute. You'd swear they have something to hide."

Amelia laughed. "You're being a suspicious cop. They're probably dissecting their latest round of golf or maybe something about investments."

She was probably right. They were wearing their golf club blazers and everyone knew Matthew Garrett looked after the investments of various Barrettsport family members. But Simon couldn't shake the idea they looked guilty as hell.

At eleven forty-five Jennifer Smith, a teenaged member of another pseudo-aristocratic Barrettsport family, arrived, and they prepared for battle. Simon stood on the dock as Amelia and Jenny fiddled with various ropes and perused the competition. He remembered that Athena was also a goddess of war, so appropriate for two warrior women who clearly treated this afternoon's race as a battle.

They cast off and sailed to the vicinity of the start line. Amelia and Jenny discussed wind and waves and weather and strategy as they munched their sandwiches while sailing back and forth through the starting area. Their discussion focused on the high cirrus clouds and the unusual wind direction. Simon relaxed and watched the mayhem as boats congregated in the confined piece of ocean.

Avoiding collisions in the increasingly crowded start line became a concern. Amelia guided *Pallas Athena* to an area where they could watch the boats starting before the Bluenoses in relative tranquility.

At twelve fifty, a shotgun blast drew everyone's attention to a small motor cruiser anchored in the inner harbour. The starting line was between the motorboat and a nearby navigational buoy. The first class would be officially racing ten minutes after the gun, with the Bluenoses starting ten minutes later. Amelia and Jenny made ready for battle, and Simon prepared to do his bit.

The Bluenose race evolved into a battle with a red boat skippered by Jeremy Witherspoon, the scion of another Barrettsport family, and Jenny's archenemy on the race course. As the race progressed, the rest of the Bluenose fleet lagged farther behind the two leaders.

Pallas Athena and the unnamed red Bluenose were neck and neck whenever their courses intersected as they flogged their way around the race course. When they converged for the final time near the finish line, they were side by side. A blast from the committee boat's gun for the winner was followed by a horn for the runner-up.

"Great race, Amelia," Jeremy called over as the crews scurried to lower the spinnakers. "Regardless of the winner, you made it tight. Drinks on me in the clubhouse."

After they had *Pallas Athena* back on her mooring with the sails and other gear tidied away, Amelia hailed the tender, and they returned to shore. Jenny rushed off to tell her friends how they'd vanquished her archenemy Jeremy, and Simon carried the jib and spinnaker to Amelia's storage locker in the clubhouse basement.

"What's with Jenny's dislike of Jeremy?" he asked. "A proper upper-class type, but is he a bad person?"

"Family rivalry. They're cousins and sailing's a big deal in both families. Jenny wants to be the number one sailor, so beating Jeremy is important. I hope we beat him, but I don't think we did."

"Because I'm such a beginner."

"Definitely not. We did the best we have all summer. Come on," she said, giving him a big kiss, "let's get to the bar and order expensive drinks on

Jeremy's tab. He'll insist on paying all afternoon. Then, you're invited to my place for dinner. I promised you a reward for a job well done."

The kiss caught Simon by surprise, and his positive reaction was further proof he shared Amelia's interest in a more intimate relationship. But things were progressing too quickly, and he had her role in his case to consider. "Wasn't I replacing someone who couldn't make it today? And I remember nothing about a reward."

Amelia shook her head. "No way. He was a summer visitor who's gone home, and you made a real contribution to our success. I don't care if I mentioned it or not, you deserve a reward. Let's go drinking on Jeremy's tab, and then..." She smiled that mischievous smile. No doubt about it, Amelia had plans for the evening.

They entered the clubhouse at four. Jeremy Witherspoon leaned against the bar with the practiced nonchalance of someone mimicking Humphrey Bogart in Casablanca or Jay from the Great Gatsby.

"This is the Witherspoon table," Amelia whispered as he escorted them to a prime table overlooking the harbour. "Mere mortals aren't generally permitted here."

"Now, Amelia, be generous," Jeremy scolded her. "I invite mortals to our table at least twice a year."

"Thank you for the honour," Amelia responded, trying to ignore that he'd caught her whispering too loudly. "This is Simon Goodyear. Simon, Jeremy Witherspoon."

"And these two ruffians," said Jeremy, looking at his two crewmembers already sitting at the table, "are Jacko Smith, Jenny's big brother, and Tony Wexler. Will Cousin Jenny join us?"

"Later. She's busy bragging about our race with her friends."

"I hope she's not too disappointed. I heard we won by a foot." He made an imperious gesture, and a waiter appeared with five full martini glasses and an elegant dispenser that looked large enough for several rounds.

"I should be happy Jenny's not here. She is too annoying. I expected a rude gesture when you crossed ahead on the first leg. You must be having success, Amelia dear, keeping her under control." Jeremy turned to Simon. "Or was it her fear of the police?"

"Are you the new police detective?" Tony asked. "The one who arrested Aunt Caroline last week?"

Simon shook his head. "I'm the one who let her go."

"And what about the murder?" Jacko added. "Did Holly's gay friends do her in?"

Jacko's comment got Simon's attention. How did Jacko know Holly had gay friends? She'd kept her friendships secret from almost everyone in Barrettsport, but Jacko had no qualms about mentioning them. Something to consider, but not until tomorrow. Today, he owed it to Amelia to stay focused on the present.

Jeremy deflected the conversation. "You know Simon can't talk about his case. Let's give him a break and consider other things, like the speed of the golden goddess. You had her going well today." Jeremy gazed at Amelia, turning on the charm. "Here's to Amelia, Simon, and Cousin Jenny who I see in the doorway—the toughest competition we've had all season. I thought you had us, and it would have been fitting. And another toast," he said after everyone put down their glasses, "to Simon, the golden goddess's secret weapon."

He then welcomed his cousin showing no sign of the criticisms he'd made earlier. "Welcome young cousin and well done, you gave us a scare. Would you like a martini? I'll give you a little one if you promise not to tell your mother."

Jenny squeezed a chair in next to Simon. "Yes, please. And I'm claiming the credit for Simon's sailing prowess. It was me that trained him."

"You may have done a good job training Simon to work with you on the boat, but you need Amelia's help with your grammar," Jeremy replied. He filled the martini glass the waiter produced for Jenny and everyone else's.

"Don't worry, Simon, you needn't arrest us. None of us will be driving home. We live close enough to walk."

Later, Jeremy refilled all the glasses except Jenny's, and when Simon and Amelia left, they had on quite a buzz. Jenny rejoined her friends, but Jeremy, Jacko, and Tony stayed for another round, or possibly two, from the apparently bottomless dispenser.

As they departed the yacht club arm and arm, Amelia gave the clubhouse a messy salute. "Thank you, Barrettsport Yacht Club, you've given me a day to remember. And the best is yet to come."

The race committee chairman had entered the clubhouse between the second and third rounds. He confirmed that Jeremy had beaten them by less than a metre, but that hadn't dampened Amelia's enthusiasm. She skipped down the street like a kid considering the wonderful treats in a candy store.

Chapter Nine

Simon willed himself to work at eight Sunday morning. It wasn't easy because he hadn't returned to his home in the big apartments until one in the morning. His refusal to succumb to the romantic attraction he and Amelia clearly shared had damaged a nearly idyllic day. But he'd vowed when he moved east to approach relationships in a more thoughtful and mature manner. And Amelia continued to be a person of interest in his murder investigation. He could only hope she'd appreciate the reasons for his reticence and allow time for their relationship to grow.

Diana's progress report, propped on his desk blotter, indicated a late morning visit from Detective Cavanaugh. As planned, he had Saturday off, she would have Sunday, and they would return invigorated to the investigation on Monday. Good plan, but they were nowhere near solving anything. Generating the necessary enthusiasm would be difficult.

He stared at the information on his whiteboard, trying to identify something they'd missed. But his mind kept wandering back to the previous evening. He abandoned work and let Amelia take over his thoughts. If he gave her an hour, it might improve his focus. He leaned back in his chair, letting his mind wander.

The previous afternoon they strolled from the yacht club to Amelia's where she placed a casserole in the oven. While dinner cooked, they wandered around Barrettsport discussing why the town appealed to Amelia. After dinner, she showed him her waterfront cottage. Then they sat in the garden on the warm late August evening drinking coffee and reminiscing about the afternoon's race until a shower chased them indoors.

Inside, things deteriorated rapidly. Amelia was clearly bedroom-bound, but Simon steered her to the living room and engaged in gentle foreplay interspersed with a discussion of where they were headed. She slowly came around as he explained why they should let their relationship develop more gradually. When he left, she seemed relieved they hadn't rushed ahead. But it was all rather tentative, and a golden opportunity had been squandered.

After leaving Amelia's cottage, Simon walked to North Point and sat near the lighthouse contemplating the mess he'd made of his first serious romantic relationship. But all was not lost. They'd agreed to sail together in the following Saturday's race, and Amelia had made it clear she expected him to take responsibility for other romantic initiatives. He walked home determined to solve the mystery of Holly Craig's murder and get on with the serious business of wooing Amelia.

Conrad Cavanaugh arrived from Halifax at 11 a.m. and dumped a stack of file folders on Simon's desk. "I've created a summary of our construction fraud investigation with links to Barrettsport highlighted. We want you to monitor relevant events and activities in Barrettsport and relay any observations you make."

Simon picked up the first report, scanned a few pages, and set it aside. "What about Holly Craig?"

Cavanaugh scowled before consulting his notebook. "She's a hardworking and resourceful investigative journalist who reported on several important stories in south-western Ontario before packing up and moving east. We found no evidence of unethical behaviour or problems in her professional or personal life that explained the move."

"That's odd. We're seeing a flighty, unethical reporter writing fluffy, frivolous stories. Also, her father mentioned nothing about her success as a journalist and said she moved here because of a love affair that went wrong."

Cavanaugh shook his head. "Looks like you have a puzzle to solve."

"Yeah."

Conrad extracted a laptop from a knapsack and dumped it on the stack of file folders. "That's her computer." He threw a CD onto the pile. "Deleted files we recovered. We've been through it and found nothing useful, but we're focused on our investigation, not her love life. Might help your efforts."

Simon nodded as he moved the disc to a safer location. "Anything else?"

"That's it. I said we'd keep you informed, and I've done so. Now, where's a convenient pub for a quick bite before driving back to town?"

After lunch at the Causeway Pub, Simon reviewed progress on his two cases. Cavanaugh's attitude—disdainful lack of concern for anyone's objectives other than his own—had been annoying, but irrelevant. He had produced useful background info on Holly Craig's life in Ontario. Simon needed to ignore Cavanaugh and focus on his two major problems, the topless protest and Holly Craig's murder.

The topless protest represented the struggle between traditionalists striving to keep the town mired in the early decades of the twentieth century, and a second faction embracing the twenty-first century. At another level, it was a struggle between the old families and the newcomers. But it wasn't a clear distinction because some of the old guard, including Mrs. Ettinger, were aligned with the newcomers.

The town's political and social structure was modelled on the New England class distinctions more than a hundred years earlier when rich families prevailed. It wasn't like the English class system where noble ancestry trumped all else. Established wealth and family longevity were the key factors. His interview with Mrs. Ettinger, his discussions with Mildred Wexler at the Tea Shoppe, and most recently, his experience at the yacht club, were a crash course in Barrettsport society.

Mrs. Ettinger was a member of the prominent families but also a leader of the push for change. She and Mrs. Garrett organized the protest as one small step in the fight to loosen up the town. She convinced Ms. Campbell and Ms. Powell, two idealistic young women who were from prominent families, to join them, and hired the three actresses. Mrs. Ettinger leaked their plans to the police and Ms. Craig. Ms. Powell was surprised by the arrests and had problems with Ms. Garrett's car. She didn't show up at the police station with their clothes when she should have. Then, Ms. Craig got herself murdered and didn't cover the story. Holly Craig brought Amelia into the action to add spice to her story.

Mrs. Garrett didn't appear devoted to the fight for social change, so her personal motives were obscure. But Simon knew she and her selectman husband were having marital difficulties, so reasonable to assume she wanted to get back at him. It appeared, however, that none of this related to the murder. *But could he be sure?*

Simon's understanding of the murder was murkier. The eyewitness observation of a gentleman caller on the morning of the murder and the discovery of an illicit lover at various motels were their strongest leads. They also suspected Ms. Craig had a lesbian relationship. They didn't know how that meshed with her male lover and her pregnancy.

They had her most recent phone bill and occasionally or frequently called numbers to chase down. Now they had her computer, so something else to investigate. Conrad's comments didn't leave Simon with much hope, but he fired it up.

Three hours later, he slammed the laptop shut in disgust. The damn thing was useless. It contained articles written for various newspapers and magazines, and related information downloaded from the internet. It had spreadsheets with expenses for various investigations and work-related emails, but no personal information. The computer was as pristine as her apartment, representing a fictitious life of all work and no play. There had to be another cell phone and another computer with emails and other records from her personal life. And why would someone make such an effort to keep her private life so private?

The hint of a lesbian lover was their most confusing new lead. The people at Crystal Crescent Beach seemed convinced Holly was bisexual, and Jacko Smith at the yacht club had referred to Holly's gay friends. But Vera Cruz was evasive when they asked her about Holly's sexual orientation. Tomorrow, he could send Diana to interview Vera's partner Christine. Perhaps she would be more forthcoming, and there was the girl with the purple hair. Vera denied knowing her, but Diana said she couldn't hide her apprehension when the girl was mentioned.

Finding her wouldn't be easy. Hair colour could be changed, and the piercings and tattoos the beachgoers described weren't distinctive. It would be like searching for a Goth girl's earring in a steampunk trash heap.

A phone call when he was preparing to leave after a frustrating day, revived Simon's enthusiasm. A cultured English voice announced, "I can identify Holly Craig's boyfriend, and it will only cost you a pint."

Chapter Ten

"Please, sir, I need your name and an explanation," Simon said when his caller failed to elaborate.

"Too dangerous. I'll be at the Rumrunner in Liverpool until seven. If you're not interested, it's your loss."

Simon sighed. The guy's attitude was incredible. "I need a name. Otherwise, how will I find you?"

"Charles. Tell the bartender you're looking for Charles, and he'll point me out."

The line went dead.

Simon approached Tom Kerry, that afternoon's duty constable. "Are you aware of an informant with an English accent named Charles? Is he reliable, someone I should take seriously?"

Tom laughed. "Everyone knows Charles Butterworth. I'm surprised you haven't run into him before now."

"So, I should ignore his call?"

"Does he want you to meet him at a pub?"

"Yeah."

"I'd go if you're not busy. He's unlikely to provide concrete information, but he's an entertaining guy, an English remittance man, but well read, and entertaining. And sometimes he surprises us."

"So, he's trying to cadge a beer?"

Another laugh. "More likely he'll buy you one. He's usually looking for an audience while he vents about the Prime Minister."

As Kerry predicted, Butterworth didn't reveal the identity of Holly's lover. But he added a new wrinkle to the investigation. How did Butterworth learn they were searching for a lover?

Monday morning, Chief DeWolfe made matters worse. He announced that circumstances beyond his control necessitated Diana's return to her normal duties as a police constable.

"Give it a week," the chief said when Simon objected. "Then we can reassess."

Before returning to his office, Simon located Diana. He needed to determine how much support she could now provide.

"Evans fell from a bloody tree," Diana announced before Simon opened his mouth. "He received facial cuts requiring stitches and a compound fracture needing an operation."

"Left forearm," Margaret Summerville called from her station.

Simon took several steps toward her switchboard. "How long will he be laid up?"

"Should know later today."

"I hope he's okay, but he picked a lousy time. We were finally making progress on our murder, and now it's bound to go more slowly." He perched on the corner of Diana's desk. "Can you find time to go through the numbers from Holly's phone and identify who they belong to?"

"I can help," Margaret interjected.

"Sort it out between you," he said, and then added more quietly to Diana, "we need names that might correspond to her lovers, male or female."

"We can do it," Diana announced loudly enough for Margaret to hear. "Margaret can link the numbers to names and addresses, and I can identify individuals who relate to our case."

"I'll visit Vera and Christine. That's the place to start if we're to establish a female lover."

Diana shrugged. "I'd do that if I could, but it won't fly."

Simon shook his head. "I should talk to them. I might also try pressing the Crystal Crescent crowd."

"Anything else we can do?"

"We need to find Holly's doctor, and Cavanaugh returned her computer. Check the content for anything I missed. But, let's not push the chief's patience too far. Sort out the phone records, and then consider trolling through the computer."

Simon returned to his office thinking the chief's bombshell would be less devastating than he initially anticipated. Diana clearly thought she would have time to pursue the case, and now they had Margaret's active contributions.

At ten thirty, he stood outside a small, well-kept house between Barrettsport and Bridgewater.

Before he rang the bell, the door opened revealing a petite woman in her late twenties or early thirties. She had blond hair and wore shorts and a T-shirt but no shoes.

"Hello, Detective Goodyear. When Amelia described you, I thought she was tormenting me with her fondness for all things Greek, but I can see you as her Adonis on *Pallas Athena*."

"That's quite the opening line," Simon replied, smiling. "I'm Detective Goodyear, and you must be Christine…"

"Nesbitt but call me Christine."

"Then you should call me Simon."

She nodded. "Come in, Simon. I'll get us coffee, then I'll try to answer your questions. Vera already talked to Officer Jackson, and I don't see what I can add."

Perhaps not a lot about Holly, Simon thought, but definitely more about her friendship with Amelia. He'd just learned they were much better friends than he'd previously realized.

A few minutes later she brought two coffees, one black and the other with cream, into the living room. She gave the black one to Simon. "Black with no sugar, that's what Amelia told me."

"You're well informed."

"She's told me about you, including your exploits on and off the race course." She paused for a moment. "Amelia and I are good friends, obviously we don't agree on sexual partners but we share our secrets."

"So, you're old friends."

"Since we were students at the Mount a few years ago."

"Interesting, but I didn't come to discuss Amelia. We need to understand Holly and her life in Nova Scotia. We're hoping you can help us fill a big gap in our knowledge."

Christine gave him a sour look. "A lot of hoping, if you ask me."

"Perhaps, but it's what we must do. We never know which investigations will lead anywhere."

"But tracking those dead ends causes innocent people grief."

"That might happen, but we can't avoid it."

She sighed with her hand to her forehead in a theatrical gesture. "Vera and I met Holly because of my friendship with Amelia. The four of us have done many things together including the visits to Crystal Crescent Beach. I've been trying to remember anything from our friendship that may be useful, but nothing comes to mind."

"Several informants told us Holly was bisexual. Any comment?"

Christine stiffened and clenched her fists. "She didn't have a relationship with me or Vera!"

"That's not what I meant. Are you aware of other women Ms. Craig was involved with?"

"I'm not."

"But you don't deny there could be other women."

"I wouldn't dispute that. But Holly was a private person and never mentioned anyone. And she didn't tell Amelia."

"Can you be sure?"

"Amelia's not one of us. Holly wouldn't tell her."

Christine's statement acknowledged she knew Holly was gay and suggested she had some knowledge of Holly's female lover. "A woman with tattoos and purple hair?" Simon asked before sipping his coffee.

"You mean in relation to Holly and a possible lover?"

"Yes, someone Holly might have known."

She looked at the ground. "I don't think so."

"Someone who visited Crystal Crescent Beach with Holly?"

"Definitely not."

"You sure? A witness placed a girl with purple hair with the three of you."

"Well, she's wrong, she wasn't there any time I was."

Christine seemed adamant, so Simon tried another tack. He would get back to Vera about the girl later.

"Do you have Ms. Craig's cell phone number?"

"Yes," she said reeling off a number from memory. It was the one Simon already had.

"Another number?"

"She had a landline at her apartment."

"Not a landline, another cell phone?"

She stood, leaving her mug precariously close to the table's edge. "I can check our phone book." She returned a minute later with a tattered address book. "There's another number written by Holly's. But this book's an awful mess." S he showed it to him. "It's hard to say if it refers to Holly or someone else."

"That number means nothing to you, someone else's number perhaps?"

"I don't think so. I'll ask Vera, she may place it."

"Please. Call me or Officer Jackson if you remember anything that may relate to Holly."

"If we have anything, I promise, we'll call."

"One last thing. Did Ms. Craig talk about her life before she moved to Nova Scotia and her reasons for coming here?"

Christine shook her head. "Not really. She was a reporter in Ontario, but I don't remember her telling us why she moved."

"Then, I should be on my way. Thank you for coffee."

Simon gave the new phone number to Diana when he returned to the station and disappeared into his office to consider the dates when Holly rented motel rooms. By ten past four when Diana stopped in his office doorway, he was cranky because of his lack of progress and hungry because he hadn't stopped for lunch.

"You look ready to explode," she said. "You should either come to the pub for a beer or visit Amelia. I'm sure she could deal with your frustration."

"Diana, is your shift over?"

"Yes, sir, I've come to report on today's progress. The number you gave me is not an active cell phone number, and I can see no link between previous users of this number and our case. Same goes for other combinations starting 221 or 223, et cetera."

"Damn," Simon replied, "I hoped that was a breakthrough."

"Sorry, but it wasn't. The numbers associated with Holly's phone are also disappointing. They're all associated with her work, numbers for hotels where she rented rooms, various newspapers, business, et cetera. Not a single private number in the whole list, except for Vera and Christine."

"But she called others, Amelia for one. So what phone did she use? And where is it?"

"The murderer probably took it e when he cleaned up the scene. He took the phone and disposed of it."

"But the phone bills and contract? He couldn't have found all those."

"Why not? He was very thorough, and she was so damned organized she made it easy for him."

"We still need the number."

"What number did Amelia or anyone else use when they phoned Holly?"

"Shit, that's right. I've just assumed they phoned the number we already had. But they didn't. I'll contact Amelia and get her number for Holly."

74

He got her recorded message. "Amelia, it's Simon. Call me as soon as you get this. It's important."

Diana smiled. "Okay, we're making progress. You look happier already."

"But I have another question. Why was Vera and Christine's number the only private one on the phone with the business numbers?"

"Perhaps they were business contacts first and became friends later."

"That's not what Christine said, but I can check into it. You should go home. You're off shift and not getting paid for this. By tomorrow morning I'll have the number and you can dig up the records. Go home and pamper your kids."

"Okay, I'll go. No point having both of us waiting for the call."

After Diana clocked out, Simon sat in his office considering Amelia's friendship with Christine. Christine, or possibly Vera, must have shot the Crystal Crescent Beach video, but she said nothing about Christine's role or their long-standing friendship. And Simon was convinced they knew about Holly's lesbian lover.

What were they hiding?

Chapter Eleven

When Amelia finally responded to his call at three thirty Tuesday afternoon, Simon's frustration was evident to everyone in the police station. They were certain Holly had a second cell phone, but without the device, it's phone number or the name and address she'd used when she acquired it, they had no way to trace it.

"Hi Simon," she said when he picked up. "I just got your message. What's so important?"

"Why didn't you call?"

"Geez, I got up early yesterday to go to Halifax, and I forgot my cell."

"Sorry, I didn't mean to jump on you. We need Holly Craig's cell phone number, and I thought I could get it from you, but now we've wasted a day."

"What about the phone company? Can't you guys access private information in cases like this?"

"We do have access, but she apparently had this phone under an assumed name, and there's no sign of the damned thing, so it's not that easy."

"Okay, calm down. I'll give you her number but then I must unload my groceries. There's frozen stuff melting in today's heat. Can you call me later?"

"Okay, but we're busy, so it may be tomorrow."

He rushed the number over to Diana's desk. "Here's the number, do your magic."

She was in his office minutes later.

"Got it sorted out already?"

"I've requested the records, they should arrive in minutes. But something more important came up. I just got off the phone with one Carlotta Ann

Leach. She called because Christine Nesbitt phoned her and said we wanted to talk. She's Holly's lover and has a computer and other stuff we might want. I said I'd go right over."

"But what about your kids? You'll be off shift in five minutes, and they'll be expecting you home."

She shrugged her shoulders. "It's okay, Travis can handle them. He's done this often enough, it won't faze him."

"Right. Travis the long-haul trucker. I forgot about him. Sounds like he's more than just a lodger."

"He is. But it's complicated, and I don't want to explain everything. I'll be back in an hour."

Fifty minutes later Diana returned with a laptop computer that looked identical to the one they'd taken from Holly's apartment, and two boxes of paper records, all properly bagged and tagged.

"Poor kid, she's despondent—twenty-one or twenty-two and grieving all alone because their relationship was a big secret."

"Christine obviously knew about it. Why wasn't she helping, and why didn't Christine tell me about her?"

Diana shrugged her shoulders. "That's for you to discover. I told her you'd be around tomorrow. But tonight, we have a treasure trove to explore."

"What about Travis and your kids? Shouldn't you be going home?"

"No way, mister. This is our big breakthrough and I'm not missing it. I phoned Travis. He has everything under control, so my evening's free."

Diana's English reserve had cracked. Simon was surprised at the childlike enthusiasm she exuded. She was committed to the investigation and giving it priority, but had her enthusiasm clouded her judgement? A secret lover, if spurned, was a candidate for their murderer. "Did Ms. Leach provide an alibi for Saturday morning?"

"Waitressing from seven until noon at the coast road diner. The owner confirmed it, said Saturday mornings are busy. He would have noticed a missing waitress."

"And the pregnancy?"

"She admitted she knew Holly was pregnant but offered no explanation."

Simon nodded at the booty Diana had collected. "We'll need confirmation of her alibi and insight into her knowledge of the pregnancy, but these have priority. Should we go somewhere to eat before we begin?"

"Let's at least catalogue everything. Then you can decide if we should keep working or leave it for tomorrow. And what about the phone records, did they arrive?"

"Yup. The current month's calls are here, and I've identified many of the numbers, so they're tonight's first discovery. But it pales compared to the computer and these boxes. Are we certain the computer was Holly's, and what about the password?"

"Ms. Leach said it was Holly's and gave me the password she used if Holly phoned her requesting something."

"Did Holly always leave it at Ms. Leach's place?" Simon asked.

"She apparently only took the computer with her if she planned to return to Carlotta's, not to her Barrettsport apartment."

"Shows how hard Holly worked to keep her two lives separate. We need to determine why. It can't have been just to keep the two lovers secret. Computer or boxes? Your choice."

"I'll take the boxes."

An hour and a half later Simon sat back and waited for Diana to finish.

She finally looked up from neat stacks of papers extracted from the boxes. "Did we find real treasure?"

"I think so, where should we start?"

"With the phone records I was chasing before I left for Carlotta's?"

"Okay, exhibit one is our investigation of Holly's secret cell phone. We have a copy of this month's traffic, and we can get the older records tomorrow. I identified most of the numbers. There were many of the ones we expected like Amelia's and various others who were probably social acquaintances. Definitely her personal rather than her business, phone. One name that caught my eye was Matthew Garrett."

"That's the husband of the Caroline I arrested on day one of this little adventure. His appearance fits with our identikit picture, doesn't it?" Diana asked.

"Pretty well. Mr. Garrett just jumped to the top of my list of contenders for the job of Holly's secret boyfriend."

"What did the computer tell you?"

"Not a great deal I can immediately link to the murder. It's mostly word files related to the construction scandal Conrad Cavanaugh's been working on. More to read, but they seem to focus on a potential Barrettsport link. Also, material downloaded from the internet."

Diana looked annoyed. "I haven't heard anything about this."

"I'm also mostly in the dark. It's an RCMP investigation involving Cavanaugh that wasn't seen as involving Holly or related to our murder investigation, so we've been on the outside. Now we have an obvious link to Holly, and we might find something that links to our murder."

"That's it for the computer, no mention of Mr. Garrett?"

"Not yet, but I haven't read every file. What about the boxes?"

"One of them contains records relating to Ms. Leach and her house, plus phone bills for Holly's second phone. They give us months of calls to and from her phone. The documents in the second box meant nothing to me, but now I realize they're linked to your construction scandal. Some predate her arrival in Nova Scotia."

"That's interesting."

"Does it suggest she worked on this before she came to Barrettsport and moved here to pursue the investigation?"

Simon nodded. "And that leaves us with a major problem."

"Why?"

"We have considerable scandal related information to pass on to the Mounties. And they'll be all over our case now that Holly's linked to the scandal."

Diana stood, shaking her head. "Having the Mounties meddling in local investigations is nothing new, and something we must accept. But as long as the murder investigation is ours, we have several new leads starting with Matthew Garrett."

"We can probably link Mr. Garrett with the motels, but not necessarily with the murder." Simon paused and looked at his watch. "It's almost seven. Let's lock everything up and go for dinner. Unless you'd rather go straight home."

"I'm up for the Causeway Pub. It's right on my way home."

"Perfect, and it's on me. Tomorrow, I'll bring the chief up to speed, and get you back on the case. We'll inform the Mounties about the link to the construction scandal."

After dinner, Simon returned to the station to copy the document files from Holly's second computer. He took the memory stick home where he read files until he could stay awake no longer. He went to sleep knowing their case was much bigger than anything he'd previously imagined without any idea where it would take them.

Chapter Twelve

Wednesday morning, Simon read more of Holly's prodigious output while waiting for a visit with Chief DeWolfe. Finally, at ten fifteen, the chief was free.

"We made progress yesterday evening," Simon began as he pulled the office door closed.

"What do you mean we, I thought you were working alone."

"I'm trying to, but Diana received a call late yesterday afternoon. It was an important witness, and we needed to treat her gently, so Diana visited after her shift ended." Simon paused waiting for the chief to stop reading the document he'd been studying when Simon entered his office. "We spent two hours going through the information the witness gave Diana before she went home. So, a few unpaid hours at her request."

"We can't pay overtime or expect staff to work without pay, so avoid any more of this." Simon nodded his acceptance, but he wasn't really happy. Evans was on sick leave so his salary should have been available to pay for a little overtime. The chief continued. "What did you learn?"

Simon tried to ignore the overtime question as he described Holly's investigations. He concluded with the immediate bottom line for the chief. "The Mounties are aware of this activity, but not Ms. Craig's involvement. We must inform them."

"Excellent. It's always good to help the Mounties if it doesn't impact our cases."

Simon shifted in his seat. Chief DeWolfe appeared preoccupied and only marginally interested with the implications. "But that's the problem. We also acquired phone records for a second cell phone Ms. Craig had under an assumed name. These records should lead us to Ms. Craig's male lover, the one she shacked up with in various motels. One of Barrettsport's prominent citizens becomes our prime candidate for the lover's role."

The chief looked up from a document he'd been perusing while Simon spoke. "Should we give these phone records to the Mounties?"

"I suspect not. I see no link to the fraud investigation so we can say they're personal phone records we need to continue our murder investigation."

"So, where's the rub?"

"We can keep the names to ourselves for now. But, once the Mounties establish a link between Ms. Craig and their investigation, they'll meddle in our murder inquiry. Then they'll demand this information."

"That's my problem. Until you hear otherwise, the murder investigation is ours, and we need to see progress."

Simon stood, anticipating his imminent dismissal, but he had one additional concern. "Several Barrettsport citizens appear in Ms. Craig's investigation. I can't say how important they are, but they're in there, and they appear to be wearing black hats."

"You sure you're not jumping to conclusions."

"Perhaps, but I didn't want to ship this stuff off without telling you."

"Your intuition may be correct. For the past year, I've been quietly investigating unethical business activity at the mayor's behest. It might blow wide open."

"Perhaps not, the RCMP investigation is an undercover effort."

"Then we have time, but a sinister cloud hangs over our little town. If I were a betting man, I'd lay odds there's a link with Cavanaugh's investigation." The chief straightened his back and slapped closed the folder with the document he'd been studying. "None of that matters right now. Call Cavanaugh, repeat what you told me, give them everything directly related to their investigation, but keep copies of everything that mentions Barrettsport or our citizens. Then get on with your murder investigation while it's still ours."

Simon frowned. Chief DeWolfe knew more about Cavanaugh's mysterious investigation than he'd admitted. *Had he been consulting that file during most of the conversation? If so, why was he keeping me in the dark on a case that was clearly relevant to our own?* "I'm on it. But I need Jackson to help with the investigation."

The chief nodded. "I'll manage it somehow. And you and I will meet Cavanaugh and the regional RCMP manager to determine how we proceed. I don't want the murder investigation to disappear if they're focused on the fraud."

After leaving Chief DeWolfe's office, Simon reviewed the material Diana categorized as Carlotta Leach's personal records. Returning it would generate another interview with Ms. Leach and further investigation of her relationship with Holly.

Simon located her house down an obscure back road in an unfamiliar part of the county. It was on the waterfront to the east of Hunter's Creek. Could the navigational buoy he glimpsed from her driveway be the first turning point in Saturday's yacht race?

A young woman greeted him after he rang the bell. "You must be Detective Goodyear, otherwise I cannot explain why you have one of my boxes."

"Correct, and you must be Carlotta Leach." She looked very young and curvy and quite attractive if you ignored her excessive pallor, tattoos, numerous piercings, and spiky hair. He was looking at the purple-haired Crystal Crescent Beach girl, but now she was a redhead.

"That's my name, but I prefer Karli or Skarlet, both with Ks, not Cs."

She reminded Simon of girls with multiple piercings, tattoos, and outlandishly dyed hair he'd encountered during his years on the Vancouver vice squad. He invariably wondered where else they had piercings, and that inappropriate thought popped into his head when he saw Ms. Leach.

"Karli Leach it is. In Saturday's yacht club race, we rounded a marker buoy on this side of the harbour. Was it the one in front of your house?"

"Like, what class were you in?"

"Bluenoses."

"You would have rounded our buoy. Were you stompin' 'em?"

"We were leading, but we ended up second."

"The yellow one with the red trim, awesome boat."

"Are you interested in sailing?"

"I, like, grew up watching them. It looked cool, but I never went sailing. You better come inside and tell me whatever bad news you have for me."

Inside, he placed the cardboard box on a table. The house was too big for one single woman but nicely furnished with solid, but worn, old-fashioned furniture. "I like your house and its ocean view. Ideal for sitting outside watching the boats."

"It was when my parents were alive and more recently when I had Holly. Now, it's dismal."

"It's hardly more than a week. A terrible loss, but it will improve."

"That's what the neighbours tell me, but I'm, like, not accepting it. I'll never be the same."

"You have friends who'll give you a hand?"

"What do you care, Mr. Policeman? The neighbours are polite because they've known me since I was little, but they don't understand how I could live with another woman."

Simon paused, wondering about her alibi and the possibility this was a crime of passion committed after Karli discovered Holly was pregnant with another lover's child. She didn't appear strong enough to have bludgeoned someone, but she was showing a certain feistiness. *Best to string her along trying to appear friendly and see if she lets something slip.*

"I'm sure you want us to find Ms. Craig's killer, and we need help understanding her, so I'd appreciate anything you can tell us."

"Here, she was Holly Kintyre, not Holly Craig. That's why I didn't contact you. I wasn't aware she was dead until Christine told me."

Simon nodded, Kintyre was the name on the cell phone bills. "Did Christine know her as Craig or Kintyre?"

Karli shook her head. "Craig apparently. We only visited Christine and Vera a few times and it, like, never came up that she was Holly Craig. She really is Holly Craig, not Holly Kintyre?"

"Afraid so. Would you like to meet her father?"

"No way, I'd rather he didn't even know I exist."

This wasn't getting anywhere. "Tell me about Ms. Kintyre? How did you meet?"

"Christine and Holly came into the restaurant one day last summer. Christine introduced us, and a few days later Holly came by the house, and you're, like, going to say she wormed her way into my life. But she was good to me. My parents hadn't been dead very long, and I was totally messed up. She taught me how to survive. When she needed somewhere to work on a secret project, I, like, let her work here. She hugged and cuddled and loved me, they were the fourteen happiest months of my life."

Simon watched as he asked his questions. Her words reflected a strong emotional involvement, but her expression remained placid. "We're looking for her cell phone and a tape recorder. Could either of them be here?"

"I'm sure they're not. I never saw a tape recorder. She had an awesome little computer that could probably record something and a cell phone. The laptop I gave Ms. Jackson almost always stayed here, but she always took the minicomputer and cell phone with her. She, like, never left them behind."

"They're both missing, so if you find one, tell me right away?"

"I won't find them. They're not here."

"What did she tell you about the project she was working on?"

"Zilch. She's, like, it's a secret and dangerous, and it's best I know nothing. But I read the stuff on the computer when she wasn't here, so I'm, like, aware."

"Did she know you read her computer files?"

"Yeah, I'm a lousy liar. She figured it out right away. She was, like, I shouldn't read them but didn't try to stop me."

"That's interesting. I wonder why she didn't keep the files password protected?"

"There was a password. I told Ms. Jackson. But anytime she phoned and asked me to check something, she'd tell me the password. It never changed."

Simon shook his head wondering about Holly's lack of concern for security. "Did anyone visit when she was here?"

"No, never."

"And did you and Holly go somewhere to meet people?"

"A few visits to Vera and Christine."

"Does the name Amelia Craddock mean anything to you?"

When Karli shook her head without commenting, Simon changed tack.

"When Holly visited, did she always drive the same car?"

"Always her blue Honda Accord. It's, like, neat and almost new. What will happen to it?"

"In the absence of a will, it becomes the property of her parents unless she has a husband or a child."

"Oh, God," Karli said, shuffling like she need to visit the bathroom and wringing her hands together, agitated for the first time since Simon arrived. "Am I ever in shit! When she first started staying here, she showed me this package, and we hid it away. She's, like, if anything happened, I should retrieve it and give it to the police. She told me never to look at it, and if I did, she would smack my bum so hard I wouldn't be able to sit down for a week. It's the only time she ever threatened me, and she was so fierce I, like, blocked it out." Sniffling was making her voice indistinct. "We better get it."

Simon struggled to contain his elation as he followed her into the kitchen where she rummaged until she found a flashlight and screwdriver. In the basement, she climbed on a wooden box and poked at a heating duct. After removing a few sheet-metal screws, she pried open the ductwork, reached in and retrieved a leather case. She passed the stiff leather package to Simon, replaced the ductwork, and returned to the kitchen. She'd been stoical until this point, but now she cried.

"Do you want to see what's in here?" he asked after she regained her composure.

"I don't. I'm sure you will tell me anything important. Please leave. I can't believe this. I forgot the only thing she asked me to do."

"You sure you'll be okay?"

"I'm, like, fine. I just need to be alone. You can, like, return tomorrow if you have more questions."

"Should I send Officer Jackson?"

"If you're too chicken shit to come yourself."

Simon wrote a receipt for the satchel and quietly left. What else could he do? He must trust her and return in the morning to continue the conversation and learn about the pregnancy. And he couldn't send Diana.

In the meantime, he had another treasure trove to investigate.

Chapter Thirteen

Simon and Margaret Summerville itemized the bag's contents before he disappeared into his office. The satchel's two envelopes had been sealed until a few minutes earlier. The one marked personal enclosed a professionally prepared, signed and witnessed will and a page of names and addresses of a lawyer, two different investment advisors, and a bank. There were also keys for two safe deposit boxes. The second envelope contained more keys and a single sheet describing a storage locker's location.

At four forty-five Simon contacted Detective Cavanaugh and described the contents of the satchel's second envelope.

"You think it's significant?"

"Definitely," Simon responded. "Your experts need to attack the computer we retrieved yesterday, and the storage locker is an unknown. So, you should come yourself or send someone, but you need to get onto it, ASAP."

"I'm on my way."

Simon next left a message for Chief DeWolfe. 'Found something new, call.'

As he walked toward his favourite pub, he thought about phoning Amelia to ask her to meet him for dinner but decided against it. She'd made it clear the previous weekend she was looking forward to formal dates. A makeshift dinner at the pub didn't quite fit the bill.

At five forty-five he entered the pub and ordered pizza and beer. After pondering the significance of the latest developments, he left another message for the chief. 'Cavanaugh will arrive between six thirty and seven. You should participate.'

Conrad Cavanaugh was talking to the duty constable when Simon walked into the station shortly before six thirty.

"Someone's been speeding," Simon suggested before turning to Constable Kerry. "Have you heard from the chief?"

"He said we're to detain Detective Cavanaugh until he gets here."

"Here's the background," Simon said as they headed to his office. "Jackson retrieved a laptop and paper records from a new witness last night. This afternoon I received additional info that should be even more interesting."

He placed the page with Holly's storage locker location on top of the cardboard box containing her second computer and investigation documents they retrieved from Karli's house. He pushed them towards Conrad. "These are relevant to your investigation, so, as per our agreement, I'm passing them on. It's now obvious Holly Craig is linked to your case, and that's why I've asked the chief to be here. Where does this leave us?"

"Exactly where we are now," Chief DeWolfe said as he walked into Simon's office. "We feed any information related to Twenty-First Century Construction to Detective Cavanaugh and keep working on our murder investigation. Any other ideas?" he asked turning to Conrad.

Cavanaugh stood with his fists clenched and his chin thrust forward. He looked ready for a fight, but his words were less belligerent. "We must consider that the murderer may be someone related to my Millennium investigation. That changes things. I don't see why I should alter the main responsibilities, but you should bring Simon into the investigation."

The chief stiffened with hands on his hips. He and Cavanaugh reminded Simon of stags preparing to fight. "You feed us anything relevant to our murder investigation, and I'll get Simon and Officer Jackson up to speed on the Twenty-First Century file. But remember, the murder investigation is ours. We've provided you with a computer and the location of the storage locker. We expect a full report on anything related to our murder."

After Cavanaugh left, Chief DeWolfe turned to Simon, "He's trying to pull a fast one on us, and he won't get away with it. But right now, I'm ordering you home. You look beat."

"I'm okay," Simon insisted. "I've had a few long days, but I can manage."

The chief laughed. "You can't cope without Jackson looking after you. But seriously, there's nothing to be done tonight. You, Jackson, and I can get together tomorrow morning."

"Welcome back, Jackson," Chief DeWolfe said as she and Simon entered his office at eight thirty on Thursday morning. The chief looked ten years younger—breaking news on the case he'd been secretly investigating had clearly invigorated him. "I've borrowed a young corporal from the RCMP to fill in until Evans is back."

"David Vickers, he introduced himself. He doesn't look old enough to be finished school, but Margaret and I will teach him the ropes," Diana responded.

The chief pressed on, clearly uninterested in chitchat. "I have an investigation that's intersected with your murder case. It's an undercover operation; you're not to talk to anyone but me and Cavanaugh. I mean it, no discussion with your colleagues, or pillow talk with Amelia or Travis."

"Fine, we understand," Simon said and Diana nodded agreement. Including Amelia in the pillow talk comment surprised Simon and reminded him of a seemingly insignificant incident on the day Holly was murdered.

The chief had expressed an interest in Amelia that now seemed prescient. Had he detected something that presaged their relationship? If so, his intuition had been correct, their relationship was serious, but it hadn't progressed to pillow talk.

The chief launched into his description of a wide-ranging RCMP investigation of Twenty-First Century Construction Corporation. He described allegations of overcharging on construction contracts in Ontario and the Maritimes, dishonest cost overruns, kickbacks, and illegal lobbying of politicians. "The investigation has been longstanding with Cavanaugh as the local RCMP lead. He calls it the Millennium case because of their blurb that goes Twenty-First Century Construction, your builder for the new millennium. It has nothing to do with the Millennium Corporation, a legitimate construction company on the West Coast."

"They're a big player in Vancouver," Simon added.

"They are big, and this investigation does not concern them. It had nothing to do with us until a year ago when Cavanaugh discovered links to our community and several prominent citizens. Twenty-First Century created an affiliate based in Barrettsport with plans to build hundreds of windmills along the coast. It's called Bluenose Wind Energy Corporation and Garrett and Adams, two of our three Selectmen are involved, as is our primary legal counsel."

Simon shook his head. "That's not necessarily illegal."

"But a company that's opaque about its operation is suspicious. And the Mounties discovered several questionable activities. They're spending more time lobbying for government contracts than on the actual windmill technology. Their publicity describes revolutionary windmill design but they have no engineers on staff and no known agreements with engineering companies who could be developing the windmills."

Simon persisted. "Couldn't this be part of business secrecy designed to keep their competitors at bay?"

"Perhaps, but their association with Twenty-First Century and the way they're working screams fraud to investigators who know more than I do."

"This is fascinating, but what does it mean for our murder inquiry?"

"I hoped it had no relevance, but we've discovered your murder victim was investigating Twenty-First Century Construction, and Matthew Garrett's name is prominent in both cases. We must consider a potential link."

Simon snorted. "Sounds like more than a remote possibility. What should we do?"

"Work on your case, not Cavanaugh's. You're not to mention anything related to our discussion to anyone, especially not someone like Matthew Garrett, but you needed the background."

After the meeting, Simon sent Diana armed with a photo to determine if Mr. Kasim could confirm their suspicion Matthew Garrett was Holly's secret lover. Simon called Garrett to set up an interview but received a frosty reception and outright refusal of an informal discussion. Garrett insisted on a formal interview with his lawyer in attendance. *Was Garrett's belligerence the normal reaction when one of the town's pseudo-aristocrats is presented with a request that's actually a thinly disguised demand? Or was it the reaction of someone struggling with guilt?*

Diana returned at twelve thirty with takeout sandwiches. "The chief says I should look after you, so I brought us something to eat. I'll get coffee and summarize my progress."

"Thanks," he said when she placed coffees next to the sandwiches. "How much do I owe you?"

"Six bucks and praise for a job well done. I have positive IDs from three hotel owners."

"Garrett refused to talk except at a formal interview with his lawyer present. I need you to compile everything. I'll check with the chief, but I think we should insist on an interview tomorrow, and if he objects, we should apprehend him. He's behaving like he's untouchable royalty and it's damned annoying. No wonder his wife was ticked off with him the last time I talked to her. He's a first-class twit."

"If he has any sense, he'll arrange to meet us at his office or his lawyer's office."

"I really don't care where."

"You want me to summarize our evidence including cell phone traffic with Holly, then what?"

"A little discrete snooping to confirm Carlotta Leach's whereabouts on the morning of the murder. I'll show her the will and watch her reaction. And we need to establish her knowledge of the pregnancy."

"I could handle that?"

Simon shook his head. "She'd consider it a cop-out. Later, I'm taking the evening off, so, you'll be on your own. Call it a day whenever you want and get prepared to battle Matthew Garrett tomorrow."

Diana gathered up the uneaten part of her lunch. "I'll do some reading to get up to speed. I was only gone three days, but a lot has changed."

Simon. noticed the absence of rings in her nose and eyebrow when he met Karli outside the diner where she worked. "You doing better today?"

"Yes, Mr. Policeman, I told you I would be. You didn't, like, chicken out and send Ms. Jackson."

He laughed. "You gave me a challenge, so I couldn't back down."

"It's good to find a cop with spunk."

"You're not a fan of the police."

"Whenever I've encountered the police, they're, like, hassling me about something."

"Well, I'm not here to hassle you. Can I offer you a ride home? I have good news for you. Promise, no hassling."

"Okay," she replied getting into his car, "I suppose you'll want refreshments."

"Coffee or tea, nothing more."

"I'm planning to sit in my backyard with a glass of wine, so you can have wine or pop, I don't have any beer."

"Wine would be nice."

She said nothing until they arrived at her place. She suggested he wait in the backyard where she would join him with the wine. When she appeared, she'd changed her waitress uniform for shorts and a tattered T-shirt promoting a rock band, and the rings were back in her nose and eyebrow. She carried two glasses and the wine bottle in an ice bucket.

He turned from gazing at the harbour. "I see you've changed uniform."

"Dimitri doesn't like the facial adornments at the diner, so I always put in my most discrete studs. I can tell you don't like them either, so you, like, get my most outlandish ones."

"Nice wine," he replied avoiding further comments on body ornaments.

"I'm glad you like it. It's a pinot grigio. I like them better than the chardonnays everyone chooses." She reacted when Simon smiled. "What's so effing funny? Never seen a girl who has an opinion about wine?"

"Not one in a punk T-shirt and numerous piercings."

"Like, don't they teach you at cop school not to judge people by their appearance? What's your favourite wine?"

"In whites, sauvignon blanc."

"I like its taste, not as sweet as a pinot grigio, but they smell weird."

Simon lifted his glass. "This is very nice wine, and I appreciate the opportunity to sit and drink wine with you. But I'm here for a reason, and I can't linger." He reached into his jacket pocket and extracted several sheets of paper. "These copies of documents from the bag you gave me yesterday include Holly's will and information about her assets. You're the main beneficiary, and if this will prevails, you might have a substantial inheritance. You should take them to a lawyer."

"I don't know any lawyers."

"Wasn't a lawyer involved when your parents died?"

"Yeah. A pompous old jerk who treated me like a freak."

"Then find another. Vera or Christine or another friend could help you."

They sat quietly and Karli poured herself another glass. She offered one to Simon, but he refused.

"It must be nice watching the boats," Simon said a few minutes later.

"Yeah, it's real cool. I sit here dreaming about boats, but I doubt I'll ever get past dreaming."

"Would you like to go sailing?"

"On a golden yellow Bluenose, perhaps?"

"Should I ask her?"

"Maybe."

"I'll take that as a yes. But I must go. Thanks for the wine and please talk to a lawyer. You never know when a good lawyer might come in handy."

That advice would prove prophetic.

94

Chapter Fourteen

Simon returned home, showered, dressed more formally than he preferred, and walked out to take Amelia to dinner at Morgan's, Barrettsport's fanciest restaurant. It was his first foray into the over-the-top wooing she expected, and he'd gone all out.

Amelia understood their destination, and dressed extravagantly, not overdressed as Simon first thought, but perfectly attired for dinner out in Barrettsport. She looked gorgeous and so sophisticated in her low-cut backless silk dress with hair piled high in a formal arrangement. The black material accentuated her modest curves in a way that sent his mind racing to fantasies best saved for later.

"Good evening, Miss Amelia," said the supercilious maître d', a person who made Simon less than happy with these pretentious restaurants. "I missed your name on tonight's guest list."

Amelia tilted her head toward Simon. "This is Simon Goodyear. He reserved the table."

"Very good, Miss. I have it. If you will accompany me." He led them into a second, more private dining room.

"Thank you, Andre, this will be lovely," Amelia said as he withdrew her chair from under a table tucked into a corner.

"Thomas will be your waiter tonight. He'll be right over."

"There's no hurry. We're anticipating a leisurely dinner."

Amelia suppressed a giggle as Andre departed.

"I guess, you passed muster," she whispered. "Otherwise we'd be sitting out front with the tourists. I'm sure he'd assigned you a table out there, and he's embarrassed there was no other in the proper dining room."

Simon snorted. "People like him are never embarrassed. And what's wrong with this table? It's one I might choose."

"None of the Barrettsport elite would. They like expansive space."

"Well, I like this; we can sit and discretely watch everything."

Thomas arrived with a glass containing a prodigious amount of Dubonnet for Amelia. "And you sir, what might I bring you?"

"Crown Royal, please, on ice," he said leaning toward the waiter, "not quite as much as Amelia's."

"Yes, sir, one small Crown Royal on ice. I will be right back."

Amelia glanced around. "Where were we? Oh, yes, a perfect location to observe others. I'll find something for us to spy upon."

"We shouldn't be spying on people."

"Yes, we should, everyone comes here to see and be seen, so we'll be doing them a favour. Anyway, spying should be right down your alley. And fun."

Simon laughed. "Okay, Miss Nancy Drew, what can the great lady detective find?"

"Ah, there's a good subject, and nearby. Two tables over, a young woman in a pale blue dress sitting with a nervous-looking young man. Have you clocked them?"

"Yes, her dress is like yours, narrow shoulder straps and no back. But she's not as beautiful as you."

She grinned while puffing up her chest. "Don't I display the perfect level of sensuous elegance?"

"Any more would get you arrested," Simon replied, shaking his head. "But what are you telling me?"

"That girl, who's the little sister of the Beverley Campbell you arrested the other day, doesn't have the posture or the self-awareness. I suspect it's her sister's dress and doesn't fit that well. She's been giving her date quite a show. He's embarrassed, but I doubt she's even aware of it."

"She might be doing it on purpose."

Amelia charged on apparently ignoring that possibility. "Another woman will approach Miss Campbell and escort her to the ladies' room. They will put a few pins in the dress and resume their seats as if nothing happened."

Thomas arrived with Simon's drink and presented him with the menu. "The third menu is a particularly good choice tonight. The sole is one of the cook's specialities and he's impressed with the lamb chops, so a win-win situation if you understand that language. I'll give you a few minutes to consider."

"Don't you get a menu?" Simon asked.

"You're supposed to order for me."

"That's preposterous; you'll have to borrow mine."

"No, Simon, we should play along with their game. How else will you learn? But if you're asking, the lamb sounds delightful. I hope you'll order that one."

"And everything works by these five menus, there's no picking and choosing?"

Amelia nodded. "Have you been watching Miss Campbell?"

"I still think she's doing it on purpose, teasing the uncomfortable-looking guy.

Amelia glanced toward the table as Simon perused the menu. "Cynthia Ettinger is riding to the rescue and peace will soon prevail."

"Okay, what's happening?"

"Mrs. Ettinger and the younger Miss Campbell have left for the ladies' room. You've had a perfect lesson in how society works, and you can now pay attention to the drink you've hardly touched.

"I'm glad I didn't order a large whiskey, this one's more than enough for me," Simon commented, taking another sip from his drink. "You've obviously made an effort to understand these people and become part of their society."

"I've studied them and tried to fit in, but I'll never be part of their society. They're polite and welcome me into their dining room, but that's all."

"And what about the yacht club?" Simon added as Thomas returned for their orders. "Ah, Thomas, Amelia and I will have the lamb chops."

"Thank you, sir, good choice. I'll return with the fish, and perhaps a white wine? I know which one Miss Amelia prefers."

"That would be perfect."

"You can do this," Amelia said, beaming. "I've worked to become accepted at the yacht club. It matters, and I fit in more naturally. But here, any sophistication is an act."

"You must be a good actress," he replied, saluting her before downing the last of his whiskey.

Thomas arrived with the fish and a bottle of white wine in an ice bucket. Later Amelia provided another etiquette lesson by telling him the lady could choose the white, but a gentleman would order the red.

After the chops were served along with the red wine Simon chose, he mentioned Karli Leach and his idea of taking her for a sail on *Pallas Athena*.

Amelia agreed without hesitation. "First nice Sunday because I plan to participate in all the Saturday races."

"There's one problem, she won't fit in at the yacht club. She has bright red hair that's clearly dyed, numerous earrings, and additional ones in her eyebrow and nose. Even a few tattoos. Will she ruin your effort to become a socially acceptable member?"

Amelia smirked. "That might be a problem. I could say she's your girlfriend and you wouldn't crew unless we took her for a sail, but it might still blight my otherwise spotless record." She paused, sipping her wine. "If you promised to come in all six races this fall, I'd risk it."

"Do you want me on board? Won't you have your regular crew?"

Amelia leaned back sporting a wicked grin Simon couldn't misinterpret. "A summer visitor who departed in the middle of August. I need crew, and you, Jenny and I make a good team. You crew all six Saturdays or no Sunday afternoon jaunt for your Goth girlfriend."

"I can't promise to be there every week."

"I'll throw in dinner and you know what in the evening."

Simon smiled, thinking she must realize that didn't change the reality of his job. "Then, I can't possibly refuse. You drive a hard bargain, but it's a deal."

As they prepared to leave, Simon looked for Thomas.

"Don't ask for the bill," Amelia said.

"Why not? Must I compute how much I owe them?"

"It's considered low class to pay for dinner, so, we're sent bills at the end of the month. I told Thomas to send it to me. I hope that's okay."

"Crazy, but if that's how it works, I suppose we must go along."

"Odd, but in its own way, it's part of the town's appeal."

"And should I quietly ask Thomas how much money I now owe you?"

"I will whisper a number in your ear when you're in bed with me and you'll be a gentleman and take my word for it."

Simon turned away so she wouldn't notice his smile. Her reluctant agreement the previous Saturday to let their burgeoning romance develop slowly hadn't changed her attitude one iota. She remained intent on getting them into bed as quickly as possible. He turned back toward her, hoping his reaction to her in bed together comment wasn't too obvious.

"I guess it's time we departed. Should I leave a tip?"

"Heavens, no! Service will be included on the bill."

Simon laughed at her inadequate attempt to sound shocked. "I have a question for you. I'll slip it in as we walk to your place."

Amelia became jumpier as they walked along the deserted street. When they were almost to her house, she blurted out, "What do you want to ask me? An obscure Hercules Poirot type of question that leads you to conclude I killed Holly. Then Inspector Jupp, or whatever his name was, will jump from an alley and arrest me on the spot?"

"Japp, his name was Japp, but what made you think my question was related to our murder investigation?"

"It is, isn't it?"

Simon smiled. "But the answer won't lead us directly to Holly's murderer. And Officer Jackson isn't lurking behind your hedge waiting to arrest you."

"Cut this out. What's the question?"

He stopped beside the narrow gap in her hedge. "The murder was on Saturday. Why would you consider Holly's request to attend the War Memorial Garden protest when you had a race?"

"Jesus, is that it? I'm almost peeing my pants, and that's all you want!"

"It's a legitimate question, and I don't like leaving loose ends hanging about. Why are you so frightened?"

"I already told you I fear being arrested. After too much wine, my fear took hold."

"Okay, but you haven't answered my question."

"Simple. I had no crew because our third crewmember had gone home to New England, and Jenny told me she couldn't come. I was ambivalent about finding a pickup crew, and Holly convinced me. Now, I suppose, you'll ask Jenny for confirmation."

"As I said, I don't like loose ends."

Amelia stepped through the gap in her hedge, glancing behind it, perhaps unconsciously expecting to find Diana lurking. She proceeded not to her front door, but around her cottage to the deck behind her living room. As she climbed the outside stairs to the deck with the hem of her dress hiked up around her knees, she looked back at Simon. He followed pondering her intentions.

She sat swinging gently back and forth in a two-person swing. Real teak with nice soft cushions, ideal for two young lovers. Those intentions appeared obvious. Simon slid in beside her and gathered her into his arms.

"Nice, isn't it," she murmured as she snuggled against his shoulder, "sitting here on a warm summer evening with a gentle breeze blowing in from the harbour."

He gazed across twenty metres of lawn and sixty metres of inner harbour waters to the golf course on the far side. "It's wonderful. A beautiful oasis and so isolated here on your deck." He leaned over and kissed her.

"More wine, coffee, something else?"

He shook his head as he pulled the pin anchoring the engineering marvel that was her hairdo. As her brown locks tumbled, he smoothed a few errant strands but resisted the urge to push her dress straps off her shoulders. He'd jettisoned the previous Saturday night's reticence, and he now struggled not to move too swiftly.

As he continued to offer endearments, he noticed a distinct change in Amelia's attitude. She'd transformed from her aggressive flirtatiousness of earlier in the evening to a more complacent anticipation, willing him to carry her off to bed.

Soon, they found themselves naked in her bed engaged in a gentler coupling than Simon anticipated. *Did it reflect his newfound determination to approach sexual relationships in a more mature manner or some last moment reluctance on Amelia's part?*

Later, with Amelia sleeping peacefully snuggled against him, he contemplated her transformation from aggressive warrior woman on Pallas Athena to determined pursuer of an intimate relationship during most of their other encounters. Then, he felt her ambivalence when they arrived in bed together.

Nicole Adams, someone he'd met during his first case, railed against the restrictions imposed upon her as a member of the ruling families while benefiting from the same social conventions. Amelia and her friend Cynthia Ettinger talked about shaking up the social structure while happily accepting the archaic customs. Nicole and Cynthia were insiders, members of the families, but Amelia was an outsider. Yet they all wallowed in Barrettsport's crazy world, accepting the dichotomies.

Simon fell asleep considering Matthew Garrett and another unsavoury aspect of the town's social structure. Matthew and the other family members expected special treatment from the law. Tomorrow, he and Diana would challenge that assumption.

Chapter Fifteen

First thing Friday morning, Simon reopened the Matthew Garrett file. When Diana arrived a few minutes later, they reviewed the situation before Simon phoned Garrett at his Town Hall office. He put him on speakerphone.

"Hello, Goodyear," Garrett said after Simon penetrated the barrier imposed by his secretary. "I've been expecting your call and have a statement regarding my whereabouts on the morning of August eighteenth. I was home having breakfast with my wife from eight, when she got up, until she left for an activity you're familiar with around nine thirty. Before eight, I was working alone in my home office."

Simon tried to keep his voice calm. "Thank you for the information, but you should let me ask the questions before answering."

"If you have questions, I insist on having my lawyer present."

"If that's your position, we'll arrange a formal interview, but you should consider the benefits of a more informal meeting."

"Don't you presume to advise me! If you want to question me, my lawyer will be present, no exceptions!"

Simon rapidly rising anger was playing havoc with his efforts to remain calm. "Would you prefer to meet here at the police station, in your office, or somewhere else?"

"My lawyer's office; Samuel Wexler, 146 Front St., ten thirty, and don't be late. I'm a busy man with no time for pointless interruptions!"

Diana shook her head after Garrett slammed down his phone. "Real gent. Why put up with that crap? I'd drag him to the station."

Simon smiled, imagining Constable Jackson singlehandedly manhandling Garrett and frogmarching him into the police station. "We will, eventually. But for now, we may learn more if he feels safe on his own turf."

At ten twenty-five, Simon and Diana arrived at Samuel Wexler's office. A secretary ushered them into a large, formal room dominated by an elaborately carved mahogany desk. Matthew Garrett and a very distinguished looking older gent who had to be Samuel Wexler sat at a matching table. Simon set his tape recorder on the table, and he and Diana took the proffered chairs.

"Do you need power for that machine?" Mr. Wexler asked.

Simon shook his head. "It will run for at least two hours."

"Mr. Garrett and I are both busy, so let's get started," Wexler said as Simon pressed the start button on his machine. "For the record, it's ten thirty-five. My name is Samuel Wexler and I'm an attorney representing Mr. Matthew Garrett, sitting beside me. He is participating in this interview voluntarily. On the other side of the table are Detective Simon Goodyear and Constable Diana Jackson of the Barrettsport Police Force."

Obviously, Wexler was taking control, proclaiming his knowledge of the procedure and telling Simon he would get away with nothing. Best, Simon thought, to let him think he was in charge. "Thank you for the introductions. Our questions for Mr. Garrett should only take a few minutes; then we can all get on with our busy days. First, Mr. Garrett, did you meet with Ms. Holly Craig at several motels within a hundred-kilometre radius of Barrettsport?"

"Time frame," Wexler interjected.

"The past twelve months. We can document when and where if that helps."

Garrett looked at his lawyer without commenting. Simon knew Garrett expected questions about the day of Holly's murder and hoped his initial question would catch the bugger by surprise. It clearly succeeded.

"Perhaps you would give us a few minutes," Wexler suggested.

"Take as long as you want. Interview suspended at ten thirty-eight," Simon switched off the machine and retrieved it. "We won't go far."

Ten minutes later, they were again seated. Simon restarted the tape while staring at Matthew Garrett. "Interview resumed, ten forty-nine."

"I met with Holly, Ms. Craig, at motels, as you suggest. I don't remember the exact times and dates but could develop a comprehensive list with the help of my desk diary."

"The reasons for these meetings?" Simon demanded.

"They were, um, how does one describe this, um, romantic encounters."

"No other reasons?"

Garrett placed his hands on the table and started to rise. "Damn it, Holly and I met for sex. Why else would we get together? There was nothing kinky about us, just plain ordinary garden variety sex I wasn't getting at home. No one else, and nothing else, was involved!"

"Did you drive to these meetings separately or together?" Simon asked as Wexler calmed Garrett.

"Separately."

"We don't have your name, or your car, associated with the motel records. Why's that?"

"She always checked in."

"Not very chivalrous, having the lady pay?" Diana suggested. It was her first contribution, and it obviously annoyed Garrett.

"She often combined business with pleasure, so she needed receipts. I used cash."

Simon resumed control. "Thank you, sir. We realize this is a rather sensitive topic. We won't make your role public if it has no bearing on the murder investigation, but we must understand her activities, especially ones that appear unusual. So, if you could provide us with the dates, times and locations of your meetings..."

"I can do that," replied Garrett, after a few whispered words with his lawyer.

Diana jumped in with another aggressive question. "Did you know she was pregnant?"

This one didn't fluster Garrett. "I didn't. Well, that's not entirely true. She was evasive when I asked her about the possibility. She denied it, but I wasn't convinced."

"Was it your baby?" Simon asked.

Garrett looked down at the table. "I suspect it is or was."

"Would you agree to a paternity test?"

"I guess," Garrett replied after looking at Wexler for advice.

"We can arrange something discreet. Did you offer Holly any advice?"

"It was hard to talk about it because she denied it's existence, but I did mention an abortion."

"How did she react?"

"She didn't say anything. She stared at me in a way I couldn't interpret."

"Were you aware of her relationship with a young woman?" Diana again, trying to get in his face.

Garrett thumped the table with a fist. "That's preposterous!"

"She visited a young woman at her residence, often staying overnight."

"It must have been a platonic relationship. Holly wasn't a lesbian."

"How would you know?"

"What the fuck does that mean? You some sort of dyke bitch?" Lawyer Wexler nearly fell from his chair while trying to shut Garrett up, but the damage had been done. They now had the makings of a credible motive.

"Explain the outburst," Diana demanded, but Garrett just shook his head.

Simon jumped back in, pleased with the success of their impromptu good cop, bad cop routine. Garrett was clearly rattled. If they lowered the intensity he might relax and let something slip. "We don't understand the exact nature of the relationship. We should talk about the morning of the murder. You told me earlier today you were home with your wife from eight until nine thirty on the eighteenth of August."

"That's correct."

"Anyone else there, family, friends, domestic staff?"

"We were alone."

"Before eight, you were up but your wife was still in bed?"

"Correct; I was up at six thirty working on town business."

Diana looked up from her notebook and Simon sat back letting her continue the questioning. "Can Mrs. Garrett confirm when you rose?"

"I doubt it; she was asleep in a separate bedroom."

"And you're certain she was there?"

"Her bedroom door was ajar."

Diana checked her notes. "She left at nine thirty, and you, what did you do after nine thirty?"

"I stayed home, still working on town business. Chief DeWolfe phoned at eleven. After that, other calls. She got home at around one thirty wearing a stupid police department T-shirt and no bra." Caroline Garrett's behaviour when she bought a department T-shirt and strutted about the station showing it off must have gotten back to Matthew. She wouldn't accept one when Simon first offered them, but later, after Lisa arrived with everyone's tops, she insisted on having one. Her top and bra ended up in a bin for used clothing the station maintained. "We had a bloody great row. I mean what the hell did she think she was doing?"

"Were these calls on your cell phone or the house phone?"

"I don't remember. Some of both?"

"We can check."

"Could any of your neighbours have seen you before one thirty?"

"If you were familiar with my house, you wouldn't ask that question. No neighbours can look in our windows."

"And you didn't go anywhere?"

"I never left the house. Caroline took her car."

"Have you visited Ms. Craig's apartment?" Simon asked, interrupting Diana's line of questioning. Garrett had recovered too quickly from Diana's anti-Lesbian attack. He didn't appear to let anything else slip.

"No, never. I've never been there."

"You know where it is?"

"The little apartment building, but not her unit."

"Thank you, that's all my questions. Anything you want to tell us, anything that might help us find her killer?"

"I don't think so."

"Then I'd say we're done. Thank you for your time. Interview concluded eleven twenty." Simon turned off the recorder and extracted the tape. "You want a copy?"

"That won't be necessary," lawyer Wexler replied. Simon and Diana collected their material and left.

"If he's our man and my money is still on him, we need to disprove his story," Simon concluded after they were on the sidewalk. "I thought you had him when you hit him with the Lesbian angle, but he recovered well. Disproving his story becomes our priority."

"If he was out early Saturday morning, someone must have seen him. I'll work on it."

"And we should confirm his wife's movements before she arrived at the park."

Thursday, after a frustrating week search for anyone who'd seen Matthew Garrett on the morning of the murder, Diana got a break.

"I've found a witness," she called out when Simon returned from lunch, "but you won't like it."

Simon stopped by her desk. "Why not?"

"Because Garrett was seen returning home at eight thirty-five."

"Give me the details."

"A repairman arriving to fix a neighbour's air conditioner saw him outside his grounds. He was crossing Shore Road when the witness, a Mr. John Stokes, who works for a heating company in Bridgewater, arrived in his truck. He had to slow down while Garrett crossed the road and disappeared up his drive."

"And he's sure about the details?"

"He recognized Garrett from a previous service call to Garrett's house. He remembered because Garrett disputed the bill and called Stokes a thief. And the time is solid because he had the arrival time on his worksheet." Diana flipped her notebook to a different page "I checked with his office in Bridgewater and the occupants of the house where he was fixing the air conditioner. It ties together, but it rather makes a mess of our working hypothesis, doesn't it?"

"It's a setback. Did Mr. Stokes say anything about Garrett's appearance?"

"He said he seemed distracted when he walked in front of his truck, but he noticed nothing unusual about his clothing."

Simon sighed as he walked around Diana's desk to check the notes she'd made. "Okay, what does this mean? The bad news is he couldn't have killed Holly and cleaned up the crime scene and himself between eight and eight thirty-five. The good news is we know his story's a lie. He was out for an unknown length of time until eight thirty-five, so he's hiding something. He wouldn't produce a false alibi if it wasn't something important."

"But it isn't necessarily related to our murder, it could be related to Cavanaugh's investigation or just another girlfriend."

"Right, but I still think he's implicated in our murder, it's just not as simple as we thought."

"But we can't just focus on Garrett now we have this eyewitness statement," Diana insisted.

"We have a dearth of other suspects."

"Amelia Craddock?"

Simon shook his head. "She's clear. Solid alibi, no motive."

"Carlotta Leach?"

"Again, solid alibi, but she's the main beneficiary of Holly's estate, so she does have a motive."

"And she may have been incensed by the pregnancy. Vera Cruz or Christine Nesbitt?"

"Possible, I guess, but they don't seem likely."

"An unknown assailant associated with the construction scandal?"

"Possible, but it would become the Mounties' problem. That brings us back to Garrett and there's something mighty suspicious about him. Why can't we find any indication of his car at the motels? He's hiding something and we must discover it."

"I'll get back to it, but I've kicked just about every tire and overturned every rock. I'm not sure where I should go next."

Simon turned toward his office. "Summarize the results of your endeavours and bring them in. We can add it to our growing pile of apparently disconnected evidence, go over it one more time, and see if we come up with anything."

"You want that today or tomorrow morning?"

"Later today if it's ready. I'm not doing anything I can't interrupt. But if it's tomorrow morning that's okay too."

Diana returned to Simon's office at five thirty with a takeout pizza and several pages of printout. She extracted two beer from the small fridge in his office.

"I didn't know you were keeping beer in my fridge. It's against the rules."

"So, arrest me," she said, aggressively twisting the caps off the two beer. "I'm so damn frustrated. My summary is great if I want to show you how hard I've been working, but it's next to useless for showing progress on the case. The only evidence I've uncovered shows us Garrett's out of the frame, and we're back to square one." She took a large swallow of beer and thumped the bottle on Simon's desk.

"It looks like you'll want a second," he suggested.

"One must do. We'll either get back to work once we've eaten or I'll be driving home. Either way, a second beer isn't ideal."

"What's next after I report to the chief you've been working your butt off?"

"I thought you'd been working on your fancy Barrettsport manners. 'Working your butt off' is not an acceptable expression."

Simon laughed. "You can help me with my manners another time. We need a breakthrough."

"But we've been through everything. Now we add one witness statement that doesn't get us any further ahead. What's the point?" Diana asked, her frustration very obvious.

"It's annoying, but you'll get used to the idea that when I get stuck, I go back and sift through the evidence again. If I find nothing, I start again."

"No wonder you ended up with an ulcer."

"That's not in order! I got ill because I couldn't cope with dealing, day in and day out, with young people whose lives were ruined by drugs and sexual exploitation on Vancouver's mean streets. Not because of my method for investigating a crime."

"Sorry. I apologize."

"Would you rather we started again in the morning?"

She shook her head but didn't appear enthusiastic. "You'll sit here all evening staring at your whiteboard. I should help."

They reviewed their evidence for the next two hours. Then Simon asked Diana what she thought was the oddest feature.

"The oddest thing?" she replied, clearly not having anticipated the question. She thought for a minute. "The lack of evidence in several important areas. First, the crime scene was devoid of any evidence that pointed us towards a killer. Now we find there's no evidence of Matthew Garrett's movements at important times when he was out and about."

"I agree, we need to understand why. And I have a third question. What happened to the murder weapon?"

Chapter Sixteen

Simon stomped around the narrow confines of his office. He and Diana had been mulling over their case for two hours and he'd just mentioned the missing murder weapon. "Forensics said it was a cylindrical wooden object approximately ten centimetres in diameter. It, along with Holly's bag and cell phone, have disappeared into thin air. Suggests the killer cleaned up without leaving a trace and took the weapon and her bag with him."

Diana continued the speculation. "That suggests a professional killing. An amateur would leave evidence for the forensic team. But it looks like a crime of passion by an obsessed killer."

Simon made a quick notation on his whiteboard. "One of several observations that don't compute."

"We also have Garrett's concocted alibi when he apparently didn't need it, and his presence at those motels without leaving a trace."

"And her mysterious pregnancy."

"What's so mysterious? It happens, and it's always difficult to decide."

"Perhaps, but it's one more enigmatic aspect of her life. Her whole existence in Barrettsport is as sterile as our crime scene."

Diana collected her belongings before finally going home. "There's one final thing."

"What's that?"

"Cavanaugh phoned this afternoon, pumping me for information on Holly's activities, and when I told him he should talk to you, he got belligerent."

"There's something wrong with that guy," Simon said.

"Yeah, he's a misogynist," Diana replied as she closed his door behind her.

Cavanaugh may or may not be a misogynist, but his temper was always barely under control. And he treated the Twenty-First Century investigation and their murder as if they were his territory. That presented another problem Simon didn't need.

He spent the evening reviewing what they knew about Holly Craig. After graduation with a degree in journalism, she worked at a London, Ontario newspaper. A minor contribution to an investigative report during her first year led to another, more substantial contribution to a second award-winning report. Her father claimed she abandoned her promising career in Ontario after an unspecified romance failed and moved to Nova Scotia to start over again.

In Barrettsport, she reported on inconsequential stories while secretly investigating Twenty-First Century Construction. A continuation of investigations started in Ontario could explain the barrenness of accommodations she considered temporary.

When she discovered Garrett's role, she could have instigated the affair to pump him for information. But the pregnancy didn't fit? If it was a mistake, as Diana guessed, why not terminate it? Uncertainty about termination didn't mesh with his picture of someone who'd devoted two years to her investigation.

Simon retreated to his own sterile apartment trying to understand the significance of the pregnancy and Holly's relationship with Karli Leach.

Simon was ready for a change when he departed for the yacht club Saturday morning. Amelia sat in an Adirondack chair on the club lawn sipping iced tea.

She pointed at the harbour as he approached. "It's already hot and sticky, and the wind's light and shifty as hell. I doubt it will pick up this afternoon. I'm expecting a slow and frustrating race, and if we're unlucky, it'll die completely and we'll be paddling in."

He laughed. "if I substitute evidence for wind, you'd have a perfect description my work week."

"Sorry about that. I can't control the weather or your case. But if we're becalmed, we can entertain ourselves by discussing our plans for tonight."

"Won't we corrupt Jenny's fertile young mind?"

Amelia smiled. "How young do you think she is?"

"I don't know, fourteen?"

"You're out of touch! She's sixteen and I'd say very aware. We'll have a hard time corrupting her mind."

"Sixteen, I would have never guessed," Simon said, genuinely surprised. The jaded urban kids he'd been accustomed to in his previous life were superficially older. If Jenny was any indication of Barrettsport's young people, their rural small-town enthusiasm hid a different sort of maturity he must acknowledge.

Jenny popped into view. "Here I am hoping to hear intimate details of your most recent night together and all you're doing is talking about me."

Amelia laughed. "He thought you were fourteen."

"Fourteen! What an insult! I'm getting a rope to whip him every time he messes up."

"Don't take long," Amelia yelled as Jenny stomped away, "we're leaving soon."

On their way to her cottage after the race, Amelia appeared down despite their good finish.

"What's the matter," Simon asked, "Aren't you pleased with coming second?"

"I am. You and Jenny did a great job keeping the boat going, but I couldn't figure the wind shifts."

"Everyone said predicting anything was impossible."

"No excuse. I kept squandering your good work. But don't worry, I'll get over it. If you and Jenny keep the boat going, I'll get my touch back, and we'll beat Jeremy. Then Jenny will be happy."

"I'm happy to participate. I don't care if we win or lose."

"You will. The first time we taste victory you'll be hooked and want to win every time."

"But tomorrow we've no worries. We'll enjoy the sun and wind and peaceful pleasures of sailing."

Amelia slowly shook her head. "I must be crazy taking you and your new girlfriend on my boat."

"She's not my girlfriend, you're my girl and you're not getting rid of me that easily."

"Perhaps not, but admit it, you're rather smitten with her and she's much curvier than I am. Must I dye my hair and get my eyebrow pierced to keep up with her?"

"You might need more intimate piercings."

"More intimate piercings? What have you two been doing?"

"I'm just guessing, but I'd bet that she has rings or bars in her nipples and other places."

"Like her belly button?" Amelia suggested.

"Well, perhaps, but I was thinking of somewhere else."

"You men can be so gross! But I'll take that bet. I bet she has no rings, bars or other appliances in intimate places. When I win, I'll exact a risqué punishment."

"And if I win, I get to choose your punishment."

"But I'll win because girls around here aren't like your Vancouver ones."

Simon laughed, but he was worried. Only a few hours earlier, Jenny had shown his perception of the local girl's behaviour was suspect. Could Karli be a good country girl beneath her outlandish Goth exterior?

Sunday morning, Simon worked for a few hours before collecting Karli at ten thirty. When they arrived at the club, they found *Pallas Athena* tied to the tender's dock. The red mainsail cover had been removed, the jib hanked to the forestay, and a bright yellow dinghy tied to the stern.

Amelia arrived a few minutes later carrying a large bag of ice. "The clubhouse machine is broken, so I went into town."

Simon made the introductions. "Amelia, this is Karli Leach; Karli, Amelia Craddock."

"Hello Amelia," Karli added, "I've been, like, so looking forward to it."

When Karli turned to admire the golden goddess, Simon knew why Amelia smirked. Karli's spiky bright red hair was prominent, but one ring and two little studs in each ear and tiny studs in an eyebrow and nostril were almost invisible.

A few minutes later, they were sailing close-hauled toward the nearest of the barrier islands protecting Barrettsport's outer harbour. They anchored in a tiny cove on the island's landward side and transported themselves and their picnic lunch ashore in their dinghy. A short walk took them across the island to a beautiful secluded beach.

After a lunch of rabbit food, sandwiches and wine, Amelia suggested a quick swim before sailing back to Barrettsport. She was wearing the same bikini she'd sported in her Crystal Crescent Beach video, but Simon and Karli were not dressed for swimming. Karli hesitated, shaking her head.

"You can go in au naturelle if you don't want to get your clothes wet," Amelia suggested. "No one will see you."

"I'd rather not," Karli replied. "I'll just wade at the edge. It's, like, freezing cold."

"Okay, but this place is totally remote and famous for skinny dipping. Come on Simon, I dare you to dive into the freezing cold Atlantic."

Amelia raced to the water's edge and straight into the waves. Simon followed, and they enjoyed a brief swim in the frigid water. Karli sauntered to the shore and waded in until the water was half a metre deep.

After their swim, they dried in the sun on two big rocks near their picnic site. Amelia mentioned the rings and bars some young people sported.

"I'll check on the boat," Simon suggested. He wanted an excuse to leave before Amelia convinced Karli to bare all and reveal her piercings.

When he got to the top of the dune Amelia hollered, waving Karli's shorts in the air. He looked toward the cove and saw *Pallas Athena* riding on her anchor where they'd left her and another boat approaching. He rushed back telling his two nutty companions to get dressed because company was coming. They didn't hurry, expecting the newcomers to take a few minutes to get anchored and ashore, but dressed and packed up debris from their picnic. Amelia was skipping and cavorting. She'd obviously won their bet.

Two young couples appeared at the top of the ridge. "Hey Amelia," one guy yelled out, "we hoped to surprise you."

Amelia laughed, apparently unconcerned about the unsavoury nature of young guys admitting they hoped to catch her naked. "You're too late and anyway no skinny dipping. We've had our swim and are preparing to leave. If you give us a few minutes, we'll be gone and you can have the beach to yourselves."

"Carlotta," one girl said. "Aren't you Carlotta Leach? Yes, you are. Do you remember me, Gloria Mulholland? We were at high school together."

"I'm, like, not sure."

"Not surprised. You were real smart and real outlandish, so hard to miss. I was dumb and mostly interested in boys, so not very noticeable."

"I do remember, you dated a football player."

"Yup, that's me. Hey guys, this is Carlotta. I knew her in high school. Carlotta, Ricky, and Tom, and that's Suzanne. You coming swimming with us?"

Karli glanced at Amelia. "It's, like, we have to go."

Gloria began shedding her clothes. "We came out here for a swim and I'm not waiting any longer." Naked, she looked toward the others. "Come on guys don't be bashful. Last one buys the beer back at the clubhouse." She stood hands on hips facing Karli while she waited for her friends. "We'll see you around the club. Have a good sail back."

"That's, like, the sort of free-spirited crap I could never manage," Karli said before following Simon and Amelia back to the *Pallas Athena*.

They sailed home with the spinnaker up the whole way. The long run gave Simon plenty of time to learn something of Jenny's role on the downwind legs and teach Karli to do his job minding the guy. When they finally arrived in the ever-decreasing wind, a mainsail and blue and yellow spinnaker were visible in the distance.

They had supper at the yacht club before Simon took Karli home and returned to Amelia's to discover what punishment she had planned for him.

Chapter Seventeen

During the drive to her Hunter's Creek house, Karli apologized for circumstances that led to Simon losing his bet with Amelia. She admitted she had rings and bars in the places Simon guessed. Holly was into them, she explained, but moved to a more modest display after she learned of Holly's death.

At her place, Karli pressed a plastic zip-lock bag containing two gold bars and three gold rings into Simon's hand. She insisted they'd been sterilized and suggested Amelia might like them. He guessed she'd never accept them, but he took them anyway, thinking they might play a role in the drama he expected when he returned to Amelia's.

On the way back to Amelia's cottage, Simon considered Karli's depiction of Holly's interest in body ornaments and all things Goth. They might explain her father's perspective when he explained her move to Simon. Easy to imagine how a father might become obsessed with his daughter's interest in another Goth girl back home and blind to her accomplishments.

Amelia peered at her driveway when Simon returned. "Where's your car?"

"My place. Shouldn't be driving after more booze."

"Idiot! You're staying the night. By morning you should be sober."

Why'd she automatically assumed he'd stay overnight? Was it part of the punishment she planned? They'd made love for the first time after their extravagant dinner date, and he'd stayed the night. That was ten days earlier, and they hadn't been together again until yesterday's race. Now she appeared to be using their stupid bet to push their relationship to another level. "Tell me what crazy activity you have planned?"

"Not, yet," Amelia said, motioning toward her sofa. "Karli wasn't like I expected. Despite the red hair, tattoos, and other adornments, she's a shy kid and a fantastic student. But she didn't attend university, and now she works in a café."

Simon relaxed. Talking about Karli suggested Amelia was reconsidering their bet. "That's about right."

"She needs a mentor, someone to help her achieve her dreams."

"Holly played that role, helped her sort herself out when she was living from day to day after her parents died."

"Perhaps Holly helped her regain control, but she didn't help her resolve her future. We should do that."

"Do I sense latent homophobia? Are you suggesting Holly lured her into a homosexual relationship, and you might change her ways?"

Amelia jumped up, raising her fists like she planned to strike him. "No way! How can you suggest that when Christine's been my closest friend for years? I don't have problems with people whose sexual orientation differs from mine."

"Sorry, I don't know why I said that. It wasn't fair."

"Apology accepted. I think you're worried about the price you'll pay for losing our little bet. Has it addled your brain?" Her voice was gleeful, the momentary aggressiveness gone. "I was considering Karli's potential. If we helped, I'm sure she could make something of herself."

Simon pulled her back down. "She needs space to figure things out for herself and decide where she wants to go. It's hard to help someone without pushing your own ideas."

"I realize that, but we must make her understand we're there if she wants us."

"She's not stupid. She knows that already."

"I hope so."

Simon stroked Amelia's hair, sorting out tangles that inevitably occurred after a day on the water. "Now, what have you planned for us?"

"I'm not sure I can tell you. Should we go for a walk?"

Simon was relieved. More delaying tactics indicated an opportunity to wiggle out of the bet and reduce the intensity of their relationship. "We could void the bet because you won on a technicality."

She shook her head. "The bet concerned appliances, not piercings. I need to do this! I just need to build up courage."

He sighed. "Let's go for that walk."

They walked along the seaside from the yacht club then inland on Shore Road toward the North Point lighthouse. From Lighthouse Park, they gazed eastward at the empty expanse of the Atlantic Ocean.

"We're looking towards the north-western corner of Spain," Simon suggested. "Do you dream of staring back at Barrettsport on a Spanish vacation?"

"You inviting me on a romantic vacation?"

"Next summer when I'm entitled to leave. Why don't we forget our little bet and dream about a trip?"

Amelia turned and started marching home along Shore Road.

In her cottage, Amelia led Simon straight into her bedroom and sat on the edge of her bed. "I want you to punish me."

"What? I lost the bet, so I'm supposed to face the consequences."

"That's what I want. Pull down my pants and smack my bum."

"That's crazy," he sputtered, hardly able to get the words out. "Why do you deserve such a thing, and why would I agree to hurt you? I'm sorry, I can't do it!"

"I need this," she insisted. "You must smack my bum until it's red and raw!"

"I won't do it. In my job I've seen too many battered women." He gave her a shove, and she fell on her side. He pushed until she was lying on her back staring at him, eyes wide in amazement. This obviously wasn't unfolding the way she expected, but it might get them around an untenable demand.

He kicked off his shoes and joined her on the bed. "Tell me what this is about."

"It's something I need you to do," she said as tears escaped from her eyes.

He caressed her thigh, inching his hand until his fingers rested between her legs. She relaxed, spread her legs and lifted her hips.

"Explain," he insisted.

She sagged onto the mattress. "This is difficult. I've only ever had one boyfriend who brought me totally, uncontrollably to orgasm. He did it by pushing his fingers in my bum during sex. But that's sinful, and sex since that guy has never been really good because I feel so guilty. You must punish me for that bad behaviour."

He snorted. "You shouldn't tell me some other guy is the only one who ever got you off if you're trying to impress me." He unfastened her jeans and unzipped the fly, then slowly moved his hand inside her pants.

"Ahhhh, that's so good," she sighed before squirming to escape his explorations. "Please, this is hard enough. I can't explain if you're tormenting me."

He removed his hand, pulled her close, and waited for her explanation. She said nothing.

"Sex hasn't been as exciting as you hoped," he suggested.

She shook her head, tears welling in her eyes again. "You're the kindest and gentlest guy I've ever known and you make me feel loved and contented. And the sex has been good…"

"But not as exciting as the guy with his finger in your ass."

"I should never have mentioned him. Until you and I got together, I feared sex, thought it was wrong. Now I want you here every night, but I've ruined everything by pushing too hard."

"Don't despair. We're here together, cuddling each other, aren't we?"

"Yeah, but I fear you'll leave at any moment."

Their conversation had taken several serious twists. Initially, he thought she was signalling an interest in pain. Then she stumbled through several other explanations, but none rang true. He needed time to consider the implications, but he wasn't planning to abandon her.

"Have you tried talking to a shrink?" he asked.

"The psychiatrist I went to attributed the problem to early experiences that convinced me sex was dirty. And when she learned my father was a minister, she became fixated on that. I couldn't convince her my father wasn't responsible."

"So, you gave up on her?" Simon wasn't impressed with psychiatrists but thought Amelia, not the psychiatrist, may be overly fixated on her father's role.

"Yeah," she replied without elaboration. She appeared more interested in hugging and kissing than talking.

"And now you're trying your own cures," he suggested between kisses.

"But they aren't working. Can you do better?"

"Definitely!" He jumped up tugging at her jeans. "You don't need punishing. You need a willing partner and wholesome adventures. Like a romp through the positions in the Kama Sutra?"

"Not in one night!" she exclaimed but didn't stop him pulling off her pants. He gave her a token smack before pushing her on her back and spreading her legs apart.

"Or I could tie you to the corners of the bed and torment you to my heart's content."

"No!" she exclaimed, but her voice contained laughter, not fear. She was enjoying this.

"Then, my lovely, should we do it on the lawn?" He picked her up and hoisted her over his shoulder. He carried her downstairs and dumped her onto the living room sofa.

"I thought we were headed for the lawn."

"Is that your choice, or would you prefer something else?" he asked, confident the crisis had passed. She beamed. She would take one of his options, or another of her own devising, but none would involve hurtful spanking or other unwholesome behaviours.

Amelia gave him the wickedest smile he'd ever seen, stood and pranced to a bookcase. She pulled out a brightly illustrated volume with ornate gold on red lettering and an erotic south Asian drawing on the cover. She scampered up the stairs clutching the weighty volume and Simon knew exactly what she was up to.

Later, after they'd checked off two Kama Sutra positions, she wiggled until her back was pressed against him and murmured, "I love you." She was asleep in no time.

"I love you too," he whispered but didn't fall asleep as quickly. He had too many crazy events to consider.

Their little adventure seemed therapeutic for Amelia. She'd relaxed and become, frankly, sexier by the end. She'd lifted several veils and appeared ready to embrace a brighter future where they could be more open, more loving, and happier. But Simon didn't think he'd seen the end of her problems. She hadn't told him why she feared arrest and mistreatment by the police, or what terrible thing happened at Mount Saint Vincent University. Her explanation for tonight's crazy request had been fragmented and illogical. Until he had a credible explanation that covered everything, he wouldn't consider the problem solved.

Amelia had gone from a reserved, sometimes overly controlling and schoolmarmy lover who now admitted she hadn't enjoyed sex, to someone looking for sexual adventures. And she'd shown vulnerability while revealing her secrets. Simon could now envisage a long-term commitment. But that would entail more openness about his own past and an honest understanding of what he desired in a relationship.

Simon had personal matters to address, and puzzles to investigate, but first, he had a real-world mystery to solve. He fell sleep contemplating Holly's murder, the Millennium investigation, and his deteriorating relationship with Conrad Cavanaugh. Something was wrong with Cavanaugh, something his RCMP colleagues in Bridgewater wouldn't discuss. They apparently neither liked nor trusted the man but weren't willing to say anything. They retreated and changed the subject whenever Cavanaugh was mentioned. Cavanaugh was hiding something, something that needed exposure. And if a crisis developed when it was revealed, Simon couldn't ignore it.

Chapter Eighteen

Simon's personal life was working out well, weird and wild, with numerous twists and turns, but it was moving ahead. He couldn't say the same for Holly Craig's murder. Their investigation was into its fourth week and they had little to show for their efforts. They'd developed a better picture of Holly, including hints she'd planned her pregnancy, but nothing that would lead them to her murderer. Some evidence suggested a crime of passion, but their investigations confirmed her friends and acquaintances weren't responsible. A witness even provided Matthew Garrett, their prime suspect, with an alibi.

On Tuesday, September eleventh, two days after Sunday's wacky adventures, things, from Simon's perspective, got much worse. Detective Cavanaugh, with the support of the RCMP brass, insisted they attach Simon's murder to the Twenty-First Century Construction fraud case and transfer responsibility to the RCMP. Cavanaugh had two arguments. First, the Halifax police provided evidence that suggested the murder was a professional hit, not a local crime of passion. Second, the evidence Simon collected linked Holly to the Twenty-First Century investigation. It included proof she uncovered at least one lead the RCMP had missed.

Simon argued against the Halifax police evidence, saying it was based on unsubstantiated rumours of an Ontario-based hitman in the area. But the validity of the evidence he'd collected at Karli Leach's house wasn't open to question. He could only argue there was no proven link between Holly's journalistic endeavours and her murder.

His efforts were in vain. The chief agreed responsibility should shift to the RCMP. On paper, Simon would remain in charge of the murder investigation because it was important to keep the Twenty-First Century probe secret. Being a figurehead leader was little consolation.

After the meeting, Conrad Cavanaugh followed Simon to his office. "Tomorrow, we plan to search Carlotta Leach's house. There's an information gap in the material you unearthed. We'll be searching for another device or a memory stick hidden somewhere. Not your business, but she's a witness you found. We'll keep you informed. In the meantime, stay focused on the local picture."

He left before Simon replied.

Diana watched Cavanaugh storm away. "What's that about?"

"What part?"

"Any of it."

Simon described the meeting ending with the proposed search of Karli's house.

Diana drew the obvious conclusion. "Karli's an innocent bystander. They can't search anyone's house based on a vague idea there might be information relevant to a surveillance operation that may be going nowhere."

"They'll presumably use the murder as their justification," Simon replied.

"But on paper that's still ours. They left you in charge to keep their surveillance secret."

"Right, I'll have a quiet word about any application for a warrant with our legal people."

"Might help."

Simon drew a hand through his hair as he watched Cavanaugh's car turn, wheels squealing, onto Second Avenue. "I'm developing a more sinister idea. What if Cavanaugh expects me to warn Karli this search is imminent? That might cause her to do something stupid like trying to leave her place with her drug supply, assuming she has one. If they bust her for drugs, they'd have solid grounds for their search."

"Or they could catch her trying to remove the evidence they're after."

"What should we do? I don't want them busting her for marijuana possession."

"Officially, nothing."

"Don't watch me too closely."

Simon met Karli in her diner's parking lot to return the rings and bars she'd offered to Amelia and warn her about the impending search. Simon identified a surveillance car and ensured the watchers observed him passing the bag of ornaments. He departed once Karli understood what she was up against. Simon avoided making eye contact with the watchers as he returned to his car and drove away, thinking he'd done all he could under the circumstances.

Cavanaugh called early the next morning.

"Judge refused our warrant, so we need her permission to look for that memory stick. She's not working today. I want you to arrange it."

He didn't mention Simon's diner visit the previous afternoon, or express any surprise or annoyance at the judge's refusal.

"I'll see what she says."

"Good, do it now, she's already up. And be convincing or we'll produce a less friendly approach."

Obvious now, they have her under surveillance and were hell-bent on making their search happen. None of it was justified, but Cavanaugh was pushing hard. He must have a compelling reason.

Five minutes from her place, Simon pulled over expecting a difficult conversation. She agreed without hesitation.

"Let the creeps do what they want to my house, we can fix it up later. When will they arrive?"

"Within minutes of me phoning, I suspect."

"Should you, like, wait until you're here?"

"I'm at the bridge over the creek. I'll phone and come straight over."

"Okay, but hurry because I had a run in with them yesterday afternoon, and I'm not looking forward to another."

"What were they on about?"

"Your package of ornaments. They wouldn't leave me alone until I showed it to them and explained why you gave it to me. I, like, called Amelia your prissy girlfriend. Not fair and I hope they don't tell her, but I was angry, and that's what I said."

"Okay, I'll call now. Let no one in until I get there, and remember, you're doing this voluntarily."

When Simon arrived, a surveillance team monitoring comings and goings from her house insisted Simon show them his ID. Ten minutes later Cavanaugh and five other officers arrived in three RCMP cars.

Simon and Karli retired with her coffee pot to a table and lawn chairs overlooking the ocean, and Cavanaugh's team began work. She'd reverted to the freshly dyed purple hair, multiple adornments in each ear, and rings in her eyebrow and nostril that Simon remembered from his first visits.

"Did you put the others back in?" Simon asked after Karli poured the coffees.

She shook her head. "Considered it, but the holes are closing and I, like, don't want to return to them, anyway. I figured my latest 'up yours to the pigs' look was perfect for today."

"So, you expected them before I phoned."

"I figured they'd burst in at 2 a.m. I didn't get undressed because I didn't want them to break in and, like, find me naked."

"What were you planning to do today?" Simon asked a little later. "You're obviously not going to work."

"I'm, like, working on a project, but until it's more complete, I don't want to describe it."

"Okay, what should we talk about?"

For several minutes, Karli stared at the harbour without saying anything. "Bluenoses. One's for sale at Shelburne Yacht Club. My lawyer says I'll inherit some of Holly's money, and I wondered if I should buy it. Vera, Christine and I could come and beat the shit out of you and Amelia."

"Good luck, Amelia's been sailing all her life and takes it very seriously. You'll have a big task beating her."

"I was joking. I'm, like, not sure I want to race but having a sailboat would be awesome."

"Amelia will help you find a good boat once we get rid of Cavanaugh and his buddies."

"You don't like him, do you? Dyed hair and lots of body ornaments help when you have to deal with people you don't like."

Simon laughed. "Not sure your defence mechanism would work for me."

They sat drinking coffee and talking about nothing important for some time. Finally, Cavanaugh arrived carrying a handful of large sketchbooks.

He swept aside the coffee cups and thumped one onto the table. It was open to a page of comic-book-like drawings. "Did you create these?"

"Yes," she said.

"Were they done while you were friends with Holly Craig?"

A curt, "No," was her one-word reply.

Cavanaugh placed a pristine sketchbook with drawings on the first few pages above the other. "What about this one?"

"I, like, started it since I knew Holly died."

"Okay, one last requirement. We must determine if you've hidden anything."

"Wait a minute!" Simon interjected. "She's agreed to a voluntary search of her house for anything belonging to Holly Craig. Invasive searches aren't included."

"You may be morally correct," Conrad replied showing his frustration and anger by letting his voice rise. "But this exercise is in jeopardy if we aren't thorough."

"I disagree. A body search implies Ms. Leach is hiding something, and you have no grounds."

Cavanaugh took a breath and turned toward Karli. He even managed a smile. "Please, Ms. Leach, a woman officer has arrived, and we'll make this as pleasant as possible."

Karli shrugged her shoulders, gave Simon a look that said 'I knew this would happen', and walked toward the house. Did she blame him for this latest development?

"This is wrong," Simon insisted after Karli and a female officer disappeared into a main floor study, closing the door behind them. He was fighting a losing battle. Cavanaugh was in the wrong, but Karli's unexpected acquiescence emasculated his arguments.

"You know damn well it's necessary," Conrad responded with the anger back in his voice.

"She's not a bloody suspect. As far as you're concerned, she's an honest upstanding citizen helping you with your investigation. You should not treat her like a criminal."

"We must find this damn memory stick, and I don't care if we trample on your sensibilities or your bit of fluff."

Before Simon responded to this latest insult, someone flung open the door to the examination room. Karli burst forth with a colourful string of expletives.

"Jesus Christ, Conrad, can't you keep your people out?"

Simon marched over, slammed the door shut, and stood guard until they completed their strip search. Finally, the young woman officer erupted from the room. She exclaimed 'nothing' to Conrad and disappeared through the front door. Was she annoyed with Karli or Conrad and his crew?

Simon held Karli in his arms while she yelled obscenities at him and thumped away with her fists. By the time she'd calmed down, she'd inflicted considerable damage.

Conrad Cavanaugh stood in the foyer when they emerged from the study.

"I apologize," Conrad said, his voice almost gleeful. "Two of my men behaved badly and I will have their behaviour investigated. But for me at least, it was worth it." He held up a memory stick in a plastic evidence bag. "Do you recognize this?"

"It's, like, fine for you to sound happy," Karli retorted. "You didn't have to submit to a strip search while others watched! I need a drink. Simon, please come and have a glass of wine." She stomped to the kitchen without answering Conrad's question.

"But what about this memory stick? Is it yours?"

"Not mine, now leave me alone. And don't blame Officer Summers, she tried to be reasonable."

Simon offered to stay, but she wasn't interested. He departed after one glass of wine and a few unanswered questions about the memory stick and what Cavanaugh's men had done. He whiled away the afternoon, avoiding the station and Amelia until the bruises Karli inflicted faded. Simon was concerned about Karli, not his bruises, but when he called her, she refused to talk.

Simon now knew why other RCMP officers avoided Cavanaugh. He played fast and loose with the rules and had no qualms about dragging others into his schemes. Not something Simon wanted to learn about someone he'd be working with.

Chapter Nineteen

Simon and Amelia didn't get together to consider her sexual hang-ups until Thursday evening. He was too busy looking for Holly Craig's killer and trying to protect Karli from Conrad Cavanaugh's stupidity. Thursday afternoon seemed less hectic, so despite Wednesday's upheavals and his still somewhat battered appearance, Simon invited Amelia out for dinner. He suggested the Traveller's Inn dining room, a formal establishment he assumed she'd like, but no private room for Barrettsport society nor supercilious maître d'. She surprised him by opting for the hotel's faux-English pub. Like pubs in English inns, it had both private and public rooms. But unlike an English pub, the hotel guests patronized the public bar leaving the private room as the local artist's hangout.

"Why did you choose the pub?" he asked when they met outside the inn.

"I preferred the anonymity of a pub, and it looks like a good choice. What's happened to you? Looks like you lost a fight."

Simon laughed. "Karli kind of beat me up."

"What!"

"I can't say too much. Two of Detective Cavanaugh's boys mistreated her, and she took out her frustration on me. I'm glad she chose me as her punching bag or she'd be in a cell subject to more mistreatment."

"Is she okay?"

Simon nodded. "We'll sort it out, and the three of us can discuss everything."

Amelia headed to a table in a remote corner of the public bar. "Right now, it seems anything but okay."

"Is it time for your big secret?" he asked when they were settled with the first beers delivered and their dinner orders taken. He tried to give her a reassuring hug, but she backed away.

"First, tell me if you're coming home with me. I've washed the clothes you've scattered around my cottage, so you need not worry about clothes for tomorrow. You now have a little drawer space and room in my closet."

"I hoped you'd invite me." He'd accepted the change in their relationship and failed to see how her revelations would change anything.

"I didn't want what I'm planning to tell you to influence your decision."

"So, you have no excuse. What's your big secret?"

She had a large swallow of beer and placed the seriously depleted glass on the table.

"In my last year at the Mount, I lived with my boyfriend in a basement apartment. I thought we were committed but as I told you Sunday night, sex wasn't as exciting as I hoped. I suggested more adventuresome approaches, and he went ballistic. He tied me to the bed and beat me. When the police finally arrived, I argued it was sexual assault, but they didn't believe me. They saw wild-living university students with crazy activities that got out of control."

"Let me move over here," Simon suggested as he shifted from his chair to the bench where Amelia sat.

"Anyway," Amelia continued as Simon rearranged the tableware. "He left me shackled to the bed. A day later, Christine came by wondering why I hadn't come to classes. She called an ambulance. I must have looked awful."

"I bet you were the cutest little damsel in distress the world's ever seen," Simon suggested putting his arm around her and sneaking a kiss.

"Hardly," she snorted without pulling away from his attentions. "Everything got sorted out, and I returned to school the following week. Christine helped me finish the term. The guy pleaded guilty to a charge related to his abandoning me and got a suspended sentence. He was a student at St. Mary's not the Mount, so I never saw him again. That's my story."

135

"It's quite the story," he said as the waitress arrived with their food. "I'm surprised you'd ask me to spank you after that."

Amelia appeared ready to cry. "Because it solved nothing," she blurted out.

"Should we continue this conversation somewhere else?"

She shook her head. "If we were at my place, you'd hug and cuddle me and we'd end up in bed."

"Wouldn't that be good?"

"It would, but we need this discussion."

"Okay, discuss away."

"It didn't solve anything."

"Maybe you hadn't found the right guy until I showed up," he suggested while offering her some fries. She'd ordered none, but the mound of ketchup she'd deposited on her plate suggested she planned to pilfer his.

She helped herself to a forkful. "The problem's in my head."

"But Sunday night was good."

"Yes, Romeo, wonderful." She reached out and caressed his hand.

"Isn't it obvious? We must generate adventures, play games, and experiment."

She slapped away the hand he'd rested on her thigh. "I'm not convinced, and definitely not here."

"Well, I'm not buying your cure or any need for punishment. We should build on Sunday night, visit a southern beach resort where no one wears clothes."

"God, you never give up. I suppose you're imagining dozens of couples merrily getting it off on the beach."

"I doubt that happens, but wouldn't it be fun?"

"Yeah, right! I can imagine explaining why I have an irritation from getting sand you know where."

"I understand that tropical beach sand is soft and smooth," he said before placing the small plastic bag with barbell-shaped gold bars and rings in front of her. "How about these?"

She peered at the bag. "What are they?"

"Karli's body piercing rings. She says she's done with them and thought you were interested and may like to try intimate body piercings. She gave them to me Sunday evening and said they were a present for you. They've been sterilized, so they're safe to use, but you'd have to go to one of those piercing and tattoo shops if you want to use them."

"No way! Your Goth girlfriend may buy into sharing such things, but I think it's totally gross!"

"So, you wouldn't use them."

She held the bag gingerly between thumb and forefinger and passed it back to Simon. "Never in a million years."

"She's not my girlfriend. You're my girlfriend and I don't need another. She's more like the little sister I never had."

"It's nice that your little sister offers me presents even if I can't accept them. And I have a gift for you."

"Oh," Simon said glancing under the table for a hidden present.

"Not a real present, some information."

"That can be just as good. Something about Holly's baby?"

"Yeah, how did you know?"

"A lucky guess. What did you discover?"

"Christine told me Holly planned the pregnancy, and she and Vera were going through legal hoops to adopt it. Also, Karli knew about the baby and their plans."

"Interesting. Diana can work on it."

"And something else. Christine told me where Holly's doctor is."

"Where?" Simon asked when she paused, apparently uncertain about something.

"Halifax clinic. I left the address at home."

"If we're done eating, we can get it."

"But I'd rather you didn't stay."

"Something's wrong?"

"I need to consider what we've been discussing and check out southern beach resorts where I can do naked cartwheels."

"Now that's an image I can handle. But what about Saturday? We're still on for the race?"

"Of course, the race and the aftermath, I haven't forgotten."

But Amelia had obviously forgotten that only an hour earlier she'd extracted a promise he'd go home with her regardless of the outcome of their conversation. He understood this subject was hard for her, and her change of heart showed the whole business had her in a tizzy. He'd give her time to sort things out while he worked on the new leads she'd given him.

Simon and Diana spent the next week trying to link Matthew Garrett's suspicious behaviour with Cavanaugh's suggestion of a professional hitman. They also expanded their look into the activities of Karli, Christine, and Vera. Amelia's revelations showed the lives of these three women were more intricately interwoven with Holly's than Simon had realized. They knew Garrett was the father of Holly's baby. Could they link Garrett with Karli, Christine or Vera?

Tuesday, one week after the Mounties took command, Constable Evans forwarded a break-in report to Simon. The chief assigned Evans the desk-bound task of managing the reports submitted by the other constables because he wasn't yet capable of performing his normal duties. He had a cast extending from below his shoulder to his fingertips, and the bruising and stitches on his face prevented him from speaking clearly.

The report described Constable Kerry's investigation of a break-in sometime between August ninth and September sixth at an unoccupied house on Elm Street. It was less than a block from their murder scene. Simon didn't understand the connection, but the time and location matched, and he and Diana were desperate for a new lead.

Chapter Twenty

A telephone interview with Mr. John Ogden, the house's owner, generated the basic story. He'd purchased the property in June but left it vacant over the summer. When he arrived September sixth to begin preparation for moving in, he discovered the kitchen door had been forced. He informed the police, and Constable Kerry's report made two important observations. First, Mr. Ogden claimed the intruder only disturbed the kitchen, and second, Kerry noticed an odour that reminded him of butchering an animal.

Simon learned of the incident on September eighteenth, a month after the murder and twelve days after Ogden discovered the break-in. He focused on his yard during the single day he was on site, and following Tom Kerry's instructions, avoided the kitchen.

With Mr. Ogden's permission, Simon began his own investigation. He sent Diana to question the neighbours about anything they observed around August eighteenth and turned his attention to the house.

Simon soon realized he needed the RCMP forensic team. He was mulling over contacting Cavanaugh when Diana arrived with news. She'd found a witness who saw a car leaving the driveway on the morning of August eighteenth. She even had a partial licence plate number. Simon now had no choice. It didn't matter how unhappy he was about the way Cavanaugh's people treated Karli. He needed to inform Cavanaugh and obtain forensic support.

Within two hours, the forensic squad was on site and Simon returned to his office while Diana interviewed neighbours. He developed a new scenario that returned Garrett to the picture. It used the empty house as a staging ground for Holly's murder. After an early morning visit to the house for the club, he could arrive at Holly's apartment at seven thirty and commit the murder after eight. He could return to the house for initial cleanup including change of clothes, and then home at eight forty-five. A return to tidy the apartment and another to the house would complete the task.

Later, when he ran his latest theory past Diana, she shook her head. "This can't be right. He had calls on his landline, so he was home from ten thirty through the noon hour. And he spent ages arguing with the chief and the mayor about the protest fiasco. Insufficient cleanup time and I doubt he has the skill for such a thorough job. And what about the car? It isn't Garrett's and there's no need for a strange car in your scenario."

"Good points. I must consider them."

"You do that, I'll get coffee."

"Here's my theory," Diana said as she placed the two coffee cups on Simon's desk. "Cavanaugh is right about the hitman. Either Garrett hired him, or someone else associated with Twenty-First Century did, and Garrett facilitated the hit. He arrived at Holly's apartment at seven thirty for a surprise or prearranged visit. He unlocked the patio door. The hitman, who arrived in our mystery car and holed up at the house, now has access to the apartment. Once he's committed the murder at say eight thirty, Garrett leaves and the hitman cleans up the apartment. After he's done, he dumps the murder weapon in the house and departs. Later, Garrett cleans up the house and deals with the murder weapon."

"It gets around your two objections to my version. But why break into a house and leave the murder weapon?"

"I agree, we need to understand why he would take these risks."

"If we accept your picture as our working hypothesis, how do we prove it?"

"Forensics might give us something."

"In several days. Isn't the car a better bet for quick progress?"

"We have a partial plate number and a description. A stolen car would point right at Cavanaugh's hitman idea."

Simon pointed his felt marker at Diana. "That's our best bet. Few cars will match your three letters and physical description."

"I'm onto it."

"I'll visit our windmill company's offices. Your hitman theory means Twenty-First Century and that links to Bluenose Wind Energy. They've been in business for weeks. There should be some activity."

"Why would you visit? We shouldn't know about links between the business and the murder."

"But Garrett's on our radar screen. I'll ask about his movements and his explanation of being seen by the air conditioner man. We haven't pursued that. It's a big inconsistency in his story, so it will appear suspicious if we don't investigate."

"We have three likely matches," Diana said when Simon returned. "Best bet reported stolen on August twentieth. The others are registered in remote areas, one in Cape Breton and the other in Amherst."

"What's the story?"

"Mazda left in the Stanfield Airport's long-term parking on August seventeenth and reported stolen when the owner returned. RCMP found it in a different location."

Simon drew the obvious conclusion. "The owner forgot where he left it."

Diana shook her head. "He had a card from the shuttle bus driver that indicated his location, and the ticket was missing."

"Kids taking it for a joyride?"

"Not likely with a modern car, and the lot's manned twenty-four seven. I'd say Cavanaugh had this one right. Learn anything at the Wind Energy office?"

"Almost non-existent, one secretary/receptionist and four unused offices. Garrett's hardly been seen. Nothing like the hoop-la during their official launching, but she didn't appear to be hiding anything."

"Nothing there for us to chew on?"

"Your murder by hitman scenario sounds more promising." Simon stepped to his whiteboard and started scribbling. "Did Garrett hire him? Crime of passion or something related to Twenty-First Century Construction? Why did the hitman need Garrett's help? Where is our murder weapon?"

"He didn't leave it in the stolen car. I suggest our hitman flew into Halifax, stole a car from the long-term lot, drove to Barrettsport, and returned it to the lot. The whole exercise could have taken less than twelve hours. The weapon is still here, or dumped along the road."

"Seems farfetched, easier to rent a car? But the evidence suggests you're right, so we keep looking for the club." He turned to his whiteboard and added 'How did Garrett get to the motels?' "Many questions to address."

Diana sighed. "They should keep me busy."

But Simon knew she was happiest with lots to investigate.

He wasn't as content. "And I'm unhappy with the whole Twenty-First Century Construction investigation. The Mounties should keep us better informed. We provide good leads and they shut us out. Where's the cooperation they promised?"

Donna's smile turned to a frown. "Be careful. Don't generate more barriers because you distrust Cavanaugh."

"Cavanaugh mistreated an important witness, and he dragged me into the whole miserable exercise, damaging respect Karli had for any of us."

"Don't let it cloud your judgement."

Simon and Diana plugged away at the investigation but their most recent discoveries strengthened the RCMP's hold on the case. They focused, as per their instructions, on Holly's friends and acquaintances and the local aspects of the case.

They received the forensic report the following Monday. It proved the sink drain contained human blood of Holly Craig's blood type, and tissue fragments that were undergoing further analysis. They failed to associate one print with any known occupant or visitor to the house. It wasn't Garrett's but it might have been their purported hitman's.

Simon sighed, lamenting that these interesting aspects were no longer their purview. He turned to Diana and her efforts to established the veracity of Vera and Christine's story.

She was equally frustrated by their reduced role. "I confirmed Vera and Christine's alibi for the day of the murder. They spent the weekend in New England at a business shindig. It's tight; there's no way they've fabricated it."

"Boring routine, but necessary."

"Vera's lawyer confirmed the adoption was signed and sealed and waiting for the delivery that never happened. I also talked to Holly's doctor. She was aware of the adoption plan. Her pregnancy was progressing well, and Holly was enthusiastic about having the baby for Christine and Vera. Where is this heading?"

"The whole scheme was sufficiently complicated to generate a motive. We must tie up these loose ends."

"The scheme, as you call it, made sense. Christine said she couldn't have a child, Vera didn't want a pregnancy because of career commitments, but she and Christine wanted a child. Holly wanted the experience of having a baby. It was an ideal solution. I don't accept it unravelled."

"All right. Holly's pregnancy is another blind alley. I thought it might lead us somewhere."

"What if Garrett discovered their plan and decided he had to keep it from happening?"

"Too thin. Would have ended their affair, but not a reason for killing her." Simon sighed, focussing on these minor details was depressing them both. "The pregnancy is another dead end."

"Look on the bright side. You've discovered a new assistant. Amelia the amateur sleuth made real progress when we'd been stymied."

"Yeah, because this crazy trio wouldn't talk to us. And I'm not happy with Amelia going from suspect who found the body to co-investigator."

Diana paused in his office doorway. "You forgot about lover. She went from suspect to lover to investigator."

Diana's parting comment reminded Simon of his personal problems. He made another unacknowledged attempt to contact Karli before spending several frustrating hours digging into Amelia's past.

Chapter Twenty-One

When Cynthia Ettinger offered for the municipal elections scheduled for Saturday, October twentieth, she became the first woman to seek elected office in Barrettsport. Amelia Craddock, Beverley Campbell, Lisa Powell, and Mildred Wexler spearheaded Cynthia's precedent-setting run for selectman. Simon remained on the sidelines convinced Cynthia's role in the topless protest two months earlier would ruin her chances. She disagreed, insisting the townsfolk's strong Bohemian streak turned the protest into a positive factor. Barrettsporters, according to Cynthia, loved eccentric behaviour, encouraging those who figuratively, or actually, let it all hang out. And anyone who'd been put off wouldn't have supported her, anyway.

Cynthia's campaign generated buzz, but she had little chance. All three incumbents were re-offering, and no re-offering selectman had been defeated in living memory. None won with less than eighty percent of the votes.

Simon tried to ignore Amelia's constant preoccupation with the fight. He helped her put up campaign signs but wasn't engaged until the twice-weekly meetings Cynthia hosted in Mildred's Olde English Tea Shoppe caught on. The meetings organized to discuss the electorate's ideas on modernizing Barrettsport without losing its unique character were a central feature of Cynthia's campaign.

For the first few, Simon arrived late and helped rearrange the tables and chairs for the next morning's business. As the meetings gained popularity, and discussion of the various proposals became the talk of the town, Simon started coming earlier and listening more carefully. Cynthia had developed a crafty election strategy. At the cost of cups of tea for the participants, she generated a forum for presenting her ideas and a sounding board for public reaction to them.

By the final week of the campaign, the crazy ideas various people presented at Cynthia's meetings dominated the political conversation. From the level of public engagement, one might conclude Cynthia would get herself elected, but it didn't happen.

One thousand three hundred and fifty-four citizens cast ballots for selectman, and each voter could vote for three candidates. David Adams was the most popular, polling 1150 votes, Kendrick Smith was second with 1096 and Matthew Garrett polled 988. Cynthia did remarkedly well, receiving 623 votes and the remaining four candidates, less than a hundred. At their election night party, Cynthia vowed to continue working for change.

The day after the election, Amelia, Jeremy Witherspoon, and two other Bluenose owners decommissioned their boats. With Jeremy masterminding things, the day developed into a season-ending party.

Simon and Amelia released *Pallas Athena* from her mooring and paddled her to a large derrick on the foreshore. They wrapped a rope around the mast and hauled it from the boat after disconnecting the stays. Later, Jeremy towed the four demasted sailboats behind his family's Boston Whaler to the boatyard where they were placed on their wooden storage cradles.

An hour later, the four boats were in their winter parking spaces next to the other Bluenoses. Jeremy, the gracious host as always, insisted on drinks before they began the messy task of washing away the summer's accumulation of algae and barnacles. A pressure washer supplied by the resourceful Mr. Witherspoon made this a less daunting task. Finally, the boats were shrouded in canvas winter covers. Simon had to ignore the freely flowing booze during the return trip to the yacht club.

It was late afternoon and cold when Jeremy nosed the whaler into the beach in front of Amelia's cottage. Amelia and Simon splashed into the foot-deep water, pushed the whaler into deeper water, and scrambled ashore. Jeremy gunned the motor and proceeded to the club while Amelia and Simon raced across Amelia's extensive lawn and up the wooden stairs onto her back deck.

"Don't you dare take those stinky algae inside my cottage," Amelia yelled from a few metres behind as Simon charged onto the deck.

"You mean leave the boots and wet gear out here?"

"I mean leave everything out here. I don't want you dripping that crud on my floors."

When Simon shed his boots and wet gear, he realized she had a point. The sleeves of his shirt and sweater were sodden and aromatic. His pants weren't much better. He stood dripping on the deck while Amelia fetched her garden hose and washed off both sides of their wet gear. She dumped it into a large bin she'd apparently left for this purpose.

"Everything else goes in here too," she said as she started stripping off her wet clothes.

Their wet, algae-covered socks, pants and shirts soon joined the wet gear. When Simon looked up, Amelia stood outside the door stripped to her underwear.

She slid it open. "Take the bin to the basement. Prop the boots upside down on the floor and drape the wet gear over the drying rack. Everything else goes in the washing machine, but don't start it. I'll set up a fire and we can hit the shower."

Simon considered their roller coaster relationship as he sorted the laundry. On the morning of the topless protest, when they were strangers, she behaved coquettishly. For three weeks she ricocheted between standoffish and blatantly aggressive, mostly the latter. Everything came to a head on the Sunday evening after they visited the barrier island. The playfully sexual approach they fell into worked, and they'd settled into a more stable relationship for the past six weeks. Did her current behaviour suggest it had become too stable? He threw his boxers into the machine with the wet clothes and hurried up the stairs.

She grinned when she stood from messing with the fireplace. "Looks like you're ready for the shower."

Clean and warm from the shower and unencumbered by clothes, Amelia pulled the quilt and pillows off her bed and led Simon to the large sheepskin rug in front of her living room fireplace. She lit the fire, and they snuggled together while it warmed the room.

"There," she said. "Isn't this good?"

"You planned it, didn't you?"

"We agreed to dream up more romantic encounters. Isn't snuggling on a cozy rug in front of a roaring fire perfect? And after we've warmed up—"

"And enjoy other things, I presume."

"Of course. After we've had our fun, I have beer and pizza ready to go. That's okay, isn't it?"

"Sounds perfect."

"You should lie back on my rug and enjoy because tonight, I'm in charge, and you'll follow my lead."

Simon smiled, ready to enjoy receiving, rather than giving, the attention. They were experiencing the varied love life they were striving for with no suggestion of Amelia being punished for her sins.

The next morning at breakfast, Simon raised Amelia's fear of arrest. "It's come to my attention—"

"Now that sounds ominous," she interjected. "Should I ask how it came to your attention?"

"Unfortunately, in a murder investigation we must dredge up background information, and I couldn't exclude you."

"And what terrible secrets did you discover?"

"Your description of the Mount St. Vincent incident wasn't complete."

"What critical detail did I omit?"

"That the Halifax police questioned your story because you had a history with them."

She set down her coffee cup and stood hands on hips, ready to pounce. "It was irrelevant and totally unfair. I participated in several protests when I was an undergraduate and arrested twice. No charges were laid, and they shouldn't have labelled me a troublemaker when the other thing happened."

"But they did, making three occasions when you were pushed around. Is that why you fear arrest?"

"Fear arrest, what makes you think I'm afraid of the police? You don't scare me one bit."

"That's what you told us when Diana and I interviewed you on August eighteenth."

She turned toward him wagging her right forefinger in an admonishing gesture. "You have it wrong. The Halifax police didn't mistreat me. An evil deputy sheriff at a New England university town where Dal's volleyball team attended a tournament caused my nightmares."

"You want to explain?"

"At our victory celebration, an idiot spilled beer over me, and I got upset. I ended up getting arrested, not the guy who spilled the beer, intentionally, I might add, but me, the innocent victim. The deputy was mean as hell and really did mistreat me."

He leaned over and gave her a hug. "Sorry, I didn't want to cause you anxiety, but I needed an explanation for that statement."

"You took long enough, and I suppose you'll dig up the report."

"Probably, but it won't mention mistreatment. If you want to elaborate, you must tell me yourself."

She shook her head as she cleared away the breakfast dishes. "Time to prepare for work."

They'd brought the sailing season to a tidy conclusion, and Simon had a new understanding of Amelia's behaviour, but the murder investigation languished. DNA analysis of tissue residues collected from the sink in John Ogden's house identified them as Holly Craig's, so the house was linked to the murder. But they found no witness who linked Matthew Garrett to the house, and renewed efforts to find the murder weapon proved fruitless. The

Mounties checked into Mr. Ogden's family but found nothing suspicious, and their mystery fingerprint matched none in police files.

Nothing they'd discovered proved or discredited Diana's murder by hitman scenario.

"We've been skirting around an important weakness in your explanation," Simon said to Diana late one afternoon while they sat in his office mulling over the case. They had no new leads, so they were spending more time discussing their jigsaw puzzle pieces than investigating.

"What now," Diana responded. Her frown revealed her frustration with his insistence on revisiting annoying details.

"Hitmen don't club their victims."

"We've been over that. He wanted it to look like a crime of passion."

Simon shook his head. "If he did, and we fell for it, it would lead us to Garrett. Why offer us Garrett?"

"They thought we would go elsewhere?"

"That doesn't wash. If they wanted to send us on wild goose chases, Garrett would have been planting clues."

"What are you suggesting?"

"We've said, ever since the hitman scenario surfaced, that either Garrett or someone in Twenty-First Century, hired him."

"So?"

"Garrett being responsible doesn't wash. That leaves someone in Twenty-First Century."

Diana leaned forward waving her pen. "And they would have Garrett as fall guy if anything goes wrong!"

"We should be searching for our perpetrator around Twenty-First Century Construction and considering why they would set up Garrett."

After their conversation, Simon rearranged his puzzle pieces and generated a new flowchart on his whiteboard. The key factor became Holly Craig's journalistic investigation of Twenty-First Century Construction. Simon now assumed Holly established a relationship with Matthew Garrett hoping he might be the soft underbelly of Twenty-First Century.

They'd previously focused on the Garrett-Craig link, looking for something so damning that Garrett couldn't live with it. Could Garrett be a secondary player, a source of information in Holly's investigations and an unwitting sperm donor for her baby?

Simon turned to Twenty-First Century and their scheme to build dozens of government-subsidized windmills. Garrett became the local frontman they needed for their scheme and Holly' secret source. Simon now had a triangle of two-headed arrows on his flow chart linking Holly Craig, Matthew Garrett and Twenty-First Century. If Garrett or Twenty-First Century learned that Holly had uncovered evidence that jeopardized the whole wind energy scheme, they may have decided she had to go. Their evidence suggested Twenty-First Century made the decision.

If Holly found damaging evidence, it should have been in the computer Diana retrieved from Karli's house or the storage locker. But the RCMP kept Simon on the periphery, providing him with no details from their investigations. His strained relationship with Conrad Cavanaugh didn't help matters, but was that the real problem? Or was someone else withholding evidence Simon needed for his investigations? And what about the memory stick Cavanaugh claimed he found in Karli's house—the one she denied knowledge of? Why were they withholding this piece of critical evidence?

Chapter Twenty-Two

The recently completed election campaign raised new questions about Matthew Garrett. Cynthia Ettinger characterized him as an ineffective selectman with few real friends, and it wasn't merely a personal dislike based on his marital problems with her friend Caroline. Simon had detected a more generalized disrespect for Mr. Garrett during the election meetings at Mildred's café.

While waiting for the RCMP's response to his latest request for information, Simon compiled background information on Matthew Garrett. A strange picture of an outsider who'd wormed his way into local society emerged. Garrett had established an investment company that managed the assets of many of the wealthy townspeople and got himself elected to council. But how did that bring them around to the Windmill scheme and Holly's murder? Were the Mounties sitting on information that might answer these questions?

Deer hunting season began Sunday morning. A call forwarded by Constable Kerry interrupted Simon's deliberations. "It's John Bell. He's on McConnell's Creek Road and says he can see a body in a ravine. He's a Barrettsport resident, so he called here, but he's not within the town boundaries. Protocol says I contact the RCMP in Liverpool. Do you want to get involved?"

"Tell Liverpool I've responded."

Simon turned onto McConnell's Creek Road ten minutes later. After a few minutes bouncing up the rough dirt road in the police force's Jeep, he spotted a man in an orange hunting vest leaning against an SUV.

"Mr. Bell," Simon said, jumping from the Jeep. "I'm Simon Goodyear, Barrettsport PD. I don't think we've met, but I understand you're one of our townspeople. We're outside the town boundary, so someone from the RCMP in Liverpool should be here shortly. While we wait, why don't you show me what you've found?"

Mr. Bell walked along the dirt road. "I was poking around while waiting for my friends. We should be deer hunting, but they're late. I looked into the ravine, and I think there's a body by the creek. I knew I should call the police and well, you guys are my police, so I called you."

He pointed into the ravine. "Isn't that a body?"

Simon's binoculars helped clarify the situation. "Have a gander. Looks like a body to me."

"City slicker," Bell responded. "No one else would venture into the woods dressed like that."

Simon retrieved a rope from the Jeep and tied it to a tree twenty metres downstream from the body.

"You stay here and wait for the Mounties. I'll see if it's someone who needs help."

John Bell gazed down the slope. "Nothing's gone down that slope recently. He's been there for a while."

"You're probably right, but I must be sure."

"A car's coming," Mr. Bell yelled when Simon was halfway down the bank. And a few seconds later, "it's only my buddies."

"Stay where you are," Simon yelled back.

At the bottom, he tied the rope to another tree and pushed his way through thick, gnarly undergrowth. Various animals had attacked exposed skin on the partially decomposed body. Simon decided the corpse was masculine without touching anything, returned to his rope, and climbed up the bank.

The hunters waited by their vehicles. "Definitely a body, Mr. Bell, and it's been there for some time. If you want to get on with your lives, I'll need names, addresses, and phone numbers before you leave."

153

Mr. Bell waited with Simon for the RCMP corporals who arrived a few minutes later. After taking statements, they called the major crimes unit in Bridgewater.

Half an hour later, a fifty-year-old RCMP detective arrived from Bridgewater. Detective Matheson was the sort of imperious officer Diana disliked, and one of Mr. Bell's 'city slickers'. He berated the two young corporals, dismissed Simon's efforts to avoid disturbance of a potential crime scene, and ignored Mr. Bell. He called for the coroner and forensic experts, then departed leaving the two young corporals in charge.

"I wish you hadn't seen that poor example of community relations," Simon said to Mr. Bell before turning to the corporals. "Any reason for Mr. Bell to stay."

One shook his head. "When we need you, someone will be in touch."

Mr. Bell shrugged his shoulders and turned to Simon. "He was only doing his job."

Simon remained at his newest crime scene.

After describing his actions to the head of the forensic squad, Simon returned to the station and the picture he was developing of Matthew Garrett's adult life. Much was speculation, but it fit the facts as they knew them. Monday morning, he tested his ideas on Diana.

"I start in 1990 with a restless young Wall Street analyst, a man with an MBA and masses of ambition, but too impatient for the job he's landed. He meets Caroline Wexler, an attractive young heiress from the obscure town of Barrettsport, Nova Scotia. Garrett concocts a scheme that involves marrying her, becoming manager of her family's wealth, and that of other wealthy families in the town. He sees it as a shortcut to fame and fortune."

"We should determine if Garrett's job in Wall Street was as dead end as you suggest."

Simon nodded. "It's not critical. I'm developing a picture where he thinks the job isn't progressing quickly enough. It may not be the truth, but he's impatient. He's a manipulator and unwilling to wait for his career to develop along normal lines. He dreams of being the financier for a whole community of dilettantes who need someone to manage their money."

"You're making him into a Machiavellian villain, but why?"

"Villain definitely, but not Machiavellian. Machiavelli was duplicitous and that's not the theme I'm developing. My villain is addicted to scheming and intrigue, a big-time manipulator. He prides himself in having everything so much under control he needn't stab anyone in the back. He'll set someone up for a fall but thinks it's less than ethical to turn on a confidant."

Diana shook her head. "You're trying to draw an unnecessarily fine distinction, but don't worry. How did you develop this picture of Mr. Garrett?"

"From listening to Cynthia and the others during the election campaign. I realized he was a more complex person than we'd appreciated."

"You've moved a long way from our position a few days ago when we didn't buy into the Mounties' hitman theory. Now you have a giant conspiracy centred on Matthew Garrett. But, carry on, you're spinning an intriguing yarn."

"I hope it's the truth, not just a yarn. I'll fast forward a few years. His scheme works out as planned. He marries the girl, sets up a successful financial management business, and becomes part of 'Barrettsport Society'. He gets elected selectman and is on his way to being mayor of his utopian City State. But he becomes far too cautious and conservative. He drifts into a life of complacency."

"Now, you're generating a Dr. Jekyll and Mr. Hyde."

Simon smiled, his enthusiasm for his story growing. "I am. His Dr. Jekyll persona is a stodgy conservative businessman and his Mr. Hyde a ruthless, scheming, badly flawed visionary. He lives his Dr. Jekyll life for many years, and then, Mr. Hyde comes to the surface. He takes on Holly Craig as a mistress and resumes his scheming ways, this time intent on squirreling away a fortune he would disappear with. Garrett would start over again somewhere else without the conservative baggage that had grown up around him in Barrettsport."

"Are you also suggesting his conservative nature bogged down the Wall Street career he escaped from by disappearing with Caroline to Barrettsport? And now it's happening again, but this time he'll disappear from Barrettsport."

"Exactly."

Diana turned, staring out Simon's office window. "Okay, I see the picture. But, is it more than unsubstantiated speculation based on Amelia, Cynthia and Miss Wexler's conversations about their main opponent during the heat of an election campaign?"

"I developed this picture of an unstable person smack dab in our murder investigation while listening to those conversations."

She rose from her chair and scrawled words describing their two key issues on Simon's whiteboard. "But that's the point, isn't it? How do these character flaws lead to Holly Craig's murder? And don't tell me you're planning to link this to the body you found on Saturday."

Diana drew thick red lines between Garrett, Craig, and Twenty-First Century and turned to face Simon.

Chapter Twenty-Three

Simon stared at the connections Diana highlighted. "Two questions. Why would Matthew conspire to murder Holly, and how do we link the murder to another body?"

"Speculation about your second body is pointless, because it may have no relevance to our case. Merging Garrett's new profile with the facts of Holly's murder might produce something useful."

"Fine. Leave the second body for now. I'll try to link my picture of Garrett to Holly's murder."

"Okay, fire away," Diana responded.

"We're up to eighteen months ago. He wants out of his marriage and his life in Barrettsport but needs money. He gets involved with Twenty-First Century Construction for the money. But they have their own problems. Cavanaugh and the RCMP are investigating their activities and Holly, the investigative journalist, is also poking into their affairs. Suppose they learn Holly is getting close to uncovering something critical. Someone concocts a scheme to permanently rid them of the threat Holly poses. It's either Garrett's scheme, or he's roped into it by someone at Twenty-First Century."

"And the Garrett Craig romance?"

"Take your pick. Holly knew about Garret's role in Bluenose Wind Energy, so she encouraged the romance to get dirt on Twenty-First Century. Or Garrett initiated the romance to gain power over Holly because she represented a threat. Or it started as a simple extramarital affair."

Diana raised her hand while shaking her head. "If Garrett hired a hitman, he would have established a solid alibi far from the murder scene."

"I would argue what happened shows a lack of trust between Twenty-First Century and Garrett."

Diana stood, turned her coffee cup upside down and shook it. "We've gone wrong somewhere. Before we step back and reconsider this, I'm getting more coffee. Want some?"

She returned a few minutes later with two coffees and a plate of brownies. "Margaret's been baking."

"Good brownie," Simon said after biting into one. "Where did I go wrong?"

"If we accept that Garrett had more sinister dealings with Twenty-First Century than the publicly acknowledged association with Bluenose Wind Energy, then much of this makes sense."

"But?"

"Not Garrett hiring the hitman. That doesn't fit your picture of Garrett the schemer and manipulator, someone with Machiavellian dreams. The hitman says organized crime and that, I suggest, points to Twenty-First Century, an organization with links to organized crime. The rest fits into place. Twenty-First Century orchestrated the hit, and they ensured they could implicate Garrett if they needed a fall guy."

"It also gives Garrett leverage. If they distrusted him, why not snuff him as well?"

Diana waved a pen in Simon's face. "They wanted rid of Holly but couldn't jeopardize the Bluenose Wind Energy deal. They need Garrett for that."

"I'll buy that. How do we prove it's fact, not my wild speculation?"

"First, establish that your history of Garrett's life is more than unsubstantiated rumours you picked up from Amelia, Cynthia, and Mildred. Should I go there next?"

Diana discovered that Matthew Garrett spent two years after college in the US Marines before joining a New York City stock brokerage as an account executive. One of his Wall Street colleagues described Garrett as a conservative plodder who'd never amount to anything. She called him a loner who bored everyone with his get rich quick schemes. When Diana asked her about Garrett's social life, she laughed saying he got nowhere with women.

"It wasn't through lack of trying," she added, "he was just uninteresting and inept."

Simon's efforts took him in a different direction. He learned from Detective Matheson that the body found in McConnell's Creek had been tentatively identified as one Bernard Cope, a known criminal from Ontario.

"Time of death?" Simon asked Matheson.

"The coroner says he's been dead for approximately two months. Forensic evidence suggests he was probably transported post-mortem and pushed over the edge. Cause of death is still under investigation, but it was not by drowning or any obvious stab or bullet wounds."

"And Bernard Cope?"

"Tough guy who worked for various criminal elements in Toronto as an enforcer starting in 1990. Arrested several times with two convictions for assault. Most recent release from prison was in 2005, no arrests since then."

"Does that suggest he left the area?"

"Our sources say he was promoted from front-line enforcement. He was implicated in a gang-related murder, but insufficient evidence for an arrest."

"Interesting. I'd appreciate it if you'd continue to share anything you can."

Matheson sighed. "We'll keep you in the loop."

Good start, Simon thought after terminating the call. They had a name for the body taken from McConnell's Creek and an approximate death date that overlapped with their murder. And Mr. Cope was a gangland enforcer from Toronto, home of Twenty-First Century Construction. Simon downloaded photos of Cope and placed copies together with a synopsis of his findings on Diana's desk.

He left for the town print shop where the proprietor was framing a large colour photo of *Pallas Athena*. When he got there, Karli Leach and shop owner Jacob Jonathon were admiring the finished product.

Karli looked up from the photo. "Yo, Simon, awesome picture. Present for Amelia?"

Simon laughed. "It's for my apartment. I'm finally decorating it. But what about you? We haven't seen you for ages."

"Better. It was, like, tough, but today Jacob and I are discussing the finishing touches to my latest project. And your mayor gave a bunch of us good citizen awards."

"It's an annual thing," Jacob explained. "The mayor singles out residents who've done something noteworthy."

"Yeah, really. I never expected a good citizen award. Like, what am I, Goth girl of the year because I provided information to your murder investigation?"

"Come for dinner. We should celebrate your success and catch up. We've missed your company."

"Like, can't. Jacob and I are busy, and I'm having dinner with them. What about after?"

"Great! Amelia's whenever you're free."

Simon departed Jacob's shop clutching his framed photo. His thoughts, however, were on Karli Leach. She'd avoided him and rebuffed his attempts to lend a helping hand in the six weeks after she was mistreated by Cavanaugh. Now he runs into her by accident and she's all smiles and friendship, behaving like nothing had gone wrong. She'd apparently worked her way through the aftermath of that traumatic event, and she'd done it without his help. He felt superfluous.

Amelia was at a school meeting when Karli arrived. She and Simon were soon enjoying glasses of pinot grigio Simon bought for the occasion.

"I'm glad we're friends again, and we, like, have to thank your funny old mayor," Karli said raising her glass and shaking her head. "Do you like my new earrings?"

Simon finally got the message. She was shaking her head to draw attention to the mayor's gift—large silver earrings featuring a square-rigged ship and the word 'Barrettsport'. "So, the mayor gave these to you outstanding citizens. They're quite handsome."

"Yes, silly, but only the women. I wondered when you'd notice. When I'm at work tomorrow, I'll be a walking advert for Barrettsport. They could put my picture on their website?" She sat up, preening. "I'd, like, look good wearing only the earrings."

"Nobody will notice the earrings."

"A low angle beach shot focusing on my head with just enough to show I was naked, a real art photo. Find me some paper, I'll, like, draw it for you."

She drew furiously and produced a drawing of a spiky-haired girl lying propped on her elbows. It was a good self-portrait. The face and hair and prominent earrings dominated the picture but her breasts were visible between her face and the sand.

"See," she said, "'naked beach girl with Barrettsport earrings'. It's, like, perfect, tits and bum are visible but you can't help focusing on the earrings. Here, you can have the sketch. If you put it somewhere prominent, you won't again abandon me for two months."

"It's beautiful, and it only took you a few minutes. I'm impressed. Thank you very much. I'll get a frame and put it in my bedroom."

"I could make a larger more finished drawing on better paper. That would make an awesome picture for your wall."

"Amelia will be jealous."

"I'll, like, do a similar picture of her, and you can have your two favourite naked women on your bedroom wall."

"Wonderful. But will she pose?"

"She's your girlfriend, so you should know better than me. If not, I can use my imagination."

Simon refilled the wine glasses. "You've been doing lots of drawing?"

"I go to work and I draw. My first graphic novel's nearly finished. A Goth girl gets brutalized by the cops and goes through hell but eventually recovers.

161

She rides into the sunset with her handsome saviour. He looks too much like you."

"I should be flattered, but why did you avoid me after our run-in with Cavanaugh?"

"Because I, like the heroine in my story, had to sort out my own demons. Now, I'm okay, and I, like, want my big brother back."

"Will you tell me your story, or must I wait for the book?"

"You should buy the book, but that won't tell you the real story. It's not an autobiography."

"So, will you tell me?" Simon asked.

"When Amelia gets here."

"I hope she isn't too long. The suspense may be hard to bear."

Karli scribbled for several minutes, filling several sheets with drawings of naked young women with prominently displayed earrings.

She sighed. "This is hard. The drawing I made for you was easy, an image I'd often imagined. But one for Amelia isn't, like, materializing?"

"Ask her what she imagines."

"Or I could ask you."

Simon picked up the rough sketches and perused them. "Discuss it with Amelia and let her choose. But not tonight. Tonight, I want to hear your story."

Chapter Twenty-Four

Amelia arrived home a few minutes after ten. Simon poured wine, and Karli started her story.

"A few days after our boat trip, the Mounties, like, came searching for stuff they insisted Holly hid in my house. Simon tried to protect me but I'm, like, stupid and let them abuse me despite Simon's efforts. When they were leaving, Cavanaugh showed me a memory stick he claimed he found during the search. I, like, knew the stick they wanted wasn't there, so it had to be a prop he brought with him. I'm, like, terrified, he hadn't found the stick, so he'd be back."

Her repeated use of the word like convinced Simon she remained traumatized. "Why didn't you tell me?"

Karli ignored Simon's question, but he knew the answer to his rhetorical question. "I got it to the lawyer who helped me with Holly's will and let her deal with it."

"How'd you manage that?"

"I'm, like, not stupid. I knew they'd be watching me so I borrowed a phone, relayed the message, and let her collect it. Two nights later Cavanaugh and the two creeps who'd abused me returned with an arrest warrant."

Amelia turned as pale as Karli. "Oh, my God."

"You okay?" Karli asked.

"Will be," Amelia replied as she cuddled up closer to Simon. "You better continue."

"They broke in at 2 a.m. and before I'm, like, awake, three men pulled me from my bed and handcuffed me. They dragged me down the stairs and shoved me into a squad car. I screamed and tried to kick and butt them, but I, like, couldn't stop them. One drove me to the Bridgewater RCMP station, but Cavanaugh and the other one stayed at my house."

"Why didn't they wait for you to answer your door, and what about their warrant?"

Karli again ignored Simon's question. "I refused to leave the car, so Cavanaugh's goon got another cop to help him drag me inside. I kicked and butted the goon, and I manage one good shot, but they, like, manhandled me inside and left me shackled to a chair. It was bolted to the floor and real uncomfortable."

"See, Simon," Amelia interjected with tears welling. "That's what happens when women are taken into custody. They get scared and overreact."

Simon sighed, wanting to avoid discussion of Amelia's arrest phobia. "It happens, but we should let Karli continue."

"A female officer tried to reason with me. She said she had to search me, and if I'd calm down, she'd remove the handcuffs. But I, like, wasn't listening, and when she got close, I kicked out at her. She called in Cavanaugh's goon and the one who helped him. She removed the restraints holding me to the chair, but not the ones keeping my hands behind me."

Karli paused, pulling Amelia into a comforting embrace. "I kept fighting, so the men held me while she pulled my pyjama pants off and cut away the top. When they had me naked, she proceeded with the searching I'm, like, rapidly becoming accustomed to, but I wouldn't stay still, and it was rough and painful. When she finished, they gave me one of those orange jumpsuits and marched me through the station to a cell."

Simon vented his frustration. "Only female officers and a private location, those are the regulations. But Cavanaugh and his team always ignore the rules!"

"Calm down, Simon," Amelia said, trying to soothe him. "You're getting more emotional about this than Karli or me. Let her continue with her story."

Simon smiled, Karli's little hug had done Amelia wonders.

"In the morning, Cavanaugh yelled questions at me through the bars. And I yelled abuse. Eventually, I told him my lawyer had the drive. He wouldn't let me phone her until much later, and she finally got me released at two thirty. She took me to a medical clinic where a gentle old male doctor checked over the scrapes and bruises I'd suffered during my struggles. Angelica, my lawyer, stayed talking on her cell phone. When Angelica took me home, we found the front door wide open, and the place trashed. I've been trying to recover ever since. I only returned to work a few weeks ago, but I drew a whole novel. It's, like, my therapy."

Simon joined the hug fest on the sofa. "What did the memory stick contain?"

"It's, like, been my saviour. Angelica, my lawyer, isn't that a perfect name, had everything downloaded and copied. It contained information Holly put together to protect her from abuse. It would have worked for me if I understood the situation and kept my cool. Angelica got the information to the right people and now everyone believes my story."

"And everyone lives happily ever after," Amelia suggested.

"Like, sort of. Carpenters repaired my house, and when I got Holly's car back, they'd fixed some funny noises it'd been making. They've paid to replace stuff we couldn't fix and Angelica's costs. They did charge me with withholding information from the police and resisting arrest. Angelica says they can't make the withholding evidence charge stick because the evidence was never at my house, and they never explained what they were looking for. But I have to worry about resisting arrest. I've recovered enough to deal with it, and I'm, like, planning to visit you two when your mayor invited me to today's meeting."

By the end of her story, she appeared unaware of tears streaming down her cheeks. Amelia led her upstairs and put her to bed.

When she returned, Amelia stood with her hands on her hips. "Stories like that make me fear arrest."

"It happens, but it's only a tiny fraction of arrests. She obviously resisted arrest, and she tried to assault several officers."

"She's not as tough as she pretends, a softy who cries easily. Can't you do something about the charges against her?"

"Not our jurisdiction, and it will probably blow over, but I'll keep a watching brief as I'm sure her lawyer will." Simon's vague promise left him with misgivings. The RCMP had kept a tight lid on the reputed internal investigation of Cavanaugh's behaviour. If the Mounties were pussyfooting around that investigation, how could he influence response to another of Cavanaugh's dubious adventures?

"I trust you'll do your best. Meanwhile, we must get to bed. I'm setting my alarm for six because Karli and I have work tomorrow, and we'll be slow getting going." Amelia turned toward the stairs but called over her shoulder. "Did you notice her new earrings?"

Simon laughed. "Not until she waved them before my eyes."

"They're great. I'm hoping someone will get me a pair for Christmas."

"Am I staying?"

"Yes, please. Karli's story was quite a downer, so I need reassurance, even if it's just gentle hugging."

The next morning, Amelia was asleep when Simon headed for the shower. She and Karli were waiting outside the bathroom door when he emerged.

Neither said anything as Simon dressed. He had the distinct impression he'd interrupted discussion of a dark secret. An outburst of giggling as he left the cottage confirmed his suspicion.

"You must be all dressed up tomorrow evening at seven-thirty," Karli called from the bedroom window. "Amelia's, like, taking us to dinner at a fancy restaurant, and we'll have a surprise for you!"

Overnight, Karli had progressed from traumatized victim of police brutality to giggling young woman.

Chapter Twenty-Five

Simon arrived at Amelia's front door wearing his best suit. He was on time for his promised outing with his two favourite women. The door swung open, revealing two young women in stereotypical 1920s flapper dresses with matching hats that resembled inverted bowls. Amelia's slim figure suited the straight-from-the-shoulders look, but Karli was too curvy for the dress she'd borrowed.

Amelia beamed. "Are we ready for the neighbourhood speakeasy?"

"I'm, like, not ready," Karli replied. "It squishes my breasts, and it's, like, too tight at the hips. We've made our show for Simon, I should put on a normal dress."

"But you can't wear the clothes you came in and my dresses will be tight on you and too long. This one's perfect, neither too tight nor too long. Your frilly panties made the material catch, so it didn't hang properly. You'll be fine."

"Provided a seam doesn't split when she sits down," Simon added.

"Cut it out, you're not being helpful. We tested it, it'll be fine." With that pronouncement Amelia grabbed her coat, picked up two packages sitting by the door and walked out, leaving Simon and Karli to scramble after her.

"Good evening Miss Amelia," Andre said when they arrived at Morgan's restaurant. "I've assigned a superb table for the three of you." He made an affected gesture with thumb and forefinger pressed to his lips. "Leave your coats here, and I'll put them away." After Amelia and Karli shed their coats, he added, "You two are delectable."

"Aren't we just," Amelia said, grabbing Karli so they could pose together. "This is our friend Carlotta."

"Welcome Miss Carlotta to Morgan's. My name is Andre and if any of my staff give you a reason to be unhappy, inform me, and I'll put it right. Please, come with me," he said taking Karli's arm and gesturing with a nod of his head. "Those two can manage for themselves."

He made a fuss getting Karli seated in the private dining area reserved for the 'families' before turning his attention to Amelia. She'd placed her packages on the fourth chair.

When it came time to order the wine, their waiter, like Thomas the previous time, suggested a chardonnay. Simon, knowing Karli preferred pinot grigio, overruled him. Amelia said nothing but gave him a salute that said 'well done, Romeo, I'll reward you later'.

During their after-dinner coffees, Amelia picked up one of her packages and turned to Simon. "You've been so good to us we decided you deserved a reward."

"Aren't we taking Karli to dinner?"

"I don't know what gave you that idea. It's always been Karli and I taking you to dinner."

Karli nodded her agreement. "Open them!"

From their shapes, Simon suspected they contained framed drawings and guessed they were two of Karli's figure drawings. "You sure you want me to open them here?"

"Like a birthday or retirement party with presents." Amelia was talking more loudly than usual, and other diners were already looking their way. Simon glanced at Karli to make sure she was comfortable with Amelia's foolishness. When he saw her look of joyous anticipation, he realized he lacked options.

More than Amelia's and Karli's eyes were on him as he unwrapped the pictures. Karli's self-portrait wasn't quite like the smaller sketch she'd drawn Thursday night. This one was more discrete with one of her forearms covering her nipples. Amelia's was also a nude, a front quarter side view showing Amelia with her bum in the air and her shoulders on the ground. Her face was turned toward the viewer, prominently displaying the town earrings.

Mayor Richard Merrick wandered by and leaned over the drawings. Everyone knew he was an art lover who considered the town's support for the artistic community one of his crowning achievements.

He addressed Karli as he peered at the drawings. "Beautiful drawings. Have you considered asking Jacob Jonathon or another printmaker to produce high quality numbered prints?"

Karli shook her head, agitating the earrings highlighted in both portraits. "I, like, made them for my friend Simon."

"Well, you should. The town will buy one of each and hang them with our Town Hall collection of works by local artists. And if you displayed them in Jacob's shop and other stores that cater to our tourist trade, you'd have an interesting product. They're quite lovely."

"And advertising for our little town," said Cynthia Ettinger as she joined the growing crowd admiring the drawings.

"Yes," replied the mayor, beaming. "Beautiful young ladies wearing beautiful earrings in our beautiful town."

Mr. Witherspoon, Jeremy's father, volunteered to buy drinks for everyone in the dining room, and the place turned, as Amelia had joked earlier, into a speakeasy. Even the crustiest members of Barrettsport society welcomed Karli with open arms, and several young debutants asked her about similar drawings of themselves.

By the time they departed, Karli was quite inebriated. She stumbled from the restaurant, stopped, and asked Simon for a ride. Simon hoisted her on his back which meant hiking her dress up to her hips and leaving her bum exposed because her jacket was short and her panties miniscule. Simon trotted down The Lane with Karli on his back. Amelia, laughing, and burdened with the two drawings, followed.

Simon and Karli arrived at Amelia's long before Amelia did, and when she arrived, they were laughing merrily on her garden swing. Amelia joined them and no one noticed it was a cold November evening. Eventually, they calmed down and retreated inside.

"I, like, can't believe it," Karli said. "I can't believe I went to such an expensive restaurant, and you could afford it. I can't believe so many people liked my drawings. I can't believe those two girls offered to undress so I could draw them. I wish I had paper and pencils with me."

"They wouldn't actually have done it," Amelia interjected. "They tease and joke, but they wouldn't do it."

"I, like, don't care, it would have been an awesome experience. I can't believe Mr. Witherspoon bought drinks for everyone, and, like, several rounds! I can't believe the mayor offered to hang my drawings in the town hall. I can't believe I got a piggyback ride mooning the whole town. I can't believe I could be this happy. I'm, like, in heaven and heaven is located at 133 Front Street, Barrettsport."

"My father's a minister," Amelia said, "and I'm not sure he would appreciate your definition of heaven, but I'll accept it for tonight."

"It's time for bed," Karli said a few minutes later stretching and yawning extravagantly. "I'm too wasted to drive, so may I stay the night?" When Amelia nodded her agreement, Karli dragged herself up the stairs.

"She's hoping you'll put her to bed," Amelia suggested after Karli left. "You should go tuck her in."

"When you get home," Karli whispered when Simon stopped in to say good night, "remove the back from the Amelia drawing. You'll find another you'll especially like. She, like, posed without fuss."

"Are you happy?" Simon asked later when he joined Amelia in her bed.

"Happy?" she asked while spreading her arms and drawing him into a naked embrace. "I know you're in love with Karli and I am too. We love her like our little sister and when you coddle her, I'm proud of you, not worried. Now, my Casanova, time to have your randy way with me."

Soon, she was satiated and sleeping the sleep of an innocent sprawled across the bed. He watched her purring like a kitten and marvelled how so much had changed in two short months. Amelia had gone from avoidance to sexual adventure. She'd managed to dispel her fear of sex and they'd resolved the issues related to her mistreatment by the police.

Most important were the insights into his own attitudes. He agreed with Amelia when she suggested he was in love with Karli. A year or two earlier, he would have reacted much more sexually and tested Karli's homosexual resolve. But he was now committed to a monogamous relationship with Amelia, and confident he could keep his feelings for Karli at a Platonic level.

He eased Amelia away from the centre of the bed, pulled up the covers, and snuggled against her. He was soon sleeping as peacefully as she was.

"I loved the drawings you made for me," Simon said when Karli and Amelia arrived for breakfast. "They're wonderful, and I'm sure you can sell prints."

"You think?" Karli asked. "Selling drawings never occurred to me."

"You'll need new subject matter," warned Amelia. "Those two girls sounded keen last night, but they might have second thoughts. And how many ways can you spin this quirky idea?"

Simon sat back considering Amelia's comments and social activities he'd observed during his short tenure in Barrettsport. Several were odd and risqué. An idea popped into his head. "If you're looking for an idea, consider a Barrettsport's Beauties Charity Calendar like the one in that Helen Mirren movie a few years ago. Lots of young women might pose for you wearing those Barrettsport earrings and little else."

"Will anyone participate?" Karli asked. "Or will it be like Amelia suggested, all talk and no action."

Simon looked at Amelia. She picked up her portrait and studied it. "If Karli makes the poses adequately modest. Yeah, if it's carefully done, a Barrettsport Beauties Calendar would be quite a kick."

Chapter Twenty-Six

Saturday morning, Simon mounted his new pictures in his living room, displacing *Pallas Athena* to a less prominent location. That left him with the third drawing, the one hidden behind Karli's self-portrait. After some deliberation, he decided to buy a mass-market frame and hang the erotic drawing in his bedroom. He then spent several frustrating and unproductive hours in the office before joining Amelia and Karli for supper.

They reported much better progress with their new project. Karli had a positive meeting with Jacob Jonathon at the print shop on Second Avenue near Amelia's Front Street cottage. Mr. Jonathon, a young man interested in computer-generated art, saw Karli as a kindred soul who distracted him from the drudgery of routine printing. They spent several hours discussing the art of print-making.

Amelia visited the mayor to discuss what he meant by his support Karli's efforts. He confirmed his offer to buy, personally if necessary, one of each print and display them in the Town Hall. The town would also promote her prints on its website.

"You should have been here a few hours ago," Amelia said shortly after Simon arrived. "We had our first drawing session and a hard time establishing a pose agreeable to Karli and our model. We needed help deciding."

"The official poser, or is that poseur," Simon suggested while shaking his head. "You'd better keep this girls only, and you must make sure they're eighteen, otherwise you might contravene child pornography laws."

"But we're making art, not pornography!" protested Karli.

"The laws don't accept that distinction. It's safer if everyone's over eighteen."

"Jenny won't like that," Amelia observed. "Are you telling us we should send her away? We're talking drawings, not photos or videos. Must we worry?"

"Karli should ask her lawyer, but it's safest."

"I, like, don't care," Karli interjected. "The hardest thing is finding ways to display two stupid earrings on not-too-naked models in ways that highlight the earrings. Ideas would be appreciated."

On Sunday, Beverley Campbell of topless protest fame, and her younger sister Amanda posed for one of Karli's Barrettsport earring drawings. Monday afternoon Amanda visited Simon at the police station.

"Ricky, my boyfriend and I saw a large red Jaguar leaving McConnell's Creek Road on the Wednesday after Labour Day," she announced without preamble. "It might have been Mr. Garrett, but I'm not sure. I don't think he owns a Jaguar."

An image of Amanda wearing an ill-fitting blue dress flashed into Simon's mind. "Around that time, we saw you having dinner in Morgan's Restaurant with a young man. Was that your boyfriend?"

She shook her head. "My parents set that up. That jerk didn't even want to look at my tits when I flashed them. You were there with Amelia, weren't you? I remember you watching me."

The crude comment from an 'in your face' young person didn't surprise Simon. "I should talk to Ricky about the Jaguar. Can you give me his full name, address, and phone number?"

She passed Simon a scrap of paper with a name and phone number. "Ricky Gaudet and he's gone to university, St. Francis Xavier in Antigonish. I know it's the right date because it was our last day together, and I was pissed because the car distracted him."

Half an hour later, Mr. Gaudet provided Simon with confirmation of Amanda's story. He prepared a report for Detective Matheson at the detachment in Bridgewater. The timing was reasonably good for Matheson's body, but they couldn't necessarily link a car on McConnell's Creek Road to Cope. But the creek road was almost unused outside hunting season and the Labour Day weekend was even too early for bow hunting season. Regular deer hunting wouldn't start until the end of October. Hard to imagine it was a mere coincidence.

But was it relevant to their investigation? Could they rely on Amanda's tentative identification of Mr. Garrett and initiate action? Flimsy or not they needed to investigate.

Simon relayed Amanda Campbell's observation to Diana. "If we continue with our assumption Cope murdered Holly, we have a problem. What was Barney Cope doing around Barrettsport three weeks after he murdered her?"

"It doesn't make sense. Professional hit men do their jobs, and they vanish."

"And the evidence from the airport's long-term parking lot is consistent with a quick departure, but we now have evidence he returned several weeks later."

"This could be a mistaken identification on Amanda Campbell's part, and we don't know Cope is our hitman."

"Two central Canadian enforcers in our area within three weeks?" Diana shrugged her shoulders as Simon returned to his speculation. "But if she's right and Cope is our hitman, it suggests Garrett and Cope met again three weeks after the murder. This meeting ended with Cope dead in a red Jaguar driven by Garrett."

"You're assuming Cope was in the car and dead before someone, Garrett presumably, drove the body to the creek."

"And that road is far too rough for the Jag. If Garrett had a choice, he would use his SUV."

Diana scowled. She clearly remained unconvinced. "So, unplanned."

"Whatever happened, if it happened, wasn't planned."

"One more thing. We've been puzzled about how Garrett got to his assignations with Holly. If he had another car no one recognized, we might solve that little puzzle."

Simon smiled, maybe he was getting somewhere. "So, we know what you'll be doing tomorrow."

"Visiting motels where Holly stayed asking about a large red Jaguar sedan. I'll need the model number, and colour, cherry red or maroon?"

"I'll check my notes. Mr. Gaudet gave me a thorough description."

When Diana returned to the station late the next afternoon, Simon had his whiteboard covered with his latest deliberations.

He turned away from the board as she entered his office. "Learn anything?"

"No one associated a red Jag with Ms. Craig's visits."

"Not surprised. I think I have the role of the Jag figured out, and having Garrett use it for his assignations is not part of the picture."

"Looks like you have new observations," Diana suggested pointing to the new entries on his board as she sat by Simon's desk. "Want to fill me in?"

Simon turned back to his whiteboard. "I started by looking in the Nova Scotia vehicle registry for late model XJ sedans."

"It's not necessarily a Nova Scotia car. Your witnesses said nothing about the plates."

"That's true but Nova Scotia registrations were the place to start, and I found one registered right here in Barrettsport."

"No one has such a car. It's distinctive, not a vehicle we'd fail to notice."

"That's right, and furthermore, this vehicle is registered to a Mr. Nathaniel Adams at a fictitious address."

Diana's brow furrowed as she bit at the end of a pen. "Nathaniel Adams? Why can't I place that? It's not anyone in Selectman Adams family, at least not anyone living here."

"I'm sure that's correct, no Nathaniel Adams has lived in Barrettsport for many years. But there were several Nathaniels in the Adams family in earlier generations."

"Where does that put us?"

"Someone, it could be an Adams but my money would be on Matthew Garrett, has set up a false registration for this car, and is keeping it somewhere nearby. It's obviously not being used very often or people would recognize it."

Diana threw the pen aside and stepped over to Simon's whiteboard. "I see where you're going. It's Garrett's car. Bernard Cope returned to Barrettsport for a purpose we have yet to discover, but one that involved Garrett. Somehow Garrett used the opportunity to murder Cope, and he used this mystery car to dispose of the body because he didn't want to use a car recognizable as his."

"That's basically the picture I developed this afternoon. Lots of uncertainty, lots of unknowns, but we should work on it."

They'd hardly begun the job of discovering who was masquerading as Nathaniel Adams and establishing links between Garrett, Cope, and the Jaguar when a new development overwhelmed their efforts.

Chapter Twenty-Seven

A storm rolled in on Thursday, November fifteenth. It was more like winter than late fall with sub-zero temperatures and snow forecast for overnight. The RCMP chose the inclement evening for simultaneous raids on the premises of Bluenose Wind Energy Corporation headquarters in Barrettsport and Twenty-First Century Construction offices in Halifax. They were coordinated with military precision to occur at 1900 hours and include apprehension of the senior managers of both companies. Conrad Cavanaugh headed the Barrettsport operation, and he assembled six Barrettsport Police Department staff and three Mounties at five thirty. Additional RCMP officers manned a roadblock at the Causeway. Simon wondered as the officers scurried about setting up a command centre why the RCMP brass would trust this operation to someone being investigated for unprofessional conduct. Did it indicate the secretive investigation was a sham? Or had a speedy review exonerated him?

Cavanaugh addressed the assembled team. "Tonight, we complete my two-year-long Millennium investigation. I've been investigating large-scale fraud at Twenty-First Century Construction in Halifax and more recently their spin-off, Bluenose Wind Energy Corporation. Tonight, I've established a roadblock to control access at the isthmus. I will secure the Wind Energy Corporation offices and apprehend their four senior managers, Matthew Garrett, David Adams, Richard Campbell, and Ronald McGuire."

"Roland," Chief DeWolfe interjected, "Roland McGuire, not Ronald."

Cavanaugh paused while checking his documentation. "Sorry, Roland McGuire. Matthew Garrett is a prime target because he's implicated in the murder of Holly Craig. Apprehending him will be the responsibility of

Goodyear and Jackson. The other three are prominent citizens so I leave it to Chief DeWolfe to organize his staff to apprehend them. I will secure the company offices, and I want the four company principals brought to the Wind Energy offices. Don't bring them here and don't let them communicate with anyone. That's it. We deploy at 1830 hours but no one moves on his target until 1900." Conrad looked at his watch. "Fifteen minutes before we move and no one uses his phone."

A phone rang. Margaret Summerville responded, listened for several seconds, and gestured to the chief. DeWolfe identified himself and listened without further comment before passing the phone to Cavanaugh. He also listened silently before slamming it down and storming out. The chief said nothing until the squeal of Cavanaugh's tires pierced the air.

"The RCMP's Regional Director has recalled Cavanaugh." He paused while the significance sank in. "Simon, you and Diana still have the job of apprehending Garrett. We also need to secure the company headquarters. I will lead that along with our RCMP colleagues. I assume they have the warrant and know what they're after." The officers nodded confirming the validity of the chief's assumptions. "We do not detain Adams, Campbell or McGuire, only request they visit their office this evening to help us. Evans, you're in charge."

A Mountie raised his arm. "We'll need someone with a key, or we must break into the office."

The chief gazed at Evans. "Tell Adams, Campbell, and McGuire we need their help with access."

"What about the secretary/receptionist? She'll have a key," Evans said.

"You contact the principals, I'll handle the secretary."

"And access to the town?" continued Evans, "is the roadblock there?"

"Road surveillance's in place."

"And beach access," Simon asked. "Anyone covering that?"

"The tide's running and last week's storm deepened the channel," Evans replied. "It isn't fordable on a night like this."

"But anyone making a run for it may not be as well informed."

"Good point," interjected the chief. "Kerry. Hit the beach and detain anyone who tries to swim the channel."

"Right, sir, I'm on it," Kerry said, grabbing his coat.

"Contact Goodyear if you see Garrett, and me if it's anyone else," the chief yelled at Tom Kerry's back.

The chief turned to the remaining officers. "It's six thirty, so we'd best be going. And, other than Garrett, no one's arrested. No strong-arm tactics, and no one moves until seven. We mustn't jeopardize the operation in Halifax. Halifax and Garrett are the focus."

"Any idea what's happening," Diana asked as she and Simon hurried to their squad car. "This is the strangest bloody operation I've encountered."

"Let's get in position," Simon replied, "before we decide how to handle this." He pondered the significance of Cavanaugh leaving the escape route around the marsh unguarded as they sped to Shore Road. It had to be intentional.

"Bloody dark," Diana observed minutes later as Simon parked the car opposite the drive into the Garrett estate.

He shivered, impatient for the car to warm up. The raindrops falling on the windshield already had the half-congealed appearance rain gets as it turns to ice. "Hopefully that's because he's alone and has few lights on. According to rumours on the campaign trail last week, his wife left him, and their two kids are away at school."

"We have seven minutes. How do we proceed?"

"I'll drop you at the front door with our warrant and block his garage with our car. If he doesn't appear through a back door, I'll join you out front. I don't anticipate trouble. He's so arrogant he'll confront us at the door."

"Only three minutes to go," Diana said as Simon's cell phone rang.

"Christ, it's Kerry," he said. "Hey Tom, what's up?"

"I'm too late, someone's on the beach almost to the channel. Looks like Garrett, but I can't be sure. I'll try to stop him, but I won't succeed if he's determined to cross."

"Do your best. I'm on my way." He turned to Diana. "Out! You're on your own. Call for backup and make sure the house is empty. Kerry says he's spotted Garrett on the beach."

"Garrett! Should I come with you?"

"He's not sure, stay and cover this end."

Diana jumped from the car as Simon roared to the only beach access on the Barrettsport side of the wildlife park. It was as far away as one could go on Barrettsport's little peninsula, but it took him less than ten minutes. Kerry's personal motorbike was the only vehicle in the beach parking lot. He slammed on the brakes by the path, leapt from the car and sprinted toward the beach. His phone rang before he'd run fifty metres.

"He's trying to swim it but the current's taking him into the marsh," Constable Kerry announced. "It's treacherous. We'll need the rope and life jacket from the trunk before I go after him."

"Okay, I'm going back. Can you get us backup?"

"Station is empty except Margaret and Evans."

"Send Evans to Garrett's house. That will free up Jackson and she can join us. And keep an eye on Garrett."

The channel water rushed into the marsh like a river in spate, pushed on by the storm surge and the waves breaking onto the shore. As he approached Kerry, Simon threw off his coat off and struggled into the life vest. He threw one end of the rope to Kerry as he tied the other around his waist, kicked off his boots and headed toward the channel's seaward end.

"What's happening?" he yelled. They stood only a few metres apart but the howling wind made communication difficult.

"Shouldn't I go? You must be tired."

"I'm doing this. Give me the situation."

"He tried to wade across, carrying a kitbag he held out of the water. When it got too deep, and I figured he'd turn back, he plunged ahead trying to swim. He made it to the other side. Around the corner into the marsh, but he reached land. I don't think he's moved. It's hard to see, but he hasn't stood."

"Okay, I'm going," Simon said, launching himself into the channel from a position near the ocean where the distance across would be shortest, but the current strongest. My God, it's cold, he thought as he struggled to overcome the urge to curl up from the shock of ice-cold water. He lost his balance, and the current swept him halfway along the channel before he convinced his reluctant muscles to respond.

The current was stronger than he expected, but he was in better shape than Matthew Garrett and less burdened by extra clothes. It swept him to the landward limit of the beach before he found solid ground.

Simon stopped to catch his breath before locating a large rock to anchor the rope. With the rope secured, he stumbled off in search of Garrett. Simon found him lying face down in the marsh vegetation near where Kerry said he came ashore. Once Simon determined he was breathing, he dragged the semi-conscious Matthew Garrett to dry ground.

Simon bellowed to Kerry, "We'll need a boat." Kerry had followed to the end of the beach closest to their location, but Simon was unsure if Kerry would hear him.

"I'm already ..." Kerry replied. "But Margaret's the ... station ... manpower ... time." The wind had garbled the message, but Kerry understood Simon's request.

"Work on it. Could the Mounties produce a vehicle from their end?"

Mention of the RCMP revived Garrett, and he started muttering. At first, he was incoherent but as the seconds ticked by Simon realized the RCMP terrified Garrett.

"For God's sake Goodyear," he begged at barely more than a whisper. "Take me back to Barrettsport. They'll kill me if they get the chance."

Simon was sure he'd heard him correctly but thought Garrett's fear irrational. But his agitation perturbed Simon. *Best to get Garrett back to Barrettsport before investigating.*

"Forget the Mounties," he yelled to Kerry. He was now yelling more for Garrett's benefit than for Kerry's. "We need to get directly back to Barrettsport so keep working on the boat."

He turned to Garrett. "Can you explain what you said?"

"Cavanaugh set me up, caused me to witness Holly's murder, and made it look like I was responsible. Now, he knows I'm onto him, and he has to eliminate me. You must get me back to town. He won't be able to get me if I'm in the town jail."

"Okay, calm down. Constable Kerry's working on a boat. Are you strong enough to walk back to the channel?"

"I guess so."

"Okay, stand up, I'll help you, and we'll go slowly. Then Constable Kerry will see us and you'll have the protection of an additional witness."

Minutes later, they stood thirty metres from Kerry across the narrow but fast flowing channel. Garrett was improving rapidly, and Kerry was not making progress getting a boat on a night that was getting stormier.

"No boat will get here from Barrettsport," Kerry yelled. "We'll need a small one we can carry from the parking lot." The message was clearer now they were closer.

Simon decided swimming the channel again was their best choice. He gave Garrett his life vest and tied him to the rope. Kerry could pull Garrett across, but Simon would be on his own. He told Kerry his plan and launched Garrett into the channel before either of them could object. Simon waited until Kerry pulled Garrett ashore. He shed most of his wet clothes, putting them and Garrett's overcoat under the rock he'd used to anchor the rope, and dove in wearing only his pants. He was much colder than the previous time, but he still managed the trip without difficulty. The thought of his dry coat and boots urged him on.

They scrambled to the squad car and then to Garrett's for dry clothes before transporting him to the safety of a Barrettsport police station holding cell. At Garrett's house, Diana took one look at Simon, left Garrett in the care of Kerry and Evans and drove Simon home. She hustled him into his apartment, deprived him of his soaking wet clothes and shoved him into the shower. Simon was shivering and his lips were still blue from the time he'd spent in the frigid ocean waters. Initially, lukewarm shower water seemed blistering hot, but as he warmed, he tolerated hotter water. Simon wasn't concerned about hypothermia. As the hot water warmed his extremities, he focused on the significance of Matthew Garrett's rambling statement on the beach.

Chapter Twenty-Eight

Diana summoned Amelia while Simon showered. When she arrived, he was yawning but impatient to return to work.

"No bloody way," Amelia insisted. "Hypothermia is serious. You mustn't venture outside until you're well and truly warm."

He refused to give in until he'd explained the situation to Diana, instructing her to protect Garrett from the RCMP until they unravelled his story. Then, Simon let Amelia put him in bed under every blanket he owned. It wasn't even 9 p.m.

"Better?" she asked after stripping off and joining him. "They say snuggling together in bed is the best way to treat hypothermia." She smiled, "naked of course, or you won't get the proper heat transfer."

He struggled to keep his eyes open. "I'm not ready for whatever you've planned." Soon thoughts of work or anything else were forgotten as he fell asleep in Amelia's arms.

Simon woke from his nap at eleven, brimming with enthusiasm and eager to investigate Garrett's allegations. He found Evans alone in the police station's main office. "I'm surprised it's so quiet. I thought everyone would still be here."

"It was busy until half an hour ago. Kerry and I brought Garrett in at nine fifteen and put him in a cell. He didn't even phone his lawyer. The crowd returned fifteen minutes later. They had no trouble with Mr. Adams or the others and learned what they needed at the windmill company's office. The chief called off the roadblock and everyone drifted home. Kerry said he'd fetch the stuff you left on the beach. He also mentioned a kitbag."

"And Jackson?"

"She's at Garrett's house, and the chief's in his office consulting with the RCMP brass. And you're okay?"

"I got incredibly cold, and it took ages to warm up. I'm surprised Garrett wasn't in a similar state."

"Hah," snorted Evans. "He was wearing a wetsuit under his clothes."

"Was he now? That's interesting because it suggests he anticipated making that crossing."

"That it does."

Simon paused considering the wetsuit's significance. Cavanaugh or another Mountie must have tipped him off. One more nail for Cavanaugh's coffin, but Garrett was his immediate priority. "Jackson came here after she sorted me out?"

"Yeah, she did but returned to Garrett's house after consulting with the chief. Says she's made an important discovery."

Simon gazed at the holding cell video output displayed on Evan's computer. It showed him Garrett was awake. "I'll talk to Garrett and then check with Diana."

"Hello, Garrett," Simon called out as he approached the holding cells. Garret slouched on a bunk with his elbows on his knees and his hands cradling his head. "You ready for a discussion, or should I return in the morning?"

"I'm okay, considering the circumstances, but what about you? I've never seen anyone as cold as you looked three hours ago."

"It took a bit of defrosting but I'm okay. Care to elaborate on our beach conversation?"

Garrett straightened his back and peered at Simon. "Definitely. I had no idea Holly was investigating Twenty-First Century Construction, and I knew nothing about their dubious reputation."

Simon questioned both statements but let Garrett continue without comment.

"They approached Adams and me about establishing a company to take advantage of the government's desire to promote wind power. We needed a money-making venture and jumped at the opportunity without adequate due diligence. Smooth sailing until early August when someone from Twenty-First Century told me to help a Mr. Timothy Jones with an important task."

"Who?"

"I have the name, a director's underling. He didn't explain or give me any choice. They could ruin me and had no qualms about doing so if I didn't follow instructions. Jones called at 6 a.m. on August eighteenth telling me to visit Holly early enough to admit him at eight."

Simon stared at Matthew Garrett when he took a breath. Simon had to press on while Garrett's cooperative behaviour continued. "Any idea why he chose the eighteenth? A relationship between this and your wife's protest?"

"Nothing I'm aware of. I followed instructions and left Holly's patio door open so Jones could enter. We were eating breakfast at her dining room table when he crept in like a ghost. He clobbered her with a club he'd stolen from my house."

"What club?"

"From my collection of ancient British weapons. He didn't hesitate for a second. He crept up behind her and crash, her head was pulverized. I had no time to react. She didn't know he was there and wouldn't have suffered."

Garrett paused, his eyes moistening. Simon needed to keep him talking. "Then what?"

"He told me to say nothing. I could collect my club at an empty house on Elm Street the next day. It was in the kitchen sink. I tried to clean the blood off it and out of the sink before I took it home and returned it to the case where it's always displayed. That's what happened. Adams, Campbell, and McGuire had nothing to do with this, and Bluenose Wind Energy is a legitimate business. They need to unravel themselves from their association with Twenty-First Century."

"Any proof Timothy Jones is his real name?'"

"That's what he called himself."

"If I brought in an artist tomorrow morning, would you help him generate a sketch of Mr. Jones?" Simon asked.

"I didn't see him clearly. He wore a jacket with a hood tied under his chin and aviator sunglasses."

"Do what you can, even a partial description will help, and I'll bring photos of known assassins."

Garrett nodded but said nothing. He'd withdrawn after describing the murder. Simon tried another approach.

"Your narrative fits the sequence of events we've put together, but it doesn't explain your fear of the RCMP."

"What I've told you so far is fact. I base my fear of Detective Cavanaugh on inferences I made when he interviewed me and Adams about the company. Things he said convinced me he, not Twenty-First Century Corp, was behind my relationship with Mr. Jones."

"We need something concrete."

Garrett looked up. "I've been trying for the past hour. I'm feeling safer now. That will help me sort it out."

"Do that, consult Mr. Wexler, and prepare a statement."

"I have a new lawyer. I'll call him in the morning."

"Good, and we'll keep you safe from Cavanaugh for the night and longer if you stay in custody. But we can't protect you on the outside. Now, I must fetch the murder weapon, so if you have no objection, I'll visit your house and collect it. Do I have your permission to enter?"

"Yes, do whatever you must."

"Then I bid you good night, and I'll see you in the morning for our sketch."

Simon called Diana while he waited for a consultation with Chief DeWolfe.

"You okay?" she asked before saying hello.

"I'm fine, couple of hours sleep, and now I'm back at work. What's keeping you at Garrett's house?"

"I've found the murder weapon."

"Let me guess, an ancient British battle club."

"When did you find out?"

"A few minutes ago, from Garrett."

"That spoils my sense of accomplishment, but what should I do with it?"

"Is it in a locked cabinet?" he asked.

"Yes, but I have the key."

"I'll be right over, we can bag it and see what else we find."

"Is that legal without a warrant?"

"I have his permission."

"I'll be here."

Simon had a brief discussion with the chief before departing for Garrett's house. He and Diana spent the next hour looking for evidence linking Garrett to the mysterious Mr. Jones. At one forty-five, they abandoned the search and Simon sent Diana home. He took the club to the station, locked it in their evidence storage locker, and returned home. He had a task for early in the morning, so he set his alarm for five thirty.

Before dawn, Simon borrowed tools from Amelia's garden shed and headed for the Upper Barrettsport beach. He'd wondered why Garrett planned an escape on foot along the beach. It only made sense if he had a hiding place or transport in Upper Barrettsport. But they'd found no keys when they arrested him. He may have lost them when he swam the channel, or in the kitbag he'd been carrying. But there was another possibility; he dumped them when he anticipated arrest.

If hidden keys existed, they were most likely buried where he'd collapsed. That section of beach was Simon's target for some early morning gardening. According to tide tables posted in the station, Garrett had collapsed two hours after low tide. The next low was 7 a.m. but ten centimetres higher than the previous evening's low. Simon figured he should dig near the water at low tide. He guessed it should be light enough to begin work by six thirty.

Simon couldn't pinpoint the spot where he found Garrett. The intervening high tide had obliterated any physical evidence, and the place looked different in the dim early morning light. He made a guess and commenced digging along the beach. Simon dug eastward without success for ten metres, noticed the tide had turned, and returned to dig westward.

He hit pay dirt after five minutes digging furiously to the west. The hiding place was only two metres from his starting point. He sat exhausted on the sand beside his dig site staring at the keys he'd found. The Jaguar symbol on the remote attached to the car key mesmerized him.

Minutes later, he realized his boots were getting wet and his tools were in the water. Amelia would not appreciate salt water on her fancy garden tools. He jumped up from his reverie, rescued the tools, and drove a large chunk of driftwood into the sand above the high tide line.

It was almost eight when he took Amelia's tools into the station to wash the salt off them. Margaret and Evans were there, along with Vickers whose shift had just ended. They made comments about westerners knowing nothing about digging clams, but Simon paid little attention. Margaret yelled something as he entered the station's single locker room, but he ignored her, thinking it was more comments about westerners and clam digging.

He should have listened more carefully.

Chapter Twenty-Nine

Simon encountered Diana when he strode into the locker room. She was drying her hair after stepping from the shower.

"You shouldn't be here," she yelled but started laughing as she fastened the towel around her torso. "Am I as hot as your friend Amelia?"

"I'm sorry," he stammered, "I didn't see the sign."

The Barrettsport police station had one inadequate locker room constructed when female officers were unheard of. When they hired Diana, they give her a warning sign to post on the door. Five years later, they were still using the makeshift system.

"It's disappeared. Margaret was supposed to warn everyone."

"She tried, but I didn't catch on. They were teasing me about clam digging and I thought it was more teasing."

"Clam digging?" she asked.

"I spent the last hour digging where I found Garrett, searching for keys hidden in the sand."

"Did you find any?"

He handed her three keys and a car remote in a plastic evidence bag.

"You should rinse off residual salt," she suggested as Margaret opened the locker room door.

"Diana, you okay?" she called from outside the doorway. "I tried to stop him."

"Yeah, it's fine, no harm's been done," Diana replied as Margaret pulled the door closed.

"I'm sorry. I'd never have barged in here if I'd known."

"It's okay. I got to strip you naked and push you into the shower last night and this morning you catch me after mine; somehow it seems fair, doesn't it?"

He watched as she returned to drying her hair. She didn't ask him to leave or make a serious attempt to keep the towel she'd wrapped around herself in place. The precariously perched towel reminded Simon of Amelia's robe on the day of Holly's murder.

"Why were you here having a shower this morning?" he asked.

"Last night, Travis pulled our bathroom plumbing apart, and it's still inoperable. Now I better have a word with Margaret or she'll be spreading rumours about us."

Simon turned his attention to rinsing Amelia's garden tools while Diana dressed.

Later, Diana appeared in Simon's doorway. "I hope you're not unhappy with my overly familiar behaviour. That wasn't professional of me, and I apologize."

"Are we discussing the same incident? I should be apologizing for walking in on you."

"You behaved appropriately. I didn't display the proper dignity, and I didn't even notice the most important fact. The car's a bloody Jaguar!"

Simon laughed. "Yeah, a Jaguar. We should forget this foolishness about behaviour and dignity and decide how to proceed."

Diana sat with her notebook at the ready. "Okay, what's our agenda?"

"First, the keys. We've shown the Jaguar is Garrett's, but where is it? And why did he hide it?"

"His escape route suggests it's somewhere in Upper Barrettsport."

"That's number one. Search for the Jag in your neighbourhood. Next, Garrett's overcoat anything useful?"

Diana shook her head. "Nada."

"And the kitbag Kerry mentioned?"

"He looked along the shore last night but didn't find it."

"Keep looking because, if Garrett was doing a bunk, he'd have false ID and credit cards."

"Also, his wallet and real ID. They could be in the kitbag."

"So, searching for the bag is priority number two."

"And his car. Their Bimmer is missing."

Simon picked up the evidence bag with Garrett's keys. "Dust this key fob for prints and wash the salt off before looking for the cars. And get help finding the kitbag from today's constables. I have an artist arriving to generate a sketch of Mr. Jones."

"Will you show Garrett Bernard Cope's mug shot? Our theory says Cope and Jones are the same person."

"Agreed. I'm making a file of mug shots that will include Cope's, and I'll ask Garrett what he's done with his BMW. Then, I'll get Garrett's war club to the RCMP for forensic analysis. I'll see what they're saying about their search for the hitman now that Cavanaugh's no longer in charge."

Diana looked up from her notebook. "Cavanaugh's been ousted?"

"From both the Twenty-First Century Construction and murder investigations."

At eleven thirty, an unhappy Simon Goodyear had a brief discussion with Diana warning her their plans to search Garrett's house had been vetoed. He also relayed the prosecutor's office decision—Garrett would be charged with obstructing a police investigation and released that afternoon. "Garrett's attitude has already changed. He was awkward about the sketch, claimed he didn't recognize Cope, and uncooperative about the whereabouts of his car. We need to find it before he's released."

"Under control. We found it in a no-parking zone with one corner protruding far enough to claim it was a traffic hazard. We're having it towed, but we lack legal grounds for a proper search."

"What's inside?"

"Clothes like you might see if someone stripped off in his car before s summertime swim."

"Hardly weather for that last night. Keys or Garrett's wallet?"

Diana shook her head. "We'd need to get inside."

"Wait a minute! Isn't it Caroline Garrett's car, the one Lisa Powell couldn't drive on the day of the stupid topless protest?"

She consulted her computer. "It's registered to Caroline Garrett."

"Good, get her to collect it and ask her about the clothes. Insist she identifies them and checks for keys and ID."

"What about the Jag?"

"We're okay on that one. Garrett denies any knowledge, so his lawyer can't stop us looking for it."

"I'll enlist Evans to sort out Mrs. Garrett and get onto the Jag. We have two constables searching the shoreline for the kitbag, so the legwork's under control."

Simon's dropped the club at the Bridgewater RCMP detachment's major crime unit. The officer on duty determined that the metre-long weapon had blood residues and removed samples for analysis in the Halifax lab. Next, Simon talked to Detective Jaimie Kim, the new officer in charge of the Holly Craig murder investigation and Barrettsport's link to the Twenty-First Century case. The chief said she was the South Shore region's first oriental detective. He didn't mention she was the region's first woman detective.

Detective Kim insisted on a late lunch at a Chinese restaurant that served dim sum. She gestured to waitresses chanting in Chinese as they pushed trolleys stacked with bamboo steamers. They were using a system popular in Vancouver's China Town that relied on the customers understanding the names of the dishes in Cantonese. Common enough in Vancouver, but Simon wondered how many Bridgewater denizens understood Cantonese.

They lingered for an hour discussing the details of Simon's murder investigation. They didn't overindulge in steamers, and, with only Chinese tea to drink, the meal was inexpensive. Jaimie insisted on paying.

Back in the Bridgewater RCMP office, they reviewed the major points of the broader Twenty-First Century Construction investigation with the officers assisting Detective Kim. The Mounties' priority was pinning the

Holly Craig murder on whoever hired Cope. A different group based in the Halifax office was investigating Cavanaugh's role and Cope's link to Twenty-First Century. Nailing Matthew Garrett wasn't high on anyone's priority list.

It was an unwelcome outcome for Simon. He and Diana unearthed the chain of events and arrested an important accessory, but the search for the real culprit, the person who hired the hitman, was the Mounties' problem. He and his Barrettsport colleagues must accept their subsidiary role in the overall investigation and focus on local leads while investigating Matthew Garrett's role in two murders.

Diana waved Simon over to her desk when he returned from Bridgewater. "I've found the Jag. I'll be in once I'm off the phone."

Chapter Thirty

A few minutes later, Diana settled into her customary chair in his office. She placed her notebook and a sheaf of computer printout on his desk.

"A cinch," she said without preamble. "Hidden in my neighbourhood just west of the causeway. Once I asked about Jaguars, someone pointed out a derelict garage. It was less run down than it initially appeared and securely locked. Two of Garrett's keys opened the door locks, but I didn't enter. The remote unlocked the Jag's doors without me going inside. I confirmed the plate number was the one you identified several days ago and left."

Simon wondered if Diana had seen the plate number without entering but avoided making a comment. "We need authority to impound it and have a forensic team search for evidence someone transported Cope's body in it. We also need to search the garage. Whose property?"

"A Mr. Cedric McNeil. He and his wife are pensioners listed as owners for forty years."

"Talk to them."

Diana nodded her head. "I will. No one was home, but the house didn't appear closed up or abandoned."

"Get Mr. McNeil's story. See if he recognizes Garrett. It will be helpful for our warrant if McNeil identifies Garrett, so tell me if he gives you a positive ID."

"I'll return this afternoon."

"Good. And the question of Nathaniel Adams?"

"That's what I was working on. I haven't found Nathaniel Adam. His name's not associated with any local records, but we have this car registration. I'll keep searching provincial and national registries. Has to be a false identity."

"Keep looking and one more thing. The Mountie's aren't giving the Holly Craig's murder, or Garrett's role in it, high priority."

"Why not?" Diana asked.

"They're treating it as solved. They want to discover who hired Holly's killer, but not interested in pursuing Garrett. They're ready to accept his story and willing to cut a deal that minimizes his liability if he helps them nail Cavanaugh and the people who hired Cope. Chief DeWolfe has agreed we should keep working on the exact nature of Garrett's involvement, but we won't get much support from Bridgewater. So, what about Mrs. Garrett's Bimmer and the kitbag?"

"Caroline Garrett confirmed the clothes were Garrett's. He was staging a fake suicide. Wanted us to conclude he stripped off his clothes, left them and his keys and wallet inside the car, and walked into the sea."

"And the kitbag?" Simon asked.

"We haven't found it, but we have a boat searching the marsh and constables walking the beaches."

Saturday morning Simon secured permission to search Mr. McNeil's garage and impound the Jaguar while they determined its ownership. They could conduct searches and take fingerprints, but not transport the vehicle for detailed forensic examination in the RCMP crime lab.

Their most interesting discovery was a briefcase containing stacks of twenties. The money suggested Garrett planned to disappear, but they found no fake IDs and credit cards confirming their supposition.

Monday, Simon delved into Garrett's marital and financial situation during a late lunch at Mildred's Tea Shoppe. He'd learned over the previous three months that Mildred Wexler was the best source for information about the lives of Barrettsport's families. He didn't expect a thorough assessment, but whatever she told him would provide a starting point.

Mildred sat at his table while Simon waited for Janice, the waitress, to bring his lunch. "Caroline Wexler's my niece. She and Matthew married in 1993's biggest social event. Caroline had recently graduated from Barnard College in New York. Matthew was a rising star in the investment world with his Harvard MBA and experience in a big Wall Street firm. It seemed like a perfect match and a real boon for Barrettsport. Matthew would bring our community into the modern age by developing an investment company that used modern technology to connect it to the world."

"Without office or employees?"

Mildred nodded her head. "Caroline's father provided their beautiful house, and they hosted wonderful parties in the first few years. Then they produced their two little boys. It appeared idyllic, but it didn't last. Everyone who invested with Matthew pretended he wasn't an uninspiring money manager. His decade-long tenure as Selectman has been just as dull. His marriage has become a hollow shell they maintain for the sake of the children."

"I thought she'd left him."

"That, young man is why I'm talking to you. You can't believe half of what you hear and now you've arrested Matthew, having the true story will be important. Their marriage is finished, but she did not leave him. Last week, she visited the children at their school in Ontario, and now, she's staying with her parents. That's just until he sorts out his immediate problems and finds another place to live. He's the one caught having a brazenly public affair. He must leave. That house is her security. It's hers and I know her father told her never to compromise her ownership."

"But it has a large mortgage against it."

Mildred jumped to her feet. "I must talk to Charles."

Fifteen minutes later, Mildred returned. "Come with me and explain this mortgage business to Charles and Samuel."

"Sorry, I'm confused. Charles is your brother and Caroline's father, but isn't Samuel Matthew Garrett's lawyer?"

"Samuel is my younger brother and the family lawyer. If what you're telling me about a mortgage is correct, he won't be Matthew's lawyer for long."

"And you expect me to reschedule my afternoon and talk to them?"

"Yes, of course. It's important for everyone."

Chapter Thirty-One

Simon pondered the significance of his latest lesson in Barrettsport family behaviour as he followed Mildred from her café to the Wexler mansion.

A butler greeted them at the door and helped Mildred with her coat. "They're in the library, Miss Mildred."

"Thank you, Johnston," she replied as she waited for Simon to give Johnston his coat and hat. "This is Detective Goodyear, he's helping us with a problem." She marched straight to the library obviously expecting Simon to follow. Caroline Garrett, Samuel Wexler and a patrician-looking older man who had to be Charles Wexler, stood in the large room.

Samuel stepped forward. "Good afternoon, Detective Goodyear, you met Caroline last summer, but not Charles. This is Charles Wexler, the patriarch of the Wexler clan, the older brother to both Mildred and me, and Caroline's father. Charles, this gentleman is Mr. Simon Goodyear, a detective in the town's police department."

"Welcome to my home, Mr. Goodyear. May I fetch you refreshment?"

"No thank you, sir, I've come from lunch at Mildred's café, so I'm fine."

Charles laughed. "The good detective mustn't drink while on duty. You must return when you're not on duty. I hear you're keeping the RCMP from running roughshod in our town, action worthy of several toasts. But that's for another time. We're concerned about a mortgage on Caroline's house."

Simon took a deep breath. "We apprehended Matthew Garrett in conjunction with the investigation we're conducting into both the murder of Ms. Craig and a potential financial scandal. When we arrived at his house, the front door was open, physically open. We received a report of a sighting and I rushed off, but my partner, Constable Diana Jackson, stayed and checked the house. We needed to ensure no one was in distress and determine if anything was amiss. After we apprehended Mr. Garrett, I returned because he told me where to find the weapon used to murder Holly Craig. The desk in the room with the murder weapon was disturbed. We needed an explanation."

"Sounds like an illegal search," Samuel Wexler interjected.

Simon stood his ground. "Mr. Garrett gave us permission. He had a greater fear of someone I'm not at liberty to mention than he did of the Barrettsport force. He was cooperating with us."

"Please, Sam, don't get all lawyerly on us," said Charles. "Let Mr. Goodyear complete his account."

"The mortgage document was on the desk. We wondered if it could be the reason for the disarray but didn't pursue it. The next day, we released Mr. Garrett, and his agreement with the prosecutors prevented further searches."

Samuel stepped forward with his hand and forefinger raised like a courtroom lawyer admonishing a witness. "Something's wrong here. You're sure the document was a mortgage on Caroline's house."

"I'm sure. A mortgage on the property with both Mr. and Mrs. Garrett's signatures on the document."

"I signed no mortgage document," Caroline said, turning to her father. "Really, Father, I didn't sign it."

"All right honey, I know you wouldn't. Thank you, Mr. Goodyear, you have provided unpleasant news that Samuel and I must investigate. If you'll excuse us, we have serious business to attend to."

"I have a few questions related to an older matter for Mrs. Garrett. Could she spare me a few minutes now, or should I return later?"

"Now should be fine. Caroline, take Mr. Goodyear to the drawing room?"

"I almost feel sorry for Matthew," Caroline said after she closed the library door behind them. "They will run him from the house and the whole damn town. And you were pretty sneaky referring to an older matter. If it concerns our little episode in the park, they'd rather not hear anything. But if you're asking me questions about this week, they won't want me to answer without Samuel's approval."

Simon ignored her qualifiers. "I noticed Mildred stayed for the family conference, but they dismissed you to talk to me."

"You're observant. They may not appreciate Mildred's liberal politics but they respect her views. I'll always be daddy's little girl, no matter how old I am. You sure you won't have a drink?" Caroline asked upon entering another formal sitting room. "I'm having one. Will you join me?"

"If you make it a small one."

Caroline poured herself a generous whiskey and a stingier one for Simon, "I'm ready for your questions."

"I'll start with the day Holly Craig was murdered."

Caroline sighed with the back of her hand to her forehead. "It's become a black day for me."

"I'm having a hard time understanding everyone's motivation, and for me, it starts with that day. Why were you making your protest? Was it your idea or Cynthia's?"

"I was mad at Matthew and his increasingly stodgy ways. He'd turned into a puritanical curmudgeon who hated anything modern or the slightest bit risqué. Cynthia's motives were more honourable. She wants to expose the town to new ideas."

"And how did your plan develop?"

"At one of our garden parties, a group of us were discussing women's rights and how we needed to modernize the town's attitude to women. Then, the younger women got frisky around the pool and most ended up in various stages of undress. Matthew berated them for their immorality. I mean they weren't his kids or his relatives, and they were just having fun. He behaved like one of those Bible-thumping preachers who see sin everywhere they look. I was disgusted with him and that, along with an earlier discussion of topless Freedom Day, made me suggest our protest."

Simon placed his empty glass on a table. "So, it was your idea. I thought it might have been Mrs. Ettinger's."

"A joint effort, but we agreed I'd be the spokesperson. I was angrier and relished the opportunity to vent my frustration. Beverley Campbell and Lisa Powell flipped a coin to see who'd manage our stuff." Caroline paused shaking her head before a smile animated her face. "Lisa messed up the logistics, and Beverley couldn't handle imprisonment."

"I noticed. Mrs. Ettinger comforted her."

Caroline stood and walked to the drink's cabinet. She pointed her empty glass at Simon's. He shook his head before she refilled hers. "I'm glad I did the protest. My anger with Matthew may have motivated me, but I enjoyed my few hours as a revolutionary."

"Okay, let's move on to your provision of an alibi for Matthew."

Caroline leaned against the cabinet and tipped back her replenished drink. "He threatened to expose activities from my misspent youth. I had no idea Matthew knew until he hit me with it when he needed an alibi."

"Sounds manipulating and devious, saving something for twenty years?"

"Please, only twelve or thirteen. When I first met him, he was a fun-loving guy and a mover on Wall Street. Then, stodgy and manipulative became better descriptors."

"When did you tell him to leave?"

"After his affair with Ms. Craig and involvement in her murder became public knowledge. I told him to leave and flew to Toronto to explain it to our kids. When I got home, he would be gone."

"And you knew nothing about the mortgage?"

"I already told you I didn't."

Simon shook his head. "You said you hadn't signed the document."

"Well, I didn't sign it or know about it."

"One last thing. A Jaguar touring car Matthew owned."

"Big stately sedan, a dark maroon colour?"

Simon nodded. "Sounds like it."

"He bought the impractical and pretentious vehicle five years ago. It sat in our garage for several years and then disappeared. I thought he'd sold it."

"He may have sold it. It isn't registered to him, but he's been using it. Presumably, it was registered in his name when he had it here?"

"I assumed it was."

"Thank you for your time. How do I retrieve my coat?"

Caroline walked to a tasselled pull cord by the door. "I ring this bell and Johnston will magically appear with your coat and hat."

"Just like a British manor house mystery."

"Thank you for not asking me what silly things I did at Barnard."

"I may have to, but not unless it's absolutely necessary."

"Somehow," she snorted, "I suspect it will become necessary."

Mildred Wexler waited by the front door, holding Simon's coat and hat. "Charles and Samuel are running Matthew off the property. I hope they don't subject him to one hundred lashes or another medieval punishment."

"Aren't they rather old for manhandling a relatively young man?"

"They have strength of character and will prevail. If we leave now and walk by Caroline's house we may see if they let him keep the clothes he's wearing."

"I'm sure you're exaggerating."

Mildred laughed, a hearty guffaw that appeared inconsistent with her aging spinster image. "He'll be gone in an hour with his clothes and other personal items. Caroline will reoccupy her home, and Samuel will handle Matthew and the mortgage."

"Will you ask Caroline to do something for me?"

"What is it?"

"Ask her not to disturb Matthew's computer or other records. Would she do that for me?"

"I suppose you'll also want an invitation to snoop?"

Chapter Thirty-Two

Tuesday morning, Simon reviewed progress with Diana before clocking out to await a furniture delivery to his apartment. He'd requested the day's leave the previous week when the case was languishing, and now when they had active leads to follow, Chief DeWolfe vetoed cancellation.

"Don't worry, Guv," Diana said, "the Jaguar's in our garage and the investigation is underway."

"Prints?"

"Garrett's are everywhere, and many of Holly Craig's. The boot has one we're trying to identify."

"Cope's?"

"The Mounties are running it." Diana paused, consulting her notes. "Records show a passport and driver's licence issued to Nathaniel Adams, and the licence has Matthew Garrett staring at the camera."

"The passport will also sport Garret's photo, and our missing kitbag will contain both documents."

"Yeah. Today, we'll step up the search by bringing in divers."

Simon glanced at his watch. "Sounds good, but I can't help because the chief won't cancel my day off. Two things before I leave."

"I'm listening."

"First, Garrett's official statement didn't alter the facts, but it omitted important details."

Diana emitted a strangled laugh. "What do you expect? He had a lawyer helping him write it."

"True, but it means they're backing off from several things, especially his fear of Cavanaugh and his willingness to cooperate with us."

"I'm not surprised. His accusation against Cavanaugh was vague. What else?"

"The mortgage is causing a big fuss."

"We must be careful how we describe our visit. We needed to secure the property, search for anyone in distress, and locate that key. That's it."

"True, we should be careful, but we have his verbal statement on tape, so we're okay. And if the print is Cope's, it destroys Garrett's credibility. But now, I must go."

By evening, it finally looked like someone lived in Simon's apartment. Amelia arrived for supper, and afterwards, they attended an extraordinary town meeting called to give the townspeople an opportunity to debate an important municipal issue. His honour, Mayor Richard Merrick, called the meeting to order at seven, not a second earlier or later.

"Thank you, everyone, for coming out on short notice. We have one important issue to discuss, but before we get to it, we have two other items on our agenda. First, I'm pleased to announce that our Barrettsport Police Force has completed its investigation of the murder of Ms. Holly Craig. They've determined a perpetrator from outside our town committed the crime and transferred the investigation to the RCMP. The whole force, especially the investigating team led by Detective Simon Goodyear, deserves our thanks."

He paused while the applause subsided.

"I have one more information item. The police have also investigated allegations of corruption in the relationship between Barrettsport's Bluenose Wind Energy Corporation and Twenty-First Century Construction of Halifax and Toronto. Chief DeWolfe reports completion of his investigation. He found no evidence of wrongdoing by Wind Energy."

The mayor paused while rumbles from the crowd subsided. The mayor's parochial take on the murder and fraud investigations puzzled Simon. Neither case had been solved, but the focus had shifted from Barrettsport. *Was that all the mayor cared about?*

"Now, to the main business," the mayor continued without providing an opportunity for comment. "Selectman Matthew Garrett has resigned only a month after his election to a four-year term. He cites personal reasons for his decision, and I have no intention of elaborating. Any clarification will come from Matthew. We need to choose his replacement, and we have two realistic options. Appoint Mrs. Cynthia Ettinger or call a special election for the open position. I open the floor to a discussion of these choices or others anyone suggests."

Many expressed their opinions, and the meeting appeared likely to drag on. Simon was more interested in the mayor's comments before he opened the discussion. They neglected several unsolved aspects of the murders and Matthew Garrett's role in them. Simon had important work to do, so he left Amelia to her meeting and returned to the station.

Inconsistencies in Garrett's story showed he had a greater role in the affair than he'd acknowledged. First, Simon had no explanation for Garrett's denial of knowledge of the Jaguar. He wouldn't realize a witness saw him leaving McConnell's Creek Road because Amanda Campbell's identification had been too tentative to use during questioning. But once they knew Garrett owned the Jag, Amanda's identification became more credible, and the link more firmly established. Second, they were building stronger links between Garrett and Cope. The investigation of a body discovered outside the town limits was the RCMP's responsibility, but Simon couldn't ignore the role it played in his investigation.

Why weren't the Mounties investigating Garrett's role in Cope's death and the disposal of his body? Perhaps they were, and Simon wasn't aware of their efforts. Or were they so committed to the Twenty-First Century case, and so dependent on Garrett's cooperation, that they turned a blind eye to inconsistencies in his story? If the print lifted from the Jag was Cope's, they couldn't deny Garrett had a larger role that demanded an investigation. Simon needed that print or some other evidence that pointed at Garrett.

And what about the timing? If he assumed Amanda Campbell saw Garrett leaving McConnell's Creek after dumping the body, it put Cope in Barrettsport three weeks after Holly's murder. How could they explain that?

Simon's workday started poorly on the morning after the town meeting. Chief DeWolfe assailed him minutes after he arrived at the station. Matthew Garrett's lawyer had filed a complaint to the RCMP about an illegal search Simon conducted in Garrett's house on the night they arrested him. Its main contention focused on the inappropriate transmission of the results of the search to his wife's family.

After twenty minutes of heated conversation, their tempers cooled. Simon reminded the chief that it was Caroline's house and convinced him they had crossed no boundaries between legitimate and dubious police work.

They also discussed Karli Leach's ongoing difficulties with Conrad Cavanaugh. Chief DeWolfe agreed they should try to protect Ms. Leach.

"But we have a serious issue," he said. "I've seen the tapes from the Bridgewater station, and it's clear she resisted with no indication the police misbehaved."

"What, they shouldn't use male officers to strip searches female prisoners."

The chief refused to back down. "Male intervention is legitimate if the prisoner resists a clearly stated request by the female officer. We must convince her to cooperate with Bridgewater RCMP and their internal investigation of Cavanaugh. She cannot fight with them. A little girl like her fighting with big officers is pointless, and it will undermine efforts her lawyer makes on her behalf."

Simon hesitated, shaking his head. "In Vancouver, I encountered dozens of young girls who were terrified of us and behaved irrationally. They were involved with drugs and the sex trade and had histories with the police to explain their behaviour. Karli's situation can't be that different."

The chief nodded his agreement. "And having the mayor on her side won't hurt. Now, let's move on."

He filled Simon in on background information related to the combined murder/industrial fraud case and provided contact names for additional digging. The new names led to a string of phone calls.

After four hours on the telephone, Simon had a deeper understanding of the overall situation. The RCMP's failure to identify the single print from the Jag's trunk was a setback. But Jaimie Kim's description of her investigation showed she was more interested in pursuing the Garrett-Cope link than Simon suspected. It may not be the Mounties' highest priority, but it wasn't a dead issue.

Simon turned next to the internal investigation of Conrad Cavanaugh. Inspector Fairbairn, the officer in charge of internal affairs in Halifax, was investigating the allegations of questionable practices used by Cavanaugh. These included mistreatment of witnesses and coercion of staff reporting to him. Two events in September brought the investigation to a head. First, Corporal Summers, the female officer who'd conducted the initial strip search in Karli's house, filed a formal complaint accusing Cavanaugh of pressuring her to falsify the results. Then, several days later, Karli's lawyer presented Inspector Fairbairn with the memory stick with Holly Craig's evidence of more serious wrong-doings. Someone in Twenty-First Century Construction conspired to divert Government money destined for Bluenose Wind Energy and place the blame on the wind energy company. The memory stick documented an impressive bit of investigative journalism but not the hard evidence that would assure convictions. Cavanaugh's role was less clear, but Holly's investigation suggested he was manipulating the investigation for his own ends.

From his own reading of the facts, Simon concluded that Fairbairn concocted his own scheme. They would blame Cavanaugh's two accomplices for the maltreatment of Karli Leach and transfer them to different RCMP detachments. He left Cavanaugh in place intending to trap him if he planted 'evidence' that implicated the directors of Bluenose Wind Energy or glorified his role in some other way.

After the November fifteenth raid, they suspended Cavanaugh pending an investigation of his behaviour and charged two Twenty-First Century Construction Corporation principals with conspiracy to defraud the government of four million dollars.

Finally, Simon learned the Bridgewater RCMP had no interest in pursuing charges against Karli Leach. In fact, they were concerned about her welfare. Cavanaugh was their target and if Karli and her lawyer cooperated, they would drop the charges. How Fairbairn sprang Karli without Cavanaugh catching on remained a mystery. But he'd succeeded because Cavanaugh continued unaware of the forces lining up against him.

Fairbairn focused on Cavanaugh's activities and other Mounties pursued the principals at Twenty-First Century Construction. Both investigations relied on testimony from Matthew Garrett. That left Jaimie Kim with responsibility for investigating Garrett's role. If Simon was to help Jaimie's efforts, he needed a witness who placed Cope at the original murder scene and something that clarified Garrett's role in subsequent events.

After talking to Fairbairn, Simon went for a quick lunch at Mildred's Tea Shoppe.

"Everything is ready for your visit to Caroline's house," Mildred said after the waitress took Simon's order. "She hasn't moved back in since Matthew departed, so nothing's been disturbed. Tonight, she's having supper at my place then returning home." Mildred placed a key on the table. "We'll arrive between eight and nine. Until then, you have our permission to do your worst."

"My worst?" Simon replied. "I promise, we'll only remove evidence related to Matthew, not Caroline, and be done by eight."

"And you, Caroline, and I can have a drink to celebrate her return to her house. Then you can drive me home."

"I'd be honoured to offer you a ride."

"Good. One more topic we need to discuss, something delicate I'll tell you in confidence."

"Careful, I won't make open-ended promises if it's something pertinent to my case."

She ignored his warning. "When Caroline attended Barnard College, she felt her father gave her an insufficient allowance. She took a job as a stripper in an upscale New York City club to augment her income. I learned about it by chance and it's been our secret for many years. Yesterday, I discovered Matthew knew all along, and he's used that knowledge to threaten her."

"Ah, I get the drift. Caroline said Matthew threatened her, and now I know how."

"This illustrates an aspect of Matthews character you must understand. It shows what a schemer he is. He observes a wealthy Barnard girl working in a sex club, takes surreptitious pictures, courts and marries her, but keeps the photos hidden away. Then when he needs them fifteen years later, he puts them to use."

Simon smiled. "Caroline told me it was twelve years and called Matthew manipulative."

"She told you about this?"

"She told me she had a secret, but not what it was."

"Perchance, I didn't need to tell you my little story. Please don't tell Caroline I've spilled our little secret."

"As I said to Caroline, not unless it's absolutely necessary."

Chapter Thirty-Three

After lunch at Mildred's Olde English Tea Shoppe, Simon returned to the station. Diana joined him in his office.

Simon waited for her to settle into her usual chair with her notebook ready. "Okay, we're back in business. I have an update on the RCMP investigation, and the chief's go-ahead to continue investigating Garrett's activities. Where do you stand?"

"First, I've found Nathaniel Adams. He was the son of David and Penelope Adams. He died in infancy and is buried in the town cemetery. His full name is Edward John Nathaniel Adams, and he was eleven months old when he died in 1970. The Jag, a 2005 XJ, was sold to Adams in 2006. The initial registration gave a Barrettsport address that was an empty house. Since then it's been changed to another empty house."

"So, we now know how Garrett established his false identity."

"Next, I checked the deed for the Garrett property, and it belongs to Mrs. Garrett. I also learned about the mortgage. Garrett borrowed the eight hundred thousand dollars from a small mortgage company associated with Twenty-First Century Construction."

"It suggests they were laundering a pay-off. Is that it?"

"More or less. I didn't get far with Garrett's business. It's a small privately held operation, no employees, no office, just him working from home. And we haven't found the kitbag," Diana concluded after glancing at her notebook.

That was Simon's cue. "I learned last week that Cavanaugh was back searching Karli Leach's house a few days after the one I witnessed. They were looking for another computer memory stick but found nothing because it was stored elsewhere. Karli forwarded it to her lawyer."

"She knew about it all along?"

"Seems so. It wasn't in her house, so she didn't outright lie to Cavanaugh. She wasn't being helpful, but she hid nothing and fabricated no evidence."

Diana smiled wagging a finger at Simon. "That girl really is trouble. What about the RCMP?"

"Bridgewater's major crimes unit is in charge and looking for our hitman. They seem reluctant to conclude it was Cope, and unfortunately, our fingerprint didn't identify him."

"Damn. I thought that print would be our breakthrough."

"I can add Garrett and his new lawyer have offered to help the RCMP investigation in exchange for easy treatment on his charges. Finally, Caroline Garrett has given us permission to search her property for evidence linking Matthew to any of these crimes. We can start whenever you can get someone to help with the technical stuff."

Diana shook her head. "Evans is the best trained, and he's no longer in a cast. He comes on at four. But Garrett had several days to sanitize the place."

"That's a problem, but he couldn't anticipate Samuel and Charles Wexler running him off so precipitously. We must try."

"And between now and four?"

"The hitman. Garrett called him Timothy Jones, but we're convinced he was Barney Cope. I suspect the Mounties are equally certain, but they're being coy. We need hard evidence that links Garrett and Cope."

"Shouldn't Garrett be able to tie together Jones and Cope? Bridgewater should show him Cope's mug shot and ask him if that's Jones."

"I've done that and he claims he cannot make the association. But can we trust Garrett to answer honestly?"

"Not likely," Diana replied. "I'll see if Cope's mug shot sparks memories with Holly's neighbours or anyone else."

While Diana searched for evidence of Barney Cope in the vicinity of Holly's apartment, Simon entered two columns of facts on his whiteboard.

The one for Matthew Garrett (MG) included:

Had secret affair with Holly Craig (HC) for eighteen months before the murder.

Business and relationship with wife both on rocks.

Has Jaguar secreted away, registered under a false name.

Eyewitness account links Jag to disposal site of body of central Canadian crime figure, Barney Cope (BC).

Claims to have witnessed murder by hitman Timothy Jones (TJ).

Sketch of TJ that MG provided looks only vaguely like BC.

Raised $800,000 illegally on wife Caroline's house.

Mortgage Company associated with 21st Century.

The one for Conrad Cavanaugh (CC) included:

Worked on same investigations as HC in Ontario, may or may not have known each other.

HC also working on 21st Century scandal over past two years.

HC had documented story of CC's illegal? involvement with 21st Century.

MG says he has knowledge of CC's relationship with TJ.

Caught trying to plant evidence at Bluenose Wind Energy.

Simon arrived at Caroline's house at three forty-five, followed by Diana and Evans in an unmarked police car. The three police officers spent the afternoon and early evening searching the property.

At eight, Simon and Diana made an initial assessment as they added three computers to boxes already loaded into her squad car.

Diana sighed. "These computers are the main result of our effort. It's like I predicted, he's cleaned up his mess."

"You shouldn't be too disappointed. We have the paperwork from Garrett's office, and we'll get deleted information from his computer. The second one you found in the basement may be untouched, and the minicomputer we located in the garage could be Holly's missing computer."

"But why would Garrett have Holly's computer?"

"And where's the bag she carried it in?"

"Too bad its battery's dead, otherwise we'd already know if it's hers."

"Get this stuff catalogued." Simon paused looking up as a familiar car approached. "I'll thank Mrs. Garrett for her cooperation and offer Mildred a lift home. Thanks, Evans, for your help."

"No problem," he replied. "It beats sitting around the office."

Mildred and Caroline emerged from Caroline's BMW sports car as Diana and Evans departed.

"Ah, Mr. Goodyear, please come in," Caroline called out rather joyfully for someone whose house had been invaded by the police. "Our timing's perfect for a nightcap." She strode to the front door and ushered Simon and Mildred into the house. Caroline led the way to a formal sitting room and filled three glasses at an elaborate bar. The tray she produced had two mixed drink glasses with generous portions of scotch on the rocks and one dainty glass of sherry. "Did you find evidence of my dissolute life?"

"We weren't looking into your life, Mrs. Garrett, so Constable Jackson only gave your suite a cursory glance. She noticed a computer but didn't turn it on. If your husband used it, we'd like a look, but we tried not to pry into your life."

"I'll get it before you leave if you'll promise to return it within a few days. Other than occasional e-mails to friends and Christmas letters, I use it for communicating with the kids."

"Thank you, I promise not to pry. We found a lot of ash in the fireplace in Mr. Garrett's office. Would you expect that?"

Caroline placed her empty glass on the table and glanced at Simon's. "The cleaning lady comes on Fridays, but last Friday's visit was cancelled because you had the place cordoned off. She'd have emptied fireplaces the previous Friday."

"We've taken the ashes and a computer with extensive external memory from Mr. Garrett's office, and another computer from the basement."

"That's Matthew's old one. We were keeping it for the kids when they come home at Christmas. It needs a new monitor."

"We'll return it long before your children return. We also found a minicomputer in the garage. Did you know about it?"

"I seldom enter the garage, but it's a funny place for a computer."

Simon produced a hand-written list. He added his signature to the bottom. "We've taken these items. We'll return them within a week."

Caroline scanned the list. "You should keep the fireplace ashes."

He laughed. "We'll dispose of them and return the rest. That's enough of business. I hope we didn't make your evening too unpleasant."

"Mildred did a superb job with dinner, and I rather enjoyed sitting in Mildred's cottage and imagining you digging into my little secrets."

Simon wondered why Caroline seemed so focused on her secrets. Was she asking him to pry? *Better to change the subject than go down that road.* "How about Mrs. Ettinger becoming our latest selectman? Amelia was excited."

"Me too," Mildred said before glancing at Caroline. "Caroline also, but she'll maintain solidarity with the families and decry the phenomenal break with our sacred traditions."

Caroline shook her head. "I won't. I'll be the first convert to the new religion. As soon as I get my life sorted out, I'll ask Cynthia how I can contribute. I want to help, but I'm done with topless protests."

"I suspect Cynthia is as well," Mildred replied, smiling as she drained the last of her sherry. "She has to embrace the selectman image. Should we be going, Simon? I trust you'll offer a little old lady a ride home, and it's getting late for this old lady."

"Oh, Aunt Mildred," exclaimed Caroline, "you can't sell yourself as a little old lady! You're remarkably active and fit, and at heart, younger than the rest of us. Mr. Merrick should have made you Selectman."

Simon spent the rest of Wednesday evening searching Caroline's laptop for useful information about Matthew Garrett without success. What he learned about Caroline Garrett left him even more confused. She conducted risqué e-mail conversations with friends including photos and video clips of various women cavorting in states of undress in and around swimming pools. They were taken at garden parties at the town's largest houses, and she had to realize he'd find them when she gave him the computer.

When he arrived at the station the next morning, he waved to Diana and beckoned her into his office. "Caroline's computer. She pushed it on me last night before I left. I've scanned it and find nothing related to our investigation. See if I missed anything before I return it. And, um, let no one else look at it."

"And the other computers."

"Have the electronics guys make complete copies of the drives and information from deleted files."

Diana picked up Caroline's computer and turned to leave. "I can handle those. Evans sifted through our pile of ashes without finding fragments big enough to be useful. We have many fingerprints to identify. He'll start on them tonight, but if you want the results sooner, I could start today."

"Leave them for Evans? Get your electronics' wizard working on the first three computers and check through Caroline's. Then I think you should return to looking for anyone who's seen Cope."

Diana returned at noon with sandwiches and coffee. "Interesting photos but nothing for us," she said, passing him Caroline's computer. "I now understand why you want no one looking at it."

"What do you think?"

"Fun and games at the homes of Barrettsport's rich and influential citizens. Your Amelia is in several."

"I didn't notice."

Diana reclaimed the computer, fired it up, and pointed at a picture. "Isn't that Amelia?"

"Could be," Simon admitted.

"If you're unsure, check out this video, it's crystal clear."

"You're right, that's definitely Amelia," Simon announced as he watched the video.

"Would you like a copy?"

"I think not."

"Too bad because I've already copied it." She showed him the memory stick before pocketing it. "And now, I need time off. Travis has bad news about his wife, and I want to be with him."

"What's this? Travis has a wife."

"It's complicated, but I should explain."

"You have every right to keep it to yourself."

"Olivia is terminally ill, living in a nursing home. He saves money to help pay for the nursing home by living with us. She knows Travis and I will stay together after she's no longer with us, but while she's here Olivia comes first with Travis. Right now, she's particularly bad, so Travis needs to be with her, and I need to play my part."

Simon sighed. Diana requesting a day off reflected their new role in what was once their big case. They were now fringe players in an RCMP investigation, and she realized they need not work extended hours. "Take whatever time you need and don't worry about the case. We'll manage without you."

"I'll be in Monday; she knows I'm a working woman."

Simon watched Diana prance from the room waving the memory stick. The town's strange propensity for exhibitionism had even infected the steadfast Constable Jackson. He wondered if something in the local water supply caused such behaviour—a small mystery to consider during idle moments. But first, his professional pride demanded he find the key to the Craig-Garrett-Cole mystery.

Chapter Thirty-Four

Monday morning, Amelia was back teaching little children and Karli was into her new drawing project. Simon was at the station working on his murder investigation. Diana arrived at nine carrying a large cardboard box.

"Our electronics guy's done with two of Garrett's computers," She announced, placing the box on Simon's desk. "He provided memory sticks with the data files downloaded."

"Hidden and deleted files?"

"He's extracted everything he can. What should we do?"

"Either you or Evans should return them and set up the office one."

"Me, then. Evans is still on nights."

"And the mini computer?" Simon asked.

"Wiped clean., We should determine if it's Holly's. Then what?"

"We keep it. It's a piece of our puzzle and not Caroline's."

"Why's it important? We know about Holly's affair with Garrett."

"He wouldn't have her computer with the hard disc wiped clean if it was merely an affair."

"True, but what?"

Simon pointed to the scribbled entries on his whiteboard. "I've been staring at my evidence against Garrett and Cavanaugh. This computer and our Jag provide key insights. If we can link them with Cope, we can show Garrett's current statement ignores a major part of the story. And what does that tell us?"

"That he's still hiding something," Diana suggested. "Something bigger than his subterfuge with the Jag as getaway vehicle."

"Which implies he's deeper in this mess than he's admitting. But I've been remiss. I haven't asked you about Travis and Olivia."

"We're okay. He left with a truckload for Ontario, and then other jobs for the next ten days. Her condition's stabilized, but she's failing. He now accepts she won't live longer than a month or two."

For several minutes, they discussed the implications for Diana, Travis, and her two sons. Then, Simon returned to their case. "I'll challenge Jaimie Kim on their progress identifying Mr. Jones and offer our help with nailing Garrett. Our big task is placing Cope here on the days before Labour Day and learning why he returned."

Diana stood, barring Simon's way to his whiteboard. "There's another consideration before you challenge Detective Kim."

"What's that?"

"The murder weapon."

"What's the problem?"

"How Cope acquired it."

Simon retreated, slumping into his chair. "How did we miss that one?"

Diana shrugged. "Too many complications."

"What are you suggesting?"

"Either Cope gained admittance without their knowledge, or one of the Garretts admitted him."

"Or Garrett took it to Holly's."

"Not likely. It's too big for him to hide if, as we assume, he walked."

"Then we need something linking Cope to Garrett's house."

"Evans is running the fingerprints we lifted from the house, and I'll look for witness observations through that Friday night. We should also search the computers for anything related to Cope."

Tuesday morning, Margaret Summerville presented Simon with a bedraggled kitbag as he entered the station. "Someone dropped it off earlier. Corporal Vickers took the young man's name and address, and details about where he found it."

219

"Thanks," Simon said as he perused the single sheet of paper Margaret offered him. "Diana can interview him, and I'll check the bag's contents."

Clothes and toiletries someone might need for an overnight trip dominated their find. A passport and wallet with two hundred dollars in cash and a driver's licence, two credit cards, and a debit card issued to Nathaniel Adams completed the haul. When Diana returned from her interview an hour later, Simon had everything carefully separated and drying on a rack Margaret set up in their interview room.

"What do you think?" Simon asked, gesturing at his display.

"Confirms our suspicions. He was scarpering."

"Looks like it," Simon replied as he rescanned Vickers notes. "What did you learn from Mr. Stevens?"

"Little more than the twenty words Vickers had from our taciturn witness, but he showed me where he found it. I've marked it off, and I can return at low tide. Our constables already walked that piece of beach, so the bag either came ashore yesterday, or it was found elsewhere and dumped."

They resumed their conversation after Diana grabbed a coffee. Simon offered another explanation for Garrett's attempted escape. "The beach was not Plan A."

"Why not?"

"He wouldn't wear formal shoes and natty clothes to ford a channel even one that's only four feet deep. And his possessions were in a bag that wouldn't survive a dunking."

"But he was wearing a wetsuit," Diana noted.

"That's because the beach was Plan B, and Kerry's pursuit forced him to ad-lib it."

"What's your scenario?"

"He took his wife's car to add confusion. He planned to drive off the peninsula, leave it at the Upper Barrettsport beach, and walk to the garage with the Jag."

"A faked suicide at the Upper Barrettsport beach, but he encountered the roadblock and didn't dare brazen his way through."

"He returned to the beach on this side of the causeway. The escape across that beach was Plan B."

Diana walked to the office window and gazed out for a few minutes. She turned back to Simon. "It explains why his car was pointing away from the causeway, and in either case, we were supposed to interpret it as a suicide."

Simon nodded. "We now have another problem. Someone tipped him off about our operation."

"But not before we established our roadblock."

"So, whoever tipped him off wasn't aware of the roadblock."

"Or didn't tell him."

"But someone tipped him off," Simon concluded, "and we must determine who."

Friday, Diana reported her progress placing Barney Cope at the Garrett residence on August seventeenth, the day before the murder. "Detective Kim tells me Cope was in Barrettsport on Friday. They have credit card purchases at the Lower Barrettsport gas station and a restaurant outside Liverpool. And no mention of Jones. They're finally agreeing Jones and Cope are the same person."

Simon looked up from the papers on his desk. "A credit card issued in Cope's name?"

Diana shook her head. "But they're confident they can tie it to Cope."

"Okay, proves nothing, but it puts him near town."

"Also, I learned from Mildred that the Witherspoon's had visitors that Friday evening, including Matthew, Caroline, and their two kids."

"So, you're using Mildred's Tea Shoppe for leads. After the mortgage fiasco, I've been careful what I said around Mildred. But wouldn't they activate their house alarm?"

"Mrs. Garrett says they don't set the alarm unless they're away overnight," Diana replied.

"Not proper security, but your story hangs together if we presume Cope was watching the premises and seized his opportunity when they left for the party. I still think someone was guiding him, but we can't assume it was a Garrett."

A meeting Simon couldn't avoid interrupted the conversation. When he returned from the departmental staffing meeting an hour later, Diana continued the discussion. "Everything you've said about Garrett rings true. He's in deep with Twenty-First Century, but you're wrong about Cavanaugh. He's just so obsessed with getting ahead he'll do anything to achieve his goal."

"But there's a dynamic between Twenty-First Century, Garrett, and Cavanaugh."

"I don't agree. Work through it without Cavanaugh."

"But why isn't Cavanaugh involved?"

"Because he wouldn't run roughshod over his fellow officers, intimidate witnesses, and twist the evidence to glorify his role if he was in with them anticipating a big payoff."

Simon stared at the new staffing chart Chief DeWolfe presented at the meeting. It provided for one new regular constable and a permanent move of Diana to Detective Constable, but it was too soon to tell her all her hard work had already paid off. "So, how does it work?"

"Garrett's corrupt, working with Twenty-First Century to make his illegal fortune and disappear. But there's another factor. Holly Craig's investigating Twenty-First Century, bent on making her mark in journalism, and she has a source in the company. She trades information about Garrett for what she needs from this source. They use the information to control him."

"You think Holly fed them what Cope needed to implicate Garrett in her murder?"

Diana paused, staring at the scribbled notes on Simon's whiteboard. "Inadvertently, she wouldn't have conspired in her own murder."

"Okay, that gives Cope an indirect source for information he needs, but doesn't tell us who tipped off Garrett."

"Cavanaugh's responsible. He wanted Garrett arrested at the roadblock. Then he would step forward and claim the credit for arresting him, and we'd look like idiots waiting at his house."

"Garrett twigged, explaining why he was paranoid."

"He couldn't come clean without admitting to his illegal involvement in Twenty-First Century," Diana added. "Which gets us to the current situation where he's playing footsy with the prosecutors."

Simon tapped a pen on his desk as he considering the implications. "It would be easier for me to imagine Garrett's schemes involving cheating, manipulation, and fraud than cold-blooded murder. Let's go with your version of the hitman."

"How do we prove it?"

"We must link Garrett and Cope, first in mid-August when Holly Craig was killed. And then in September when Garrett and his Jag were seen on McConnell's Creek Road by Amanda Campbell and Ricky Gaudet."

"A witness says he saw a stranger lurking around the Garrett residence on the evening before the murder. But he didn't finger Cope when I showed him a bunch of mug shots."

Simon shook his head. "Not solid enough."

"And less when we attempt to link them in the first week in September. An indistinct print on the trunk of the Jag that isn't definitively Cope's and a sighting of the Jag near where the body was found."

"But that's what we have, and it's difficult to generate a better explanation for Garrett being on that road."

"The picture we've developed has Garrett murdering Cope. How does a pudgy middle-aged stockbroker murder a professional hitman, especially one who doesn't trust him? That will be hard to explain."

"He was in the Marines before his MBA, and he may have been a martial arts enthusiast."

"Nothing in his house suggests an interest in martial arts."

"But he's interested in weaponry, even if they're medieval. It's not great, but it's what we have. I'll talk to Jaimie Kim. We can't dig into this, so I must convince Jaimie it's in her interest."

Chapter Thirty-Five

An unproductive interview with Matthew Garrett had Jaimie Kim seething. "The guy's a total asshole," she blurted into her cell phone. "Why do they coddle him? The prosecutors need help nailing the principals in Twenty-First Century, but he has zero credibility."

"But what did he say?" Simon asked.

"He helped Cope look for property."

"So, Garrett's now a real estate agent, but he's admitted Cope was Holly's assassin?"

"He hasn't. He said Cope got his name from someone in Twenty-First Century Construction. They were surveying the country inspecting farmland when Cope collapsed and died."

"That's it, no supporting evidence, and no explanation of why he didn't call nine-one-one."

"Nope, his lawyer wouldn't let him elaborate. It's so obviously false and so frustrating, but they won't say one damn thing unless they get something in return."

"It's annoying but consider this. He's admitted to stealing from his friends and colleagues in Bluenose Wind Energy, conspiring with Twenty-First Century Construction to defraud the government of energy development money, and aiding and abetting the murder of Holly Craig. Add concealing the death of Barney Cope and disposing of his body. It's quite a list."

"We'll see, but I fear his fancy lawyer will wiggle his way out of most charges."

Garrett was living up to Simon's picture. Garrett was scheming to the end, and given his track record, and his current legal team's reputation, he might get off easy. The fraud allegations relied on dicey evidence provided by Cavanaugh. And his lawyer would argue Garrett helped Cope murder Holly under duress. Chances of extended jail time were slim.

No one was addressing two glaring questions. Why had Cope returned to Nova Scotia? And why was Garrett helping him?

"Oh, Christ, it's obvious," Diana exclaimed when Simon finally posed the critical questions. "Cope took Holly's laptop and cell phone after he murdered her. Something on those machines told him Holly had incriminating evidence hidden somewhere. He, or more correctly, his bosses at Twenty-First Century, needed to find it, and they enlisted Garrett to help him."

"Holly's storage locker, or the computer at Karli's house. They got wind of those."

"Nothing related to Ms. Leach, because we'd have learned about it. And Garrett's surprise when we revealed Holly's lesbian affair was genuine. It must be the storage locker."

Simon grabbed his jacket. "Get our photos of Garrett and Cope. We're headed for the Bridgewater self-storage facility."

Two hours later, they'd located the correct witness. "Yup, they were here around Labour Day. They asked about a certain storage locker and pushed their weight around. The shorter guy, the bald one, had a medical problem and collapsed. I offered to call nine-one-one, but his buddy bundled him into their car and raced toward the hospital. Baldy was sitting in the passenger seat trying to look confident, but he was definitely suffering."

"Do you remember the make?"

"Big fancy foreign thing, red. Not a Mercedes, sleeker than that."

"Jaguar," Diana suggested.

"Yeah, big red four-door Jaguar, not a sports car, a big elegant sedan."

They'd located the last piece in their puzzle.

Once they'd established the link between Garrett, Cope, and the Jaguar, the RCMP were all over the Jag languishing in the Barrettsport Police department garage. Their crime scene investigators found fabric fragments in the trunk that matched the clothes Cope was wearing. They became a key factor in Jamie Kim's ongoing investigation of Garrett's role in Cope's death.

A few days later, Simon's involvement in the investigation ended during a meeting he and Chief Reginald DeWolfe attended at the RCMP detachment in Bridgewater. Inspector Fairbairn of the Internal Affairs Department spoke first.

"Detective Conrad Cavanaugh has admitted to numerous infractions. We've agreed not to pursue charges provided he cooperates in the case against Twenty-First Century Construction. These are the relevant facts. First, he planted evidence in the house of one Carlotta Leach of Hunter's Creek and provoked her to lash out against his colleagues. Second, he threatened Corporal Janet Summers of the detachment here in Bridgewater to force her to falsify evidence. Third, he tried to plant evidence implicating a Mr. Matthew Garrett of Barrettsport in the offices of the Bluenose Wind Energy Corporation. Officers from the Bridgewater Detachment and the Barrettsport Police Department thwarted that attempt." He nodded toward Simon and Chief DeWolfe before opening the floor to questions.

"Will these admissions jeopardize the cases against Garrett or Twenty-First Century?" Jaimie asked.

"They won't affect the Twenty-First Century case because his actions changed no facts. He twisted the records to glorify his role but nothing more."

"You mean he did this to steal credit for solving the crimes?"

Fairbairn nodded. "We have everything documented. You can pursue your investigation without fear of cross-contamination."

"And the case against Garrett?" Simon asked.

"That's more problematical. I'll leave it to those responsible for the Garrett inquiry."

The regional commander stood. "We need not discuss Mr. Cavanaugh any further, but the last question leads us to Mr. Matthew Garrett. Sam, the floor is yours."

Samuel Myers, the commander of the Bridgewater Detachment rose. "First, the murder of Holly Craig. It's clear Barnard Cope, a low-life with a long rap sheet associated with various crime syndicates in Ontario, murdered her. Someone in Twenty-First Century Construction hired him to eliminate her because she'd learned too much about their criminal activities."

"Do you know who?" Simon asked.

"That's our priority. Garrett admitted involvement in setting up the hit, but denies responsibility."

Simon was back on his feet. "Cope died in September. A witness thought he had a medical emergency. Has that been confirmed?"

"We thank you for your efforts. We haven't reached a firm conclusion about how he died. It's another aspect of our investigation of the relationship between Cope and Twenty-First Century." Myers paused, looked away from Simon, and had a large swallow of water. "Our ongoing investigation involves teams in Bridgewater, Halifax, and Toronto." His implication was clear, the RCMP didn't welcome Simon's input.

"Garrett is next," continued Myers. "He coordinated the interaction between Bluenose Wind Energy and Twenty-First Century. He siphoned off money for himself and several principals in Twenty-First Century. Garrett also concealed and disposed of Cope's body. The basic facts are not being contested. Cavanaugh and Garrett are cooperating with our investigation of Twenty-First Century Construction. That's it. Questions?"

"Is Bluenose Wind Energy being investigated?" Chief DeWolfe asked.

"Nothing suggests they committed any crimes. They formed a dubious partnership, and it got them in difficulty. Several of Garrett's activities are being scrutinized, but the company remains in operation. They're not under criminal investigation."

Myers wrapped up the meeting after additional desultory questions and non-committal answers.

"More unanswered questions than answered ones," Simon said outside the station. "And I'm reluctant to pass our whole investigation over to them."

"It's nothing new. We start an investigation, but if its scope expands, it becomes the Mounties' responsibility. Not satisfying, but that's the role of a small-town police force."

On the highway to Barrettsport, Simon resumed their conversation. "Here's an explanation that neatly resolves our case."

Chief DeWolfe laughed. "That's what I heard before we hired you, you always had a theory."

"The Twenty-First Century bosses sent Cope to eliminate Holly and destroy the incriminating evidence she'd gathered. Garrett participated but not willingly. Cope's use of Garrett's club shows a lack of trust between Garrett and Twenty-First Century."

"I agree. It appears Garrett was willing to defraud but not to murder."

"Cope took Holly's laptop and cell phone because he thought they contained the evidence he wanted to destroy."

"Devices you and Diana spent weeks searching for."

"We never found the phone, but the computer showed up, eventually. One of them led Cope and Garrett to the storage facility in Bridgewater. Cope's collapse at the storage facility may have been the result of a medical condition, but Myers would have acknowledged it if the autopsy report supported that idea. More likely, Garrett orchestrated Cope's collapse. Remember, Garrett was a Marine, so he would have known how to incapacitate someone."

"That makes more sense than anything else I've heard, and it suggests Garrett orchestrated Cope's death. But it doesn't change our perspective. For Barrettsport, the two important facts are clear. Cope murdered Holly Craig, and Bluenose Wind Energy is not in any serious trouble. Matthew Garrett committed several crimes but bringing him to justice is no longer our responsibility. If Garrett was responsible for Cope's death, Detective Kim will try to prove it. We must leave Matthew and Twenty-First Century to the RCMP."

Simon shrugged his shoulders but said nothing. An unsatisfactory outcome, but he had to accept the Chief's arguments. Time to cut their losses and move on to other things.

Simon pondered his future as he walked the few blocks from the police station to his apartment. Much had changed in the four months since the dog days of summer. He'd established a good working relationship with a highly competent partner who would soon be available for full-time collaboration on criminal investigations. A growing group of friends and colleagues added to his sense of wellbeing. He'd even made inroads into the exalted halls of Barrettsport society. He and Diana may not have resolved their case to his satisfaction, but his overall work situation was in good shape.

And Amelia Craddock, could she be the love of his life? Circumstances had pushed them together, and he'd initially gone along for the ride. It transformed into a much more serious relationship. He suspected she still hid secrets from earlier in her life, but they no longer seemed pressing.

Was he destined to share his life with her, spending their days together without a single consideration of anyone else? Would they go on vacation, climbing the Eiffel Tower to the top, or sit on a tropical beach watching the sun go down? Would they have and raise kids? Could he and Amelia do these things together for the rest of their lives? He couldn't imagine anything else.

And that little minx Karli Leach, simultaneously tough and vulnerable? One minute they're frolicking together like siblings who'd loved and trusted each other for years, and the next she's shunning him completely. What if he was a cop, and she'd tried to beat up four of his Bridgewater colleagues? She was like family, he would defend her against all comers. That's what you did for your family, especially at Christmas time.

Deck the hall with boughs of Holly, fa, la, la, la, la, la, la, la, la!

Epilogue

Conrad Cavanaugh resigned from the RCMP rather than fight charges he mistreated and corrupted subordinate officers, intimidated and harassed witnesses, and tampered with evidence. The investigating officers discredited Garrett's accusations of corruption and conspiracy to commit murder. Cavanaugh joined a private investigation agency based in Halifax.

Matthew Garrett pleaded guilty to several charges related to Holly Craig's murder and received five years in a minimum-security prison. He cooperated with the crown in their case against the owners of Twenty-First Century Construction including testifying at the trials. Evidence provided by Garrett and Cavanaugh led to several convictions.

Two years into Garrett's prison term, when the likelihood of parole was on the horizon, the crown had laid no charges related to Barney Cope's death.

Matthew agreed to an uncontested divorce from Caroline. She secured sole custody of their children, her house, and most of their communal assets. She also gained control of his investment company. Despite what Mildred Wexler said, an audit showed a successful business with numerous happy customers who valued conservative, risk-averse investment advice. Caroline hired a manager and kept the business going without changing its investment philosophy.

The End

About the author:

Alan Kemister is the pen name of a Halifax Nova Scotia based scientist experimenting with creative writing. He has a keen interest in environmental science and dabbled in yachting and golf before turning to fiction after retirement. He's written a baker's dozen of published short stories and one poem. Several of these stories appeared in two anthologies produced by Halifax's Evergreen Writers Group: *Out of the Mist: 22 Atlantic Canadian Ghost Stories* released in 2014, and *Off Highway: Journeys of Nova Scotia Writers*, in 2017. A third Evergreen Writers group anthology of short stories is in preparation.

A Body in the Sacristy was Alan's first novel, and the first of the Barrettsport Mysteries featuring Detective Goodyear and the fictional South Shore town of Barrettsport Nova Scotia. *Tilting at Windmills* is the second Barrettsport Mystery, and future novels in this series are planned.

Links:

E-mail: alkemi47@gmail.com

Facebook: https://www.facebook.com/Phil.Yeats47

Website: https://alankemisterauthor.wordpress.com

Tilting at Windmills, A Body in the Sacristy, Out of the Mist: 22 Atlantic Canadian Ghost Stories, and *Off Highway: Journeys of Nova Scotia Writers* are available on Amazon in paperback and e-book formats.